WITHIN THE ISLAND'S HOLD

A NILE VALLEY MYSTERY

GLENNIS GOODWIN

First published in 2025 by Blossom Spring Publishing
Within the Island's Hold © 2025 Glennis Goodwin
ISBN 978-1-917938-11-2
E: admin@blossomspringpublishing.com
W: www.blossomspringpublishing.com

Notes to Reader

In antiquity, the Island of Philae, and the temples and structures built upon it, sat in the south of the Nile River, close to the First Cataract. However, since the building of the Aswan Dam between the years 1960 and 1970, this island now sits submerged below the waterline. For visitors to Egypt since that time, the relocated Temple of Philae, dedicated to the Goddess *Isis*, sits downstream of the dam in the lower reservoir on Agilkia Island.

For reading purposes, this book is loosely based on where it sat in ancient times and aspects of the Ancient Egyptian worship that may have taken place there.

PROLOGUE

In the clear sky, the seagulls soared on outstretched wings, their harsh cries carried on the wind blowing fresh from the sea. Below them on the stark white sand, a young girl lay looking up, her eyes following the sweep and swoop of the birds across the deep blue. She had been lying there for uncounted moments, her mind not wishing to think of the hour to come. Instead, she focused on the memories of her younger years. The sand was where her father and mother frequently brought her as a child and the Red Sea, which stretched out from the shore, fascinated her with its blue-green waters.

Occasionally she stood witness to the change of colour as the exotic blooms of algae died back and the reddish-brown waters lived up to their name. But mostly it kept its clarity and often she bathed in its warmth.

The girl was called Heba. This meant 'gift', as it was many years after their marriage that her mother gave birth and their only child was looked upon as a blessing from the great gods. But now, at fourteen, she had reached an age when she must leave behind her family and be schooled in the ways of the temple.

"Heba! Heba!"

A voice rang out further up the beach and, raising her head to look across the bleached stretch, the girl witnessed her mother stopped at the top of the shore. She was gazing the other way, standing on tiptoe, her hand held over her eyes to shield them from the glare. As she spun around, Heba dropped back and flattened herself in the sand. She held her breath, but as the minutes passed with no further call, she let out a deep sigh and relaxed.

Time passed, but she knew she could not put off the

1

inevitable any longer. Rising from her soft bed, she walked slowly up the beach and entered the village from its top end.

Arriving at the baker's stall, she dodged past a group of women haggling over the flatbreads and, nipping down the side, came to a brief standstill where the dusty road wound its way through the labyrinth of back gardens.

Taking the first turn on the right, she moved one way and then the next, easily navigating the alleys that snaked behind the low, reed-covered, sand-washed buildings.

Arriving home, Heba took a deep breath before pushing open the creaking door. A silence met her. Until, letting the door close noisily, her mother looked up.

"There you are." Her voice came strained. "Didn't you hear my call?"

"No, Mother," the young girl lied.

Slipping off her sandals, Heba washed her hands and, keeping her head bowed, let her eyes fix on cleaning her ragged sand-engrained fingernails. She avoided looking at the visitor, whose presence filled the room. Yet as the dirt and sand sank slowly to the bottom of the basin, she could put it off no longer. Drying her hands, she turned to face their guest.

Beside the table, the fat man known as Khalid sat enjoying the figs and wine placed before him. He had returned to take Heba away and watching as the young girl moved around the room, his eyes never left her.

It had been many years since he had been there when Heba was only a few years old, but he had seen something in the girl. Noting her name, he put it forward for the Temple of Dendera and the villagers, looking on it as a blessing from the gods, rejoiced in her choosing.

The Temple of Dendera, dedicated to the Goddess

Hathor, accepted only a few novices for instruction in the ways of the temple and Heba had been told she was fortunate to be chosen to stand and serve within the great halls. All the people around had said how favoured the village was in having one picked from within their community. However, the girl did not feel fortunate or favoured in the moment. In fact, the opposite feeling fell upon her.

Her mother busied herself, not wanting to reach the time to say goodbye. But finally, she stopped, her hands becoming still as she hardened her heart for the coming moment. The time had arrived and she must let her only child go.

Her father had not even been able to remain behind to say his farewells, for the seas were full of fish and the sweat of the common man was needed to drag the nets along the shore and gather its bounty to see them through the winter. He and the young men of the village had left many days ago to walk the sands in the south and would not be returning until the seas were harvested.

"Get yourself ready, girl." The voice of Khalid broke the silence as he rose and pushed back the chair. Standing squatly at the door, he waited as, with bowed head, the girl disappeared behind the curtain that separated the rooms.

Collecting the small bag of possessions from her bedside, she took a quick last look around, holding the image in her memory. Her father had made the bed and, although not gifted in carpentry, he had done his best. The mattress was thin, and when the wooden slats had given way under her growing weight and they had punctured the straw-filled pallet, her mother had sewn a patch over to hold back the stuffing.

Folding the blanket back, Heba felt beneath the hard

wooden form that acted as a pillow, and pulling out a small carved heart-shaped stone she found on the beach, she kissed it and placed it on top of the bedding. To her, it was a token of her great love for her parents, and she hoped they would use it to remember her.

Finally, she could put off leaving no longer, and seeing her mother standing silently at the open door, she lifted her head and walked through.

Heba sat on her donkey as the villagers stopped to watch her pass. Hands were raised and voices followed along the dusty track. Her mother walked beside her all the way to the village's edge before she could bring herself to let go of the girl's hand, but seeing the stunted palm trees give way to the open sands, she planted a kiss on the girl's cheek and let her go.

Eventually, the village and its wishes of farewell faded at their backs and Heba, fixing her eyes on the growing dune rising before her, let her thoughts turn to the future.

CHAPTER ONE

In the dawn's morning light, the wooden felucca pulled slowly away from the eastern reed-lined bank. Seated within, the figure of a young woman sat motionless, her shaved head covered by the hood of her cloak. She stared down. Around her, the other occupants placed their baskets of offering at their feet and, sitting back, let Basim, the ferry owner, and his oarsmen struggle to move them out from the rushes. For the Priestess Nofret, the weeks of travel along the Nile into Upper Egypt were finally coming to a close. Yet unknowing of what lay before her, these passing days had seen both the rise of concern and expectancy as she neared her destination.

Once out in the water's darkness, the white square sail was raised high and the soft winds filled the fabric and pushed them silently along. The crew sat back, and as Basim and his assistant stood tall in the stern, they guided the craft along the well-travelled course.

Ahead of the boat, the Island of Philae lay flat in the distance, while at its back, the growing light spread pink along the eastern skyline. On the temple isle, the grey weather-bleached sanctuaries of the gods slowly rose above the walls as they sat mirrored in the water's brilliance. Around and among the colossal buildings, the palm trees waved in the breeze and the harsh call of birds interspersed their sighing as they cried out their alarm from the reeds.

The boat, having first moved south, headed directly for the boulders that stood menacingly out of the water and lay about the island's edge. However, just before they hit, Basim deftly turned the rudder and the craft, sliding between two of the jagged rocks, came to a stop in the calm on the sheltered side. Above their heads, at the top of the bank, the torches held by waiting figures lit the sky.

The woman remained seated as the supplicants picked up their gifts to the gods and, leaving the boat, they climbed the rough-hewn steps and followed the blaze from the leading torch. Their hushed voices disappeared along the well-worn track between the palms.

Rising slowly, Nofret covered her lower face before passing across her bag and, taking the proffered hand of the ferryman, she stepped out onto the island. She thought she may have sensed something at that moment. Yet, looking up to the heavens, her lips could only move in grateful thanks to the gods for her safe arrival. A lone torchbearer waited, and coming down the steps, he took her bag, and the small man introduced himself.

"Welcome, priestess. I'm Abbas." He dropped his bare head in recognition of the person who stood before him. "I'm one of the *wab* priests of *Hathor* and am here to serve you."

"Thank you, Abbas," Nofret replied, as he led her upwards and, reaching the top of the bank, they stepped through the wall which ringed the island's edge. Pausing, she took her time to straighten her robes before smiling at her attendant, who waited eagerly to do his duty. Following him along the palm track, they left the boatmen to their rest.

Abbas escorted Nofret to where the first of the large temples spread across the expanse of the Island of Philae. Here the Temple of *Hathor* stood in its surrounding of palms and, although being one of the smaller shrines that graced the isle, it held its own in the pantheon of the gods. The temple's walls rose high on this side of the island, but beyond, on the western edge, lay the sprawling intermingled complex of buildings dedicated to the Osirian Triad, the God *Osiris*, his wife, the Goddess *Isis* and their son *Horus*. These three had, of late, become the most worshipped throughout Egypt and here on the sacred island, the Goddess *Isis* took predominance over those of lesser worth.

Nofret knew that protocol meant she must present herself before the High Priest of *Isis*, even at this sacred hour of the morning, and waiting while Abbas dropped her bag in the temple's shadow, she followed his lead as they walked the sparsely grassed path before reaching the far buildings.

Ahead, the recognised sounds of chants along with the singing and rattle of sistra rang out, and the lights of a winding procession made their way between the girdle wall and the ring of palms that filled the centre of the island. The two stopped as it passed. Waiting for the end of the snaking line, Nofret and Abbas joined the march as the pageantry played out. The torches of the parade lit up the temple and the statuesque figures of the great gods carved upon the walls looked out across time above their heads.

High Priest Teos, the *hem-netjer-tepi*, and foremost servant to the triad, led the way south to the grand opening in the wall and entering through the monumental gate of the first pylon, the expanse of the forecourt spread out. Continuing on, his imposing figure slowly climbed the steps, and leading through the second gateway, the parade entered the hypostyle hall and the sanctuary of the gods. Here, *Isis*, the Spell Maker, received the veneration of the people alongside her husband, *Osiris*, Lord of Silence, and their son *Horus*, God of the Sky.

Beginning his ritual of the morning offering, Teos's hard voice echoed strong and loud as he entered the covered area. Around the carved columns, his words of invocation disappeared into the painted ceiling, where the sacred words governed the world of man and the great gods looked down in witness.

Teos was a Nubian, and the island had long been his home. He had come many years ago as a lector priest from a simple temple in the south and had found work as a scribe and secretary to the then high priest, Ahmose. However, on Ahmose's passing, the younger man had received overwhelming support, and stood uplifted above the heads of others. Delighting in his position, he had, over the years, collected around him those thought worthy in his eyes and now basked in their everlasting devotion.

Gradually, the singing died away and Teos and his four main lector priests stepped forwards and entered the inner temple. Here the flare of the torches shone their light to guide the way, while around the darkness hung heavy in the corners and beneath the high roof the smoke gathered and tumbled in the disturbed air.

Standing before the granite statue of the Goddess *Isis* that sat in its niche, Teos waited as first his lector held up the small dish holding the blessed water of the Nile. Dipping his long fingers, he wiped them over the hands and feet of the Goddess of Magic and whispered the words of custom known only to himself. Next, an exquisitely carved grey and white crystalline jar containing perfumed oil of blue lotus replaced the water bowl and, lifting the lid on the aromatic unguent, the high priest anointed the stone hands and feet. A length of fine linen cloth was then presented and wrapped around the waist of the statue in the final commemoration of the goddess.

Seeing the completion of the service of dressing, the worshippers slowly passed down their many offerings and, along with the prayers that came with the gifts, the lector priests of the Goddess *Isis* placed them reverently at her feet.

The service then moved on to performing these same rituals for *Osiris* and his son *Horus* and, on completion of the dedication to the triad, outside in the growing light, the sweet singing of birds immediately began in the bushes and reeds.

Finally, as Teos turned to one side, he stepped behind the gilded screen at the side of the altars and, opening an elegantly carved door, he entered the realm of the gods. Leaving the priests, priestesses and supplicants standing for many moments as the light of the new day began its resurrection, he performed the rituals witnessed only by himself.

He reappeared some time later, his eyes wide as if in a dream, and standing before the triad, the service moved on in his many invocations, before, as the rays of the risen sun lay crossways over the island and the tall columns of the temple stood out against the skyline, his cry of "May the gods be pleased" rang out in the hall's roof. He bathed his face in the blessed waters of the Nile and, lifting his eyes skywards, his lips moved slightly as his whispered words to the heavens met the growing day.

Finally, dropping his head, the ceremony reached its end and Teos stood before the congregation and gave them their leave. The faithful worshippers, having dutifully given their offerings and gratefully received the prayers and thanks of the gods, then began their slow file out of the temple where the new day's light greeted them.

Departing the shrine, the supplicants headed back to where Basim and his crew remained in wait. There, the swiftly rowed boat returned them to the constant sameness and worries of their everyday lives. On their leaving, the island exchanged its ceremony of song and dance for a peacefulness and the dominion of the priests and priestesses returned to its silence.

Beneath the swaying palms, the *wab* priests began their routine of tidying up the temple and knowing the gods had received the spirit and essence of the offerings, these were taken away to be enjoyed later. Sweeping aside the sand trodden through on the feet of the supplicants, the priests made way for the escort of Teos on his walk back to his home at the northern edge of the island.

Emerging out of the forecourt to where the massive carved pylon stood at their back, the high priest glanced over to where Nofret had stopped in wait.

Gesturing her forwards, he greeted her.

"Welcome to Philae!" The man's voice was high-pitched and somewhat childlike, his everyday speech at odds with the one spoken in the temple. "You must be the Priestess Nofret." His eyes stared wide and dream-like after being in the presence of the gods. "We have been waiting a great time for your arrival!" he declared, his voice still holding its authority.

He swept past before the woman could reply, leaving her standing alone. But as the last of his retinue followed, a tall young woman turned back.

"He will see you later." Her dark-rimmed eyes looked deep into Nofret's. "When the light of *Ra* reaches its zenith, then you may present yourself."

The Priestess of *Hathor* watched as the end of the line

disappeared and, following behind, walked back along the girdle wall. Her authority of the Goddess of the Sky awaited and, seeing the small figure of Abbas standing in the sun's warmth before the shaded entrance, Nofret headed that way.

The *wab* priest stood in wait, his bald head shining in the rays of *Ra*. Seeing his priestess emerge out of the shade into the brightness, he bowed slightly and, gesturing for her to enter, he walked before her and guided her beneath the painted doorway.

The Temple of *Hathor* bore little comparison to the massive buildings at Dendera, which held the same name. For in having only a large forecourt that was first entered before the smaller hypostyle hall led beyond, it stood diminished in its overall size. However, within the interior, as expected, the sprawling structures of carved columns stood surrounded by the highly painted walls, and the overall decoration depicted the Goddess *Hathor* in her many embodiments.

Abbas led the way along the columned walkway to the very front of the temple and, leaving Nofret at the shrine, he stepped aside to allow her some privacy.

The enormous granite statue of *Hathor* rose high central to the altar, the headdress of cow horns sitting atop her head. On either side, etched in the walls, the elaborate depictions showed the many names given to her, along with her maternal and celestial features. These stood out, surrounded by their hieroglyphs. At her feet, bouquets of dried flowers slowly burned and gave off their incense. To her left and right, further along the ledge, the representation of the goddess sat squatly in two smaller figures, while before these, along the front of a lower shelf, the many carved stone statuettes in all her forms stood facing outwards.

Reaching to her belt, Nofret removed the tiny alabaster flask she had carried with care close at her side and, dripping the waters from the sacred lake at Dendera over the feet of the goddess, she blessed the statue. Looking up into the finely chiselled face, she asked for guidance as she took up her new position in the temple.

The silence fell around as she whispered her words, until, lifting her head, she declared, "*Ánuk pau ḥem.tã*," – I am your servant.

Rising, she turned to her priest and let him lead her past the altar. Leaving through the side doorway, Abbas gestured to the small building which was adjoined to the temple by a covered walkway. Dropping his head respectfully, he took his leave and Nofret stood alone.

Retiring to the private area beyond the temple, she passed along the small open corridor that united the two buildings before entering the rooms that would become her home.

Looking around the space which once belonged to the last Priestess of *Hathor*, she remembered hearing that her name was Safiya but knew little else of the person in whose rooms she now stood.

The area sat clean and tidy, made ready by her *wab* priests and, as Nofret let the hood fall from her shaved head, she placed her bag upon the bed and removed the few items held dear to her. A peace and calm fell around and moving across to the low window in the east, she stared out through the palm trees to the reeds of the water line below.

Ten years had passed so swiftly since the girl she knew had left the shores of the Red Sea. She was now a woman and rarely thought about the name given at her birth. The simple life of Heba was of the past and they had named her Nofret, the beautiful one!

On looking out, her gaze fell to the east and suddenly her thoughts turned to her mother and father. She wondered if they were still alive.

She had left all those years behind her, along with her name, for as soon as she and Khalid had reached the Temple of Dendera, a new existence of duty and prayers had been found. From that moment, her whole life became bound in service to the Goddess *Hathor* and all the ceremonies and rituals learned along the way governed the hours of her day.

She had settled in the north, and her life became one of custom and observance. Contentment had wrapped her in its hold and her sudden posting to oversee the Temple of *Hathor* in the southern great Nile waters had come unexpectedly into her daily routine. However, she had been pronounced greatly favoured to be chosen and with that, there was no way to decline the position.

Abbas eventually disturbed her reflection and, wishing to introduce the other *hem-netjer*, the Priests of *Hathor*, he left her to reposition her hood to cover her bald head before returning her to the main part of the temple. Here, four linen-robed priests stood in wait in the large house of prayer, the columns dividing the area into two with an ornately tiled passageway between.

Essam and Ramy were first to step forwards, being the lector priests to the temple while Musa and Kheti, who were *wab* priests like Abbas, were the last to be introduced. However, they all let their heads drop as their priestess passed, and each presented her with a lotus flower.

Essam was the oldest priest, having arrived from

Nubia as a boy. And in giving his younger years to the goddess known in his homelands, he felt there was little he did not know about the revered work of service in her name. Since the last priestess had died, he had taken it upon himself, as the senior lector, to continue the blessing of the altar. Yet in his ministrations to *Hathor*, he was limited to certain sacred duties and knew it should be a woman who held the position above him. However, in hoping that the gods had blessed them well with their new priestess, he kept faith that the supplicants would soon return and again pay homage to the goddess.

***

High Priest Teos had requested that Nofret should attend upon him. And after changing her travelling clothes for those of her temple attire, and decorating her eyes with crushed green malachite powder, she applied the red of the carmine beetle to her lips before stroking the dark kohl around her lids. Finally, she placed the black wig atop her shaved head.

Pushing the many beaded bracelets up her arms, she felt suitably dressed as she stepped out, and along with Essam and her four priests, they left the Temple of *Hathor* to settle into the warmth of the late afternoon.

Walking the short distance to the island's northwestern edge, they passed the homes of the priests and priestesses before arriving at the house of Teos. This sat amongst a low walled garden of greenery surrounded by its boundary of bleached sand.

The man sat in wait in the courtyard to the front of the house while behind him, an array of sharp stubby palms poked out of their decorated clay pots and dropped their tiny flowers around his feet. His domain encompassed him and he sat in his chair like a king.

Before him, the offerings presented in the temple lay on a low table where a young man, wearing only a white linen schenti around his hips, sat dusting away the ever-present flies with a woven fan.

Teos gestured for Nofret to sit and watched as she lowered herself to the mat with a rattle of her beaded wrists while her priests sat down at her side.

"Please eat." The high priest smiled, his eyes never leaving the woman's face. "The gods may have taken the spirit of these offerings, but the reality of them sits before us and we honour their names in our indulgence!"

The principle was not new to Nofret, for the priests and priestesses at Dendera had never gone hungry in all the time she had been there, but to her, it always felt wrong. The offerings brought each day were mostly taken from the tables of the workers and market sellers and they and their families often did without in order to placate and praise their gods.

However, in seeing Essam stretch forwards and pick up a scrawny leg of a chicken, Nofret quickly realised she had not eaten since last evening and her hunger made itself known. Reaching over, she picked a honey cake from its woven mat.

***

Later, as the sun began its heading into the west, the Priestess of *Hathor* left her priests continuing their enjoyment of the donations and she strolled alongside Teos as he escorted her around the gardens. Showing off his estate, where the figs and dates grew in abundance, they eventually reached the back of the house. Here, a walkway led to the waters of the Nile. Marching forwards, the high priest walked the smooth slipway before reaching the water's edge.

Further out, the heads of the hippopotamuses rose slowly, disturbing the flat of the river, and behind them in the reeds, the dark shapes of crocodiles slid from off the far bank. Suddenly, a splash close by alerted them to the closer presence of these reptiles and Nofret stepped back.

"The Nile here is certainly abundant," the woman exclaimed, her dark eyes swiftly glancing to where the thick reeds sat close beside her. The Temple at Dendera did not sit directly on the banks of the Nile and these two creatures, although known in their godly forms as *Sobek*, the crocodile god and *Taweret*, the hippo goddess of fertility, had rarely been encountered. It was only on her journey along the great river that she had become more closely acquainted with them.

"Yes, we are surely blessed by the gods," Teos replied with no fear in his voice. Turning away from the wonders of the Nile, he changed the subject. "You know that we are pleased to have you here, Nofret!"

The woman dropped her head in acceptance of his words before replying, "And I am favoured to be here!"

The high priest smiled, and leading her along the bank, they let the warm wind lift the sand at their feet.

Stopping at the boundary of Teos's domain, they let the courting call of the cicadas add their song to the silent surroundings as they looked left across the thatched rooftops to the temple buildings beyond. Here, a complex of structures filled this side of the island. After some moments, Nofret asked the question which played on her mind.

"What happened to the last Priestess of *Hathor*?" She

knew the woman she replaced had been dead for many long months, going on a year, but she needed to clarify her mind about that event.

"She died," Teos replied softly, his high-pitched voice vying with the call of the insects.

"I know she died, Teos, but of what?"

Nofret knew she held a position below that of the high priest and hoped her tone would not cause offence. But in asking, she wanted to fully understand her reason for having had her peaceful life of routine disrupted. She needed to know why she was there.

"We don't rightly know!" Teos eventually answered.

The man looked over the water as it passed below them and, watching a huge crocodile move northwards in the flow of the Nile, he finished, "Safiya's body was found on the rocks on the southern border. It appears she may have fallen to her death."

Pulling his eyes away from the ripples, he straightened up and, forcing a smile, took the woman's hand and led her away from the bank. "But let's not dwell on the past."

Returning to the rear of the house, Teos guided the woman into the dark of the cool interior, where the smell of burning incense met them.

"We have a good library here," he continued his instruction, before adding, "That is, if you should need to check a reference at any time. Or if you wish to further your knowledge."

Opening the double doors with some vigour, the man eagerly strode into the smoke-filled room. The fusty smell of old papyri filled the air and, at the tables, the beeswax candles dripped down in their exquisitely carved alabaster holders.

"My scribes can be of service, should you require

them." He held out his hands to encompass the bowed heads of the men seated at their desks.

"I can write," the woman softly replied, surprised that the man should ask. "And read!"

"Yes, of course you can."

The library was far smaller than the one at Dendera, Nofret considered, as she left Teos standing in the doorway. The one there held many papyri and had become a part of the life of the young girl Nofret. Yet, as she wandered around the small tables, she noted the boxes poking out from the shelving and the rolls lying atop the desks and thought them slightly inferior to those of the greater temple.

Stopping where a scribe worked, head bent in the light of his candle, she watched the precision of his hand as he painted in the lined drawing of the God *Thoth* which ran down the edge of the papyrus. The man never hesitated, but keeping his head bent, he concentrated his steady hand on illuminating the image of the god.

The next desk held a scribe who was writing hieroglyphs across the width of a small papyrus and, often dipping the nib of the split reed into the black of the palate that sat before him, the words appeared scratched across the yellowed surface. The noise repeated itself at other tables around the room and in the library's quiet, its scratch and susurration sounded loud in the silence.

There appeared little else to be gained from this room and eventually, after looking up and down at where the carved containers held the writing of the past, Nofret arrived back where the high priest stood by the door.

"Thank you for showing me around, Teos."

Returning outside, Essam and her priests remained in wait, and the Priestess of *Hathor* extended her hand and gestured for her men to rise. Turning to the high priest, she made sure he understood her eagerness and devotion to the obligation placed upon her. In essence, she was his equal in the ministries she would perform for the goddess, and in her last words, she wanted to show her strength.

"Tomorrow the Temple of *Hathor* will be open to those who wish to pay tribute," she said fervently, as she made to leave. "And I shall begin my residence with a special morning blessing in honour of her name and the deeds that surround it."

Teos dropped his head in recognition and, returning to his seat to continue his enjoyment of the offerings, Nofret led her priests away along the short walkway and returned to the front of her temple. Stopping to look up at the grand façade dedicated to *Hathor*, she called out to Essam before he disappeared into the interior, and awaited his return.

"Walk with me, Essam," she instructed her senior priest. "You must show me the island."

The Island of Philae was not overly large, being roughly 857 cubits in length and 285 cubits across, but the two took their time as the older man pointed out its main features.

The temple built for the Goddess *Isis* took up the greater part of the buildings and gloried in its ceremonies, while around, the smaller ones seemed somewhat dilapidated and disused. Reaching the westernmost aspect of the goddess's temple, the Nilometer, which calculated the clarity and water level of the river during the annual flood, stood below them on the island's edge. Steps led down to the well-like structure and descended to where the water line fluctuated in its annual rise. Here, in the season of *Akhet*, the period of inundation, the priests monitored the day-to-day level to determine the summer flood. If the waters rose well and spread their richness across the lands, then taxes could be increased and the common man would expect to pay more as his harvest swelled. At present, in the season of *Shemu*, the water stood low, but come the hoped-for deluge, the river would rise and flood the lands with its outpouring.

Nofret looked down and noting the water below her, saw the marks on the side of the well where the heights of the Nile, in some years great while in others small, had been recorded in the past. She knew the gods would be called upon to grant their favour of a good flood and an equally good harvest and, aware she must play her part in invoking them, she stood tall at the lip of the well and turned to stare over the sacred island.

"Tomorrow, Essam, I want Musa to be present when the boat arrives. We must announce that the Goddess *Hathor* can once more be petitioned!"

Returning to her rooms behind the altar, Nofret put aside her worries and, concentrating on the power given in her posting, she let the authority wrap itself around her as she vowed to continue her life in tribute to the great Goddess *Hathor*.

***

In the night, Nofret awoke from her dreams to the sound of scratching at the bottom of her door. Rising, she put her ear to the wood but hesitated to open it. It was known that these islands were rat-infested and, not wishing to share her room with these pests, she returned to her bed. Staring up at the white of the ceiling, she lay awake until the noise eventually stopped.

CHAPTER TWO

The scratching noise, along with the stifling heat, awoke Nofret a further three times in the night as she passed in and out of her dreams, until, as the darkness turned grey, she left sleep behind. Rising to prepare for the morning, she began the routine which governed her life.

Last, as the greyness was pushed to the corners of the room, she fixed her wig, and staring into the polished metal of the small hand mirror, appeared satisfied with her presentation. Picking up her sistrum, she opened the door. The passageway beyond was in darkness, but on stepping out, a clay light had been left at one side and, lofting it, the shadows fled.

Suddenly, a cry was heard at her feet, startling her. She instantly froze, and lowering the lamp, a cat danced in the silhouette of the flames. Brushing itself around her legs, it purred noisily.

Nofret had no fear of these creatures, for the Temple at Dendera was overrun with them, but this was the first seen on the island. Reaching down with a rattle of her beaded wrists, she touched the animal lightly on the head.

"Have you been scratching at my door?"

The cat purred even more loudly, and after stretching up at her stroke, it again wrapped itself around her legs.

"Well, next time, make yourself better known."

She pushed the cat aside with her sandalled foot, and closing the door, raised the torch. The cat skittered before her along the walkway, and on entering the small hall of columns, it disappeared into the dark.

***

In the early hours, Musa, the youngest of the *wab* priests, had walked, torch in hand, to the arrival point of Basim's boat and, standing alongside Samir the priest of the Temple of *Isis*, he waited beneath the overhang of the palms.

The white sail grew in his vision as it neared the landing place and as the voices of those bringing offerings disturbed the quiet, he stepped forwards and made his announcement.

"The Temple of the Goddess *Hathor* is once more open," he fervently declared as the greeted devotees made their way up the bank. "And prayers and donations may again be given in her name!" He repeated the mantra twice before ending, "The Priestess of *Hathor* awaits and gives praise to those who come to make offerings to the gods!"

However, he knew that these last long months, when the temple had been without its priestess, the offerings had fallen away. The commitment of the local people had moved to the worship of the Goddess *Isis* and her temple had prospered as the other diminished. It therefore came as little surprise that the line of men and women fell in behind Samir.

Musa followed dispiritedly, but as the last woman looked back, she stopped to wait for him to catch up. Holding out her hand, she presented the priest with a small basket containing dates, and atop this, she placed a circle of intertwined flowers from around her wrist.

"For the Mistress of the Sky," she said hurriedly, before running to catch up with the others, leaving Musa standing alone.

***

The Priestess of *Hathor* stood in wait outside the doorway to the temple courtyard and, watching the line of witnesses to the morning rituals pass by, she stood staring expectantly out from the shaded entrance. Musa finally arrived, carrying his offerings and Nofret, realising there were to be no devotees for *Hathor* that morning, turned away and began her service.

Entering the large forecourt, she rattled her sistrum as she led the men in song. Their voices rose as they walked towards the hypostyle hall and once entered, they crossed the tiled floor and their chant disappeared into the heads of the columns. Here, at the top of each hieroglyph-adorned pillar, the many carved representations of *Hathor* looked down as the echoes of the mantra answered back and filled the covered space.

Essam and Ramy, the two lector priests, carried the water and sacred oils to anoint the statue while Abbas and Kheti carried the white linen dress between them. Musa brought up the rear, holding the meagre offerings.

Passing into the smaller hall, the priestess brought them before the altar of *Hathor* and quietening her sistrum, the blessing of the goddess's statue was passed over to her men. Being a woman, it limited her sacred duties to the goddess, and so she stood to one side as the lector priests came forwards.

Essam carried the water and, dripping the liquid on the hands and feet of *Hathor*, he waited for Ramy to hand over the oils. Likewise, the limbs of the statue received a blessing with the fragranced pomade before the white linen dress passed forwards. Here Essam and Ramy stood on the raised steps on either side and dressed the goddess in her finery. Stepping down, the two made their chant and entreaties to *Hathor* and after the words known to all had been spoken and released into the world, they dropped their heads.

The last part of the service was then performed, and the small offering was brought forwards. Bowing his head, Musa held out the small basket of fruit topped by the flowers and Essam, taking this reverently from his hands, placed it at the foot of the goddess.

The service was soon coming to its end and after she had given the sacred rites, Nofret, as the Priestess of *Hathor*, entered the innermost shrine to the left of the statue and spoke her words in the goddess's presence. Muttering her invocations, she waited as *Ra*, the Sun God, was reborn into the world. Staring up to where this roofless building opened to the pale sky, she watched as the heavens turned to blue above the heads of the palm trees and, once again, she stood as witness to the birth of a new day.

***

The sun was rising further when the ceremony came to its end with the lighting of incense bouquets at the goddess's feet. And Nofret, leaving her priests to go about their duties, walked along the passage to her rooms.

Her obligations were over for the moment and, removing the wig, she let the cool air fall around her shoulders as she stood at the window. Her neck ached, and staring over at the bed, she remembered the discomfort and heat of the night. Dragging the couch away from the wall, she repositioned it opposite on the left side of the room and placed the small table at its side. This brought the head of the bed directly beneath the window, where the feel of a fresh breeze blew.

She then moved the remaining sparse furniture, first to one corner and then the other, until she felt happy with its position and that the room was hers. Finally, she placed around the few things she possessed before taking her lipstick, kohl and mirror through into the smaller wash area.

Sitting on the bed, she pulled her legs up and made herself comfortable, her back resting on the roughness of the cool wall beneath the window. But suddenly she realised she must show herself and, at least in these early days, be seen out and about as the new Priestess of *Hathor*. Standing, she replaced her wig, and after checking in the mirror, reapplied her lipstick before emerging into the fresh air.

The passageway to the temple had openings on either side, where the short tufted grass of the island grew in abundance, and a soft breeze met Nofret as she stepped out. Walking briskly, she passed along the western side of the temple, before reaching the front, where the lines of men and women, their hands now empty of gifts, were making their slow way back to the waterside and off the island.

The ceremony of offerings in the Temple of *Isis* had been much greater than those given that day to *Hathor* and time had passed as gifts were presented and many prayers said in hope of answer. It had only just come to its end.

Raising her hand to shield her dark eyes, Nofret called out to those passing.

"The Temple of *Hathor* is open to any wishing to honour the Goddess of the Sky and place their donations at her feet!" She paused for a moment, seeing no acknowledgment of her words, before looking up to where the sun shone brightly.

"The daughter of *Ra* awaits," she added, her voice rising, "and in the giving of her blessings she wishes to aid all those who ask for her help!"

There was still little reaction, the congregation eager to leave the island and return to their daily life. However, the young woman who had given Musa the dates lingered as the others strode past. Hesitating to approach, she shouted over.

"I'll make it known in the village that the Temple of *Hathor* can again be called upon, priestess." The girl smiled and turned away.

"What's your name?" Nofret eagerly called back.

"Yara!" the shout came over her shoulder.

"Thank you for that, Yara," the priestess replied. "The Mistress of the Stars is eternally grateful, and I'll say a special prayer in blessing for you!"

The young woman stopped and, bowing her head in acknowledgement, quickly ran to catch up with the group, who were heading beneath the palms. Here, their shadows lengthened before blending into the rising mist at the island's edge.

Nofret remained standing for many long moments as the tail of the procession completely disappeared and the island returned to its silence.

It seemed it was going to be a bigger task than expected. But she would see the name of *Hathor* once more spoken aloud and rejoiced, and the offerings lying at her feet would be increased in her name. Remembering the simple offering of dates given that morning, along with the ring of flowers, she knew she could certainly do better.

However, leaving that for the coming days, she

retraced her steps taken with Essam and, letting the shadow of the girdle wall guide her, she headed south.

Reaching the southern edge of the island, Nofret looked down at the place where she had been told her predecessor had met her death. The rocks here were huge. They rested on the island's fringe, having been carried down the first cataract on the annual inundations in the long past, and there any further travel stopped. They now formed a mixture of large granite boulders with smaller jagged stones built up in between. Here and there, greenery sprouted where the silt and soil of the past Nile risings had collected around them and the bees droned lazily amongst the flowering heads of the weeds.

The drop was deep, yet Nofret wondered if a fall would have killed someone. She was thinking of stepping down onto a small ledge which jutted out of the bank when a voice disturbed the silence.

"Priestess! Priestess!" The wind carried the voice of Musa, and rushing up, he waited for a moment for her to turn around and acknowledge him.

"High Priest Teos, wishes you to attend him!" He bowed his head in respect. "He seeks your immediate advice."

Nofret heard the words of command. But as a child, she never enjoyed being ordered around, and in her grown life, that had not changed. She knew her title was subsidiary to the high priest and she could be called his inferior, but she was unwilling to be rushed. Her thoughts at that moment remained with Safiya and, for some unknown reason, she wondered about the woman.

"Was the Priestess Safiya well liked, Musa?" She looked back at the rocks as the young *wab* priest reached her side.

"Yes, as far as I know." The young man stared over the rocks. "I liked her," he added. "She was highly thought of on the island and had been serving the Temple of *Hathor* for many years. We were all so upset when she went missing."

"Went missing?"

"Yes, she was gone many, many days before we found her body!"

The man glanced down and the image of the woman, her head caved in on one side, suddenly flashed before his eyes.

"She was there, just where that darker rock meets the water." His long finger pointed to the boundary of the jumbled boulders someway out from the drop, where at that moment, an ibis stood looking intently for crayfish and frogs.

"Was it you who found her, Musa?"

"No, it was Abbas. He says he heard words in a dream which led him here!"

Nofret stared long at the river-scoured rocks. Safiya could hardly have fallen to her death from the bank, yet be found so close to the water's edge. Imagining the body spread across the hardness of the headland, she ended, "Tell Teos I'll be along shortly."

***

Nofret walked slowly along the southern border, her mind still on the fate of the woman, but the scene was not giving anything further and the Nile moved past in its perpetual flow.

Leaving the water, she took the route through the outer halls of the Temple of *Isis*. Here many cats wandered through the walkways or else lay asleep in the temple's shade. The cool of the building gave instant relief from the outside, but she did not stop or linger and quickly left the temple behind. Crossing the sandy space which was interspersed with the homes of the priests, and passing between the ruins of an ancient building, she met the wall that surrounded the side of the high priest's home. Following it around, she found Teos awaiting her in the front courtyard and could immediately see his agitation as he paraded up and down.

"I thought to see you sooner!" he said, watching the priestess enter his gate. He stopped his pacing and stood in wait. The man was obviously angry, his dark eyes shining his frustration.

"Did you not get my message?"

"I did, but I was otherwise engaged, Teos!"

The man was holding a papyrus and handing it over, he added, "The nomarch is wishing to pay homage to the new Priestess of *Hathor* and in his capacity of governor, he wishes to make a visit."

"Does he say when?" The request came as a surprise and Nofret wondered about the man's interest.

"No, he asks only when it would be convenient." The high priest looked again at the hieroglyphs spread across the papyrus. "He's left it for you to decide!"

"Then tomorrow in the afternoon will be favourable, if it suits the nomarch."

Teos nodded his head and, turning to where a young boy stood invisibly in wait, he raised his hand and waved him over. Given his instruction, the young lad scurried off to where a boat awaited the reply.

The high priest, having seen the intrusion into his ordered life dealt with, then gestured for the woman to sit beneath the shade of a palm where two stools and a low table stood in wait. His attitude slowly softened and, watching the chickens emerge from beneath the bushes and pick their way through the sand, he sat back and let out a long sigh.

Nofret, however, was thinking of the following day and as the silence gathered, she voiced her concern.

"Is it usual for the nomarch to make a visit, Teos?"

"Not usually, but he does occasionally come on special feast days and, of course, he always takes an interest in the season of *Akhet*!" He held out a woven platter containing honey cakes while a ring of dates sat around its edge.

"Well, of course he would!" Nofret accepted the offering. "Taxes must be assessed and paid."

"Yes, we are all subjugated by the need for wealth," the man reasoned. He took a bite out of a cake and let the crumbs fall to the ground. "But now let me ask. How are you finding your new position? Was the service to the Goddess *Hathor* to your satisfaction?"

"It was given in honour of the goddess and in that it was fine," Nofret guardedly acknowledged, not wanting to show her disappointment in the absence of devotees. "And my thanks for your asking."

"Perhaps the offerings, or lack of them, were not as expected?" The high priest looked knowingly at the woman.

"Perhaps." Nofret let a smile cross her face. "But I foresee that to change in the coming days."

"Well, people move on and their prayers are said to those who listen. However, surely the interest of the nomarch will play in your favour and the word will be passed around."

"He'll be made most welcome!"

"Good! Now, let me show you the ruins of the Temple of Augustus."

The high priest stood and, eagerly leaving the shade, he led the way out of his gate. Taking great pride in his knowledge of the history of the island, he escorted the young woman around the fallen walls of the temple. Nofret followed and listened with great interest as the rise of the Philae Island complex was further explained.

She left Teos later in the day and, holding a woven plate of fish and flatbread which had been gifted, she returned to where her priests awaited. That evening, the dates given in offering to *Hathor* were enjoyed along with the fish and bread and after the oblong grid of a board lay scratched in the sand, Nofret watched Essam and Ramy play a game of senet with their black and white stones. Essam eventually won after the white tokens deftly moved off the board in his favour and, accepting the praise of the small assembly, the evening was deemed almost over.

There remained one last service to the goddess to be performed and as Nofret stood in witness, she watched as Essam and Ramy took down the white linen wrap from around the statue. Folding it over their arms, they blew out the smouldering incense.

Leaving the goddess to the dark of the temple, the only light came from a solitary flame that stood at her feet and reflected upwards to where her finely chiselled face looked out into the dark.

***

The Priestess of *Hathor* slept better that night, the slight breeze from the window giving some relief from the stifling heat. But before she did, the scratching noise began at the door. On reaching it, she pressed her ear to the wood before cautiously lifting the latch.

The dark, sleek shape of the cat shot through and disappeared beneath the bed and, after swiftly closing the door, Nofret cautiously lay back down. Within a short time, the cat's weight felt heavy at her feet. Slowly, as it made itself comfortable, and the woman turned on her side, it came to rest in the lower part of her back. The deep purr eventually subsided, trailing off into a silence as the two slept.

CHAPTER THREE

On waking, Nofret found she had the bed to herself, although the cat appeared to have only recently left, and the small area where it had rested still held a modicum of heat. She assumed it had gone through the window, but on kneeling on the bed and looking out, there was no sign of paw prints in the sand. The cat had simply disappeared.

She rose, hopeful that the morning would see a bigger assembly in the name of *Hathor* and singing to herself, she prepared her face and made ready for the service to her goddess. Fixing her wig, she checked her mirror before pulling over her robe and wrapping it securely around her waist. Picking up the sistrum, she rattled it to loosen the metal pieces before opening the door.

The passageway was windy as she stepped out and the desert's smell blew through, along with the shifting of the sands. The greyness that surrounded her led through into the hypostyle hall where a dark stillness met her, but here she did not linger. Carrying on across the tiled floor, she walked out into the courtyard and headed towards the main door. She thought Musa would again await the devotees and, wondering how he was doing and hoping he had better luck this morning, she stared out along the line of palms.

Musa had, as expected, joined Samir in wait for the boat, and watching as the craft emptied, they both called out in the name of their deity. As the day before, most organised themselves behind the Priest of *Isis*, but three young people stood next to Musa. Two were young women and the other a man, who looked to have only recently left his youth behind.

The young *wab* priest was relieved, and standing

beside Samir, they waited for the first glimpse of the sun at their backs on the eastern horizon before moving along the oft-trodden walkway.

The Priestess Nofret never let her eyes waver from the line of sand beneath the palms, and waiting at the door, her heart uplifted to see Samir and Musa walking side by side in the growing light of the new day. Letting the delight fill her face, she rattled the sistrum and let her welcoming chant fill the air. The line for the Temple of *Isis* was still far longer than that for *Hathor*, but it was a start, she thought, and in her soul, she felt a gratefulness rise alongside the feeling of relief.

Reaching the temple, Samir led his line past as Musa stopped and, as he stepped aside, the first person Nofret saw was the young woman, Yara. She was holding a basket of flatbread and dates in one hand while the other held tightly to the hand of the tall man at her side. Behind them, the other girl carried a small plate of silvered fish delicately crisscrossed over each other.

"It's good to see you here this morning, Yara." The welcoming voice of the priestess rang out in the morning's stillness.

The young woman bowed her head in acknowledgment and, holding out her hand, she presented her donation.

"We're here to give an offering to the Goddess of the Sky." Turning to the man at her side, she declared, "This is my husband, Abasi!" Looking behind she added, "And this is my sister, Basma."

Welcoming the three, Nofret turned away to face the doorway to the temple, and the witnesses fell in behind. The Priestess of *Hathor* began her chant and along with the rattle of the metal rings, she escorted them through into the courtyard and on into the hypostyle hall.

The ceremony in the name of *Hathor* played out before her statue. However, this time, on seeing the offerings placed at the feet of the goddess, Nofret accepted the pleas of the devotees and took their words into the sanctuary and appealed their case to the gods.

The words for Yara and Abasi were especially meaningful, and Nofret passed on their supplication to her goddess at length. The young couple had been married for some years and the disappointment seen on their family's faces, as each month passed, was disheartening. They had expected to be starting a family by now, like others who had married alongside them, but as yet, nothing had happened.

Disappointed, they had come to the island many times to appease the gods, but on eventually finding the Temple of *Hathor* closed, Yara had turned to the Goddess *Isis* in her desperation. Yet, still, her pleas had gone unheard. However, now the temple of the Cow Goddess had reopened, her petitions, she felt, would be better placed at the feet of one well known for giving aid to women who desired children.

The priestess had heard these words many times at the Temple of Dendera, for *Hathor* was one of the most widely worshipped deities and was often called upon in these circumstances. However, here they seemed just that more touching as, passing forwards her offering, the tears ran down the young woman's face.

Nofret returned from around her screen, the effects of the blue lotus showing in her shining eyes, and holding up her hands declared, "The great Goddess *Hathor* has heard your petition, and in the receiving of your gifts, she notes your words!"

The ceremony came to its end and, leaving her priests

to extinguish the dried blue-lotus-infused bouquets, Nofret walked alongside Yara and her husband and guided them out of the darkness of the temple where the brightness of the forecourt met them.

"You must keep faith in *Hathor*," Nofret instructed, taking hold of the woman's hand. "But remember, once she has answered your prayers, you must shout her name loud within your community!"

Knowing she could do little more, and hoping the couple would soon rejoice, she watched as they disappeared, hand in hand, beneath the doorway.

***

Mysis was the nomarch and administrator to the First Nome in Upper Egypt, the territorial division where the Island of Philae sat surrounded by the lands of the Nile valley, and in his governance, he likened his role to that of pharaoh in his own small world.

He had held the position since taking over from his father nearly twenty years ago and had brought about many changes of benefit to his collection of farmers and fishermen who lived and worked the nome. With this, their families were ever grateful for his authority.

He was well respected and his two wives had given him numerous children, which added to his reputation of abundance. He was, however, strict on taking taxes. Yet, in times when the inundation had been low, and the fields left dry and barren on their outskirts, and the farmers had seen only a pittance in the harvest of their hard labour, he had never taken advantage. With that, nevertheless, he also expected full payment when the gods had been good enough to lift the waters high! He was an honest and fair man and, more importantly, he always saw that his people did not go without.

Basim and his crew rowed Mysis over in the heat of the day and, landing at the island, he clambered up and stepped out beneath the palms. There, Essam met him. The two knew each other of old, but on this occasion, a ceremony was called for and respected on both sides, and Mysis awaited his invitation to follow the priest.

"The Priestess of *Hathor* welcomes you," the lector solemnly announced, "and wishes you to join her. She awaits you in the great temple."

Essam led the way as Mysis walked behind and in his hands, he carried a tray of washed figs upon a square of white finely woven cloth. He held them out before him as if they were precious jewels.

Reaching the temple, Ramy greeted them at the doorway and the two lector priests ushered the nomarch into the forecourt as behind, Abbas and Kheti followed, with Musa bringing up the rear. Around them, the columns topped with the heads of *Hathor* looked down as they walked her holy ground.

The party came to a halt at the far end of the forecourt as Essam raised his hand and, gesturing for Mysis to sit beneath the gaze of *Hathor*, the lector priest alone entered the hall.

Inside, the incense was drifting high, enveloping the statue of the goddess in its fragrance, and as Essam walked towards the altar, he came to a stop and dropped his head before his deity. Reaching out, he touched the left hand of the statue where the *ankh*, the symbol of life, was held and whispered his words.

"Praise to the Goddess *Hathor*, Mistress of the Sky and the Stars. Let her words of wisdom be heard and known throughout the lands!"

Stepping back, he lifted his head and called out, "Are you there, priestess?" His voice echoed around the chamber.

Nofret was in the shrine when she heard the voice and, aware Essam was bringing news of the nomarch's arrival, she rose from her knees and straightened her dress. Blowing out the incense under which she had been communing with her goddess, she stepped out and stood tall over the smaller man, her authority falling around her.

"The nomarch awaits, priestess."

"Thank you, Essam."

Nofret walked into the light of the courtyard, her flimsy dress enveloping her slim body and in her wake, the fingers of incense followed and cloaked her in a veil of mist. The fresh air filled her lungs and the lightness in her head slowly lifted as the sun shone fully upon her face.

The nomarch stood on seeing the woman.

"We are surely blessed to have someone of such beauty to represent the temple." The man let his head drop slightly, but his gaze never left the dark-rimmed eyes that stared back. "And the Goddess *Hathor* is favoured by your presence."

"The Goddess *Hathor* is beyond beauty, my lord!" the woman rebuked. "And it is I who am favoured by her approval."

"Of course. I meant no disrespect." The man laughed as he held out the figs which glistened in the sun.

"You have gifts for the goddess?" Nofret happily asked, on seeing the gesture. "Come, let us place them at her feet."

Leading the way, the priestess returned to the columned hall, and the two approached the altar. The nomarch bowed his head as he placed his offering, but on staring up, he gazed at the goddess before him and Nofret saw his lips move as he spoke his words of prayer and petition.

The offering given, the two moved back as the incense of blue lotus clouded the air and enveloped them in its lingering vapour. Its effect slowly heightened and, wishing to replace it with the clearness of the day, the nomarch hastened to leave.

"Shall we sit in the sun?" he whispered. He coughed as the fragrance hit the back of his throat and, for some moments, felt a euphoric lightness fill his head.

The Priestess of *Hathor* knew the incense had little effect on those used to its action upon the senses, but realising the man was feeling its impact, she led him back into the forecourt. Carrying on through, they left the goddess and her temple behind. Seated on the grassy edge beneath the palms opposite the great doorway, they let the lingering fumes of the lotus drift away in the breeze.

Above them, the wind whistled high, but here on the ground, the only sound heard was the constant call of the cicadas as they disturbed the silence.

"We're pleased you arrived so quickly, Nofret," the nomarch eventually began, making himself comfortable on the sand. "You must know our village has been lost without the guidance of this temple!"

"I feel the Temple Priests at Dendera were loath to leave this island without its priestess for long." She left a few moments between her words before continuing, "But the Temple of *Isis* has surely benefitted!"

"Yes, I can agree with that." The man let his eyes

wander over to the temple in the west. "Most have turned to her in their prayers, for we have never, in my time, seen this temple without its priestess." His eyes came back to where Musa was brushing the windblown sand away from the temple door.

"But now we have you, and *Hathor* can again receive our appeals!" He patted her hand in a fatherly way before finishing, "I'll send words of thanks to the High Priestess at Dendera when I send my next report down the Nile."

"I'm sure they will be gratefully received!"

Their talk turned to the affairs of the nome and Governor Mysis gave Nofret an insight into the amount of people she could hopefully entice back to the temple. The area sat on both sides of the Nile, but in the main, the east side was more densely populated, being where Mysis had his main family home.

Around him, he explained, the village spread in its messy disorder of streets and workshops, and briefly, Nofret thought of her own home by the sea with its rat run of lanes and feeling of enclosure.

"Our village was here before the island held its temples," Mysis explained, "and we have served the priests and priestesses for as long as the worship of the gods has taken place here."

He spoke of the *wab* priests who had been born in the nearby village and who served the Triad of *Isis*, *Osiris* and *Horus*, along with those dedicated to the Temple of *Hathor*.

"Kheti and Musa are both from the close by banks of the Nile," he further explained, "and you must realise that at certain times during *Akhet*, when the rivers rise and run full, they will be absent to do their share of the work on the land."

This was nothing new to Nofret, for the work of the *wab* priest was known throughout the Nile and in some places, they came and went on a daily basis. However, speaking of the village, Nofret wondered if Safiya was known there.

"Did you know the last priestess?" she tentatively asked. "Was she also from the village?"

"She was not from here," the man said, shaking his head. "I think like you, she came from Dendera."

"The Priestesses of *Hathor* are all trained at Dendera," Nofret explained. "But they come from far and wide across the country. I was born on the edge of the Red Sea and of low birth, but that did not stop me from attaining this position!"

"Well, all I can say is that, from my knowing, Safiya was highborn." The man shuffled around on the soft sand. "But then, as we only met on certain occasions, I can hardly form an opinion!" He stared out over at the temple building, before adding, "However, I have been told she was well-liked in her service to the gods and did her duty to the temple."

"And nothing else?"

"What else is there for a priestess to do?"

Nofret knew the world of the temple and its priests could sometimes be a separate entity to the world around and, at times, neither they nor the people who worked the Nile wished for the intervention of the other. Most seemed happy to enjoy their lives in their separate ways and to call upon the gods in their need, and Nofret could not argue with that. But she was surprised that the nomarch had so little to say about the priestess and she turned her attention to her recently gained knowledge.

"I understand she went missing?"

"Yes, but as far as I know, it was not for long." The man leaned back against the tree and, stretching his legs, he relaxed in the woman's presence. "Teos made me aware she was absent, and he seemed unconcerned."

"But she was found dead!"

"Yes, eventually," the man conceded, his words being chosen carefully. "But in my understanding, one of her priests found her on the island and that was surely temple business!"

"Then there was no inquiry?"

Nofret reasoned that as nomarch to the area, Mysis would have needed to make his record and let the news travel down the Nile to be documented and, if need be, investigated.

"No, I felt it wasn't required and left it in the hands of Teos."

"But you let the Temple of Dendera know about the need for a replacement?"

"No. That I also left for the high priest."

Nofret stared at her hands and let the words sink in. There had been no investigation regarding Safiya's death and she could not help feeling that was lax on the part of the governor.

The silence filled the space between them, and in it, Mysis took advantage. Feeling he was being assessed on his lack of control and judgement over the situation, he hoped to move on and change the subject.

"I understand my son, Abasi, and his wife gave an offering this morning?"

"They did," Nofret slowly acknowledged, suddenly aware of the couple's connection. "And I have spoken their words to *Hathor*!"

"Good, I hope the goddess will have heard." He leaned

forwards and stared once more at the temple walls, where the carved images of the Cow Goddess sat surrounded by her hieroglyphs. "Then let us hope we'll soon see an increase in Yara's waistline!"

The meeting appeared to be over with these last sharply spoken words and Mysis rose stiffly from the ground. Brushing the sand off his clothes, he stared again at where the Temple of *Isis* stood on the far bank. The sun was heading into the west, passing over and letting its rays fall on the glory of the buildings. Shading his eyes, he watched as an ibis sailed down to sit atop one of the carved pillars.

He stood frozen for some moments until Nofret coughed and he lowered his hand. Holding it out, he gestured for the priestess to lead the way. Smiling into the dark eyes, he finished, "Now let me talk with the high priest and enjoy some of the bounty of this great island!"

***

Teos had been waiting patiently, filling his time in watching his scribes continue their constant scratch across the papyrus, but eventually, the sound began to irritate and the stuffiness of the sanctuary clouded his mind. He sought the freshness and quiet of the gardens, and walking out through the back, reached the edge of the island and peered across the ever-flowing Nile.

The hippos were there as usual in their recognised group, and the enormous head of the dominant male sat perched across the shoulders of one of his subordinates. He looked as if asleep, a deep smile of satisfaction covering his face, while his beady eyes were tightly closed. His ears occasionally twitched, giving him a comical look, as the mosquitos played up from the water. Teos smiled at their contentment, knowing the ferocity of these beasts.

Suddenly, the male yawned widely, showing off his tusks, and let out a roar that disturbed the group. The water, without warning, became alive with activity before an order of sorts eventually returned and they slowly settled back into their slumber.

The Nile appeared sluggish in the heat of the day yet continued in its forever flow past the island, and the high priest, having stared out at the familiar scene for some time, turned away. Feeling he should check on the whereabouts of the nomarch, he headed around to the gate. He was hoping the meeting between the governor and his new priestess would have gone well.

Nearing the wall, he saw, in the distance, Nofret leading Mysis across the sandy stretch of the island. The two seemed deep in talk and, waiting beside the garden path, he let them come to him.

"Welcome, Mysis." Teos held out his hands as the figures reached the gate. "The Goddess *Isis* gives her blessing at our meeting!"

"Many welcomes to you too, Teos." The governor graciously bowed his head.

The high priest and the nomarch met as old friends and Nofret, with a quick nod to both men, left the two to their talk. Passing through the gateway, she heard a laugh along with a lightness in their voices. Looking back, she paused and watched as, with arms thrown around each other's shoulders in companionship, they disappeared into the shade of the house.

Leaving behind the high priest's home, she was unsure of her thoughts on Mysis. In this first meeting, he appeared genial enough, but she had noted his shortness in speaking of his son's wife and wondered why that should be. *Perhaps it was her lack of providing a grandchild.* She knew how important family was to those who worked the soil of the Nile and, as a young novice, had received tuition in their expectations.

As a Priestess of *Hathor*, she had often been called upon by the high and the low in their need to thrive and prosper. Yet in her short lifetime, this was her first meeting with a nomarch of the Upper Nile, and she felt unschooled and with little insight into the dealings of governance along its stretch. She felt out of her depth in this aspect and, hoping to improve her knowledge, she vowed that the following day she would seek advice from the library of Teos.

However, one thing she had learned was that the death of Safiya had been dealt with by those on the island, and wanting to find out more about this, and find where the body of the priestess lay, she went in search of Essam.

CHAPTER FOUR

"What happened to the body of Safiya?" Nofret directly asked, on finding Essam seated behind the Temple of *Hathor*. He was eating a ripe melon, spitting the seeds to his side, and the collection had formed a small pyramid of pips.

"She's buried beneath the temple." The lector priest nodded his bald head towards the Temple of *Isis* and, placing the empty rind aside, he wiped his hands on the cloth that covered his knees. "All the priests and priestesses of the island are there."

Nofret gazed to where the light of the day lit the magnificently carved walled statues of the gods. It seemed odd to her that the departed lay here on the island when the west bank, the land of the dead, sat so close.

"Can you show me?"

"The catacombs are kept locked." The man seemed surprised at her asking, and cautious in his reply, he glared up at the woman. "For the most part, priestess, we leave alone those who have passed on to their rest and the contentment of the Field of Reeds."

Nofret knew it was usual for catacombs to remain closed and the dead left to the peace of the afterlife. However, on certain festival days, they were opened and friends and family members could celebrate their loved ones and pay homage. With this in mind, she thought she might use it.

"Yes, I know they're kept locked, Essam. But, as Safiya's replacement, I'd like to show my respects to her."

The lector looked doubtful. He did not want to be doing this at this moment and in hoping to delay the event, he finished, "I'll need to ask Teos first."

"Do you have to?" Nofret did not wish to disturb the high priest and his visitor, and making known her station, she held her head high and stood tall above the man. "Surely, as Priestess to the Temple of *Hathor*, you can do as I request? Can't you just show me where she lies?"

Essam remained reluctant, but slowly unfolding his legs, he stood and impassively dropped the cloth over the pyramid of pips. "Very well. But I'll need to collect the keys."

The lector priest led the way, and the two walked the dusty space between the palms before entering the Temple of *Isis* through the pylon. There they carried on across the deserted forecourt. The priest went straight ahead and, climbing the short stairway, he moved to the right and led his priestess into the shadow of the hypostyle hall.

It was the second time Nofret had entered the temple since joining the procession on her arrival, but on her first, her attention had concentrated solely on the grandeur of the ceremony as they paraded down the middle. There, in giving homage to the triad, she had been in the moment and witness to the ritual. Now, however, standing to one side of the main walkway, she had time to look around.

The temple, at this time of day, was silent, the echoing chants of the priests, priestesses and supplicants given over to the hushed voices of the lowly *wab* priests who brushed away the constant wind-blown inundation of the sand from the foot-polished floor. Ensuring the columns with their carved figures and hieroglyphs remained free of bird droppings, the servants of the temple tidied around their feet and readied the sanctuary for the next service. It was a full-time job, for above their heads, at the top of the roof where the clerestory windows directed the sunlight down, the doves and pigeons hid from the scorching mid-afternoon sun and occasionally added their droppings.

At Nofret's feet, the skinny cats of the island also sought the shade and lying on the coolness of the temple floor, they lounged around the polished bases of the tall statues and darted between the rising columns. They were everywhere, but in their presence, they graced the gods.

Halfway down the echoing temple, Essam raised his hand and Nofret came to a stop. The walkway here was criss-crossed by the light of the upper windows, but oil lamps sat placed low between the feet of the statues that lined the walls and their glow added to the place's mystery.

"Wait here," he whispered, and leaving her in the light beside a carved column showing the rising figure of *Horus*, the lector priest disappeared into the gloom.

Nofret peered up to where the god arose, his beaked head staring into the west. The deep carvings surrounding his richly painted name stood out, and the words in his celebration disappeared into the gloom of the expanse rising above her head.

Reaching out to the cool of the stone, she hesitated to touch the declarations as her fingers hovered over the sacred words. Her education at Dendera had included the reading of hieroglyphs and, whispering the inscriptions that sat beneath her fingers, she muttered the incantations that sat around the reds, blues and golds of the colossal figure. Many cartouches held his name and stood well over a hand span across. In one he was called '*Horus* the Great' and in another '*Horus* in the horizon' while alongside, the ornately carved hieroglyphs showed the *Wedjat* eyes of *Horus*, the right representing the Sun God

Ra while the left represented the moon along with aspects of healing, well-being and heavenly protection.

Nofret slowly let her hand drop and, leaving the god to continue his stare across time, she followed the wall along. The surrounding columns rose high and the many pillars, each topped with a polychrome floral capital, led down the length of the hallway. The temple in the north, Nofret reckoned, was far bigger than this, and with its mud-brick wall which surrounded its might, it gave a sense of enclosure. Yet, here in the southern reaches of the valley, the worship of the triad of gods could not be called lacking, for the exaltation of the three within the colossal structure had grown in the citizen's favour.

Essam eventually returned, having fetched the keys to the entrance from the high priest's side office. Finding Nofret seated before the gods, he pushed aside a cat that lay stretched at her feet and picked up the oil lamp from the niche opposite. Leaving the cats to the silence, they left *Horus* and the other gods in the gloom.

The two stepped back into the brightness of the day and, heading to the right around the wall of the temple, Essam walked directly towards the sparkling water of the river. Reaching the island's edge, he stopped and looked over to the west bank where the pod of hippos basked in the sun. The catacombs lay below the temple, an ornate metal-worked gate locked and barred from any outsiders. Yet, as he held the keys at his side, the reluctance to enter the place again came over him.

"Are you sure this is necessary?" There was a reticence to his voice, along with something Nofret did not recognise. *Was it fear?* she thought as he ended, "Do we really need to disturb the dead?" He looked directly at her, his eyes wide.

"I need to give my respects!" Nofret firmly maintained. "And I'm sure I'll not be offending the dead." Gathering several corn poppies that straggled the boundary of the island, she bunched them together and tied them around with a strong slip of grass.

Essam knew he could not avoid the request of his priestess and, reluctantly stepping down, his foot found the small flat ledge which jutted out. The stairway was invisible unless standing directly over it and Nofret, knowing she had passed this way on her tour of the island and obviously not seen it, carefully leaned out over the bank. The steps could easily be mistaken for a build-up of the roughly tumbled rocks that ringed the island unless you looked to where the well-worn path led down. Essam, knowing the way of the dead, moved from one stepping stone to the next before his head disappeared beneath the overhang of the island's edge.

The priestess, wrapping around her long dress, hesitantly followed, her right hand grabbing hold of the tufted boundary while her left hung on to her tribute. She felt any moment she could slip and fall between the boulders, but watching where she placed her feet, she steadily dropped out of sight.

Reaching the point where the lector priest had vanished, she discovered an open-roofed tunnel between the rocks and, entering, found it stopped inwards of the river at a small steep stairway. Essam was standing at the top, the light held high and, seeing Nofret raise her head, he gestured for her to follow.

He seemed in no hurry to open the gate and, bringing his hands to rest on the ornate metal of the outer barrier, he waited as the priestess arrived at his side.

Nofret noted there was a double door into the bank

and after Essam swung open these first railings, a wooden wall beyond filled the entire opening. It was solid wood but inset within, a small door large enough for a sarcophagus stood outlined. The second key opened it. Essam stepped back as the build-up of trapped air escaped before he wedged the door open with a large rock and let the breeze blow away the musty smell of the catacombs.

Lifting the light, he stepped over the threshold and took the flight of chiselled steps downwards. The darkness was instantly overpowering after the brightness of the day, and the unexpected chill of the lower caves of the island gave the feeling of enclosure. Nofret, being tall, kept her head bowed and followed the smoking light held by Essam.

The steps were steep, the walls alongside cut and highly polished, and they took them straight to the bottom where the tunnel flattened out. Here the walls became interspersed with many ledges surrounded by carved and painted depictions of the Weighing of the Heart Ceremony, along with images of the Field of Reeds.

Inside the dark sills, the caskets of the long dead lay stretched out on the flat-backed shelves cut from the syenite rocks and, climbing high on either side, the slit-like portals sat one above the other. The sarcophagi here were ancient and lay with their feet facing west, back over Nofret's shoulder, so that as the spirits of the dead arose, they would be guided over the water and onto the west bank of the river.

These were as the priestess expected, but suddenly being so close to the Nile, she briefly wondered about flooding. Looking down in the pitiful light, the dusty floor appeared untouched by water, and the painted walls which stood floor to ceiling were undamaged.

Around her, extensions to this main corridor had been added over countless years, the rocks first roughly hewn out to be used elsewhere, before the master craftsmen had polished the walls and richly carved them in their hieroglyphs. However, over time, the passageway had changed from being the lining of burial openings, to instead becoming whole rooms excavated out of the island's structure. These still held those who passed into the realm of eternity, and within them, the sarcophagi remained sat within their enclosures.

The catacombs wound on and on beneath the Temple of *Isis* and Nofret, her hands held out on either side to brush the walls, tried to remember their twists and turns. But, she eventually lost count of the right and lefts they took as the surrounding darkness closed in on their backs. Occasionally, the light before her threatened to go out and a sudden fear gripped her. Essam, however, quickly blew on the embers to reignite the flame.

The corridor came to its end at a solid polished wall, bringing them to a stop. But at its side, two entrances loomed, one on the right and the other directly opposite. Essam raised his lamp, and treading carefully to the left, he let the flame guide him through. Nofret stepped in after him and stood within the crypt.

Two funerary boxes lay within, one near the wall while the other sat squarely in its middle. They looked as if painted only yesterday. Around them, and over their colourful lids, rings of dried and desiccated flowers held a hint of colour. No niches, as yet, had been started in these walls and the two sat flat on the dusty, stony ground. The ceiling felt low to Nofret and instinctively she dropped her head.

"These are the latest to find their rest here. Safiya and Jomana." Essam's voice echoed around the confines of the chamber. The place seemed to hold a fear for him and his agitation grew as the smoke of the flame thickened, and the light continued its threat to go out once more in the near-airless room.

"Which one is Safiya?" Nofret whispered, staring at the two sarcophagi.

The man, holding his hand over his face to ward off the miasma of death, pointed to the one beside the wall. This casket was not overly decorated, but the painted face of the dead priestess stared out ornately from the wooden surface, and her pale hands with their long fingers sat entwined and crossed at her chest. Below these, the body of the box was painted a plain bright white, apart from where a line of black hieroglyphs bled down its middle.

Stooping, Nofret walked over and waved Essam to follow. Standing at her side, the lector priest raised the meagre light as his priestess knelt and read the funerary texts. These appeared to be the usual words which accompanied a body on its journey into the afterlife, but the cartouches at either end detailed Safiya's names and titles.

The container held the mummified body of the priestess but remained sealed to those who walked beneath the Eye of *Ra* and Nofret respectfully placed her offering along the coffin top. Bending her head, she took time to whisper her words.

Yet, on finishing her blessing of the woman she had never known, the new Priestess of *Hathor* knew there was little else to do or see apart from the grave goods that accompanied the casket. These lay scattered at the base of the sarcophagus, but appeared to be the usual items given for a priestess's last journey. Most were jars of unguents needed for the day-to-day rituals and, alongside, a set of combs and many strings of coloured beads sat within the gathering dust.

Last, the priestess picked up and turned around a small pot of tiny malachite stones that sat alongside the slate palette needed to grind them. There was no inscription and after taking out the stopper and having a quick sniff, she placed it carefully down.

However, looking along to where the foot of the sarcophagus faced west, she noted an exquisite wooden senet board seated in the dust. The four throwing sticks lay alongside, all facing white-side up. On the thirty cedar and ivory squares which sat in rows along the top of the board, two carved pieces remained in play. One, a conical-shaped tower sat upon house number 28, 'The House of Three Truths', while the other, a small, flat token, sat on number 15, 'The House of Rebirth'.

Nofret had often taken part in this game at Dendera, her choice of using the flat token over the shaped one directing her play, and fleetingly she wondered which side Safiya had picked. The remaining pieces lay about the board, the four flat tokens collected at one side, while the same number of towers sat randomly in the dust. Unknowing why, she retrieved the painted throwing sticks and tossed them into the musty air. They came down three white and one black. Reaching forwards, she plucked away the conical piece and placed it down beside the others. The game was over and after wiping off the last disc, the senet board sat ready for the next play!

She sat back on her heels. There appeared nothing further to see and, although she had not known what to expect, Nofret felt a disappointment.

"Let's leave the departed to their rest, priestess." The voice of Essam filled the silence and, as the light of the flame flickered, threatening again to leave them in the dark, Nofret rose and turned away.

They made their hurried way out and a feeling of relief swept over Nofret as she saw the pinpoint light of day appear at the top of the steps. Reaching the doorway, she took in a breath of the fresh Nile air and waited as its sweet smell filled her lungs. Essam was quick to follow her through and, closing off the chambers, he locked the door and left the dead to their peace.

***

The heat of the afternoon met them as they returned to the edge of the island and, climbing the steep-sided slope, the fresh smell of the river breeze was welcoming after the suffocation of the caves. Nofret sat for some time on the sandy grass, letting the warmth of the air chase away the chill, as Essam sat at her side.

Across on the west bank, a laden donkey and its rider had seen the figures appear from beneath the island and, wondering who it was, had stopped to look across. After lifting his hand, the young boy shouted over his greeting and, seeing the raised hand in reply, he urged his mount on. Nofret watched the boy ride away and he and his donkey eventually disappeared into the overhanging palms.

"Are the dead dealt with on the island?" she eventually asked. She turned her gaze away from the river's flow as she thought of the chambers beneath her feet and the simple coffin of the dead priestess played in her mind.

"Yes, we have two *sem* priests on the island, Atsu, the

elder, and Garai, his assistant." Essam slowly stood and, towering over the seated woman, he finished, "They are under the administration of the Temple of *Isis* and High Priest Teos."

"Do they also serve the wider community?"

"Yes," the priest nodded in confirmation. "The banks of the Nile are also under their guardianship." Lifting his eyes to take in the sun's position in the sky, he saw its dip into the far horizon. A growing urgency to prepare the temple for the evening ceremonies arose in his thinking and stepping back from the island's edge, he finished, "Now, priestess, please forgive me, but my duty calls. *Ra* moves ever on, and I must be about the work of *Hathor*."

Leaving Nofret to continue her stare across the Nile along with her pondering on Safiya's end, Essam rushed to the temple. The path of the sun was heading westwards, and the lector priest, being delayed in his routine, had work to do.

***

Governor Mysis, on his return to the river crossing, passed the Temple of *Hathor* and, seeing Musa seated in the wall's shadow, he shouted over.

"Is Lector Essam around?"

The *wab* priest was casually peeling back the leaves off some corn, which lay in a heap at his feet and, placing the cobs aside, he appeared happy in his work. On hearing the shout, he looked up.

"Essam, is he around?" Mysis repeated, his hand raised to shade his eyes.

Musa nodded his head towards the temple entrance and, watching as the nomarch stalked across the sand before he disappeared through the temple door, he then went back to his work.

Inside the temple walls, Essam prepared the altar of *Hathor* for the evening's service and ensured the smaller statuettes that sat at her feet looked out on the assembly. Often, he found that these had moved slightly out of position and, thinking them disturbed by the attentions of Kheti or Abbas as they cleaned around the feet of their goddess, he carefully straightened them. Taking his time, he worked quietly in *Hathor*'s presence.

Mysis stood at the temple entrance and watched the man as he performed his ritual. But on seeing him bow his head and turn right towards the side doorway, he quietly followed. Stopping before the statue, he bowed his head and, finding a few grains of wheat in his pocket, he scattered them around and gave an offering.

Leaving behind the cool of the hall, Mysis found Essam at the back of the temple where he was washing himself in a stone bowl of cold Nile water. He was cleansing himself, splashing it over his head and hands. As the nomarch appeared, the priest moved away to sit in the shade and let the water drip onto the sand.

"Has the new priestess been greeted well, Essam?" Mysis dropped his hands into the refreshing bowl and, feeling the cool of the remaining water, he washed it up his wrists.

"Order is restored in the temple, Mysis." Essam raised his dripping hands to the sky, "And the 'Mistress of the Stars' is once more commemorated."

"Good." The nomarch shook his hands to flick off the droplets and, placing his damp fingers behind his head, he felt a brief respite from the swelter of the day. "Let's hope there'll be no more mishaps!"

Mysis joined Essam to sit and, being friends of old, the two talked the afternoon to its end.

Meanwhile, Nofret had continued her stare across the Nile and let her worries gather. She had a sense of something not quite right in Safiya's death, but as her thoughts bounced around, she could not give it a name. However, as Priestess to the Temple of *Hathor*, she thought she needed to be wiser in the island's history and, now being aware of the catacombs, she felt a duty to know more about them and their occupants. Remembering the papyri that filled the library of Teos, she felt a visit there might prove useful.

Finally, her mind resigned to finding out more, she left the Nile to continue in its forever flow and, following Essam's footsteps, returned to her ministrations in the temple.

***

The sleek brown Abyssinian cat was asleep on the bed when Nofret later entered and, seeing her by the light of the growing gloom, the priestess noted her age in the sandy greyness of her mouth. She was curled tightly near the wooden headrest that acted as a pillow, but her long tail dangled over the bed's edge.

"Am I to feel grateful for your presence?"

The cat opened an eye and, lifting its head, let out a soft chirrup in greeting. For its welcome, it got a pat on the head.

The priestess, taking off her wig, placed it carefully down and let the twisted tresses lie flat. Her scalp and neck were hot and the feel of the warm breeze from the window felt refreshing. Nofret hung her head and let the light wind cool her as she thought about the day.

Concern remained for Safiya. Yet not knowing why and feeling unable to shake it, she undressed and let the darkness creep around her.

Tomorrow she would visit the library and hopefully get more details on the island's underground and also seek to speak with Atsu, the *sem* priest. But feeling the tiredness of the day weighing heavily, she stretched out beside the cat and rested her hands over her tattooed stomach. Letting the cool evening breeze fill the room, the contented purr of the animal sent her to sleep, and she lost herself in her dreams.

CHAPTER FIVE

Yara and her husband attended the morning service to *Hathor*, and along with her sister, it included three more devotees. Seeing them, as Essam led his priests and the small procession followed, Nofret's thanksgiving to the gods soared. She did not doubt that the girl would return, and it looked like she had kept her word in making known the reopening of the temple.

The priestess's voice was uplifted as she welcomed them and after the goddess of the sky received her due veneration and offerings came forwards to be placed in honour at her feet, the ceremony moved on to Nofret taking with her the pleas of those present and conveying them directly to *Hathor*.

On her return, the blue lotus giving her the usual gentle euphoric gratification, Nofret raised her hands to the tall statue on the altar and, pledging her words of devotion to her goddess, the service ended.

The priestess followed the group out into the courtyard and, walking beside them as they headed to the ferry, the fresh air filled her body and chased away the overpowering essence of the flower's perfume.

"The Goddess gives thanks for your gifts, Yara, and has heard your words." She took the hand of the young woman and, holding it lightly at her side, finished, "But you must continue in your prayers and give homage in her name."

Tears filled Yara's eyes as they strolled along the path, but reaching the waiting boat, she stopped and planted a kiss on Nofret's cheek before stepping down. "Thank you. *Dua netjer en etj*!" the girl repeated.

Nofret nodded her head in acceptance and, as she

watched the felucca move away, her hand lifted. To those who sat within the boat, her figure on the shoreline became a silhouette beneath the palms, before, finally, as the craft turned away in a sudden gust, her shadow disappeared.

The Priestess of *Hathor* did not return to the temple. Instead, feeling invigorated by the lotus and the service to her goddess, she walked past its doors and turned towards the house of Teos.

On the opposite side of the island, the ceremony in the Temple of *Isis* continued in its grandeur and as invocations were being given to the triad, Nofret hurried on with purpose in her step. For the moment, she was unsure of her concern for Safiya and, wondering if she was being silly about it, she did not as yet want Teos to know of this. However, he would feel nothing amiss, she thought, if the new Priestess of *Hathor* took an interest in the island and its temples.

Finding the door to his house thankfully open and the hallway deserted, she stepped through and headed to the library.

The room of scrolls was almost in darkness, a lone scribe seated in the light of a semicircle of flames as he finished an urgent missive to the Nomarch of Heliopolis, 'the City of the Sun' in the north. He appeared in complete absorption of his work, his head bent low over the parchment, but hearing the door close, he briefly looked up.

Nofret entered the gloom and, not knowing where to look in the walled expanse of papyri, stopped at the table and asked if there were maps of the island showing the temples and their surroundings. She was directed to the dark of the far corner and advised to look on the very top shelf. Giving her thanks, she lifted a light and left the man to his concentration.

The shelf was reached easily enough and bringing down a box that held a few dusty scrolls, Nofret blew on them and scattered the collected years of cobwebs and fine powder.

Seated with the papyri along the top of a desk, she untied the first and rolled it out. Spread out, and with the smooth stones of past use placed at each corner, it stayed flat and showed the outline of the island squarely on the page, along with the west and east banks drawn raggedly down each side. Between the two, the great Nile River sat indicated by the groups of hippos that the scribe had drawn lying beneath the water, their ears, eyes, and nostrils shown above the waterline. And on the banks, the scrawled crocodiles sat overly large in relation to the size of the island. The temples, though, were drawn in an artistic hand and sat surrounded by lines of light green painted palms. They were exquisite in their representation, but gave no detail of the exact size or shape of the buildings.

Nofret was unsure of what she sought, but thinking back to the climb down the bank of the island, she recognised the difficulty of getting a cumbersome coffin down that way. It was not impossible, and she knew the tomb diggers had their secrets. Yet, thinking of the many burials there, it was, apparently, a routine that had been performed many times. But, briefly, a thought crossed her mind.

What if there was another way in?

The first scroll gave no help on this, and hastily she rolled it away. The next two gave no insight either, but rolling out the fourth, the actual structures of the temples sat before her, drawn in an educated hand. These were more like architectural drawings, their lengths precisely measured and written along each plane. It had faded over time, but despite that, the linear lines filled the scroll, and as she peered down through the flicker of the flame, Nofret noted the side elevations of the Temple of *Isis*.

This scroll was the only one, she thought, *that might give any understanding*, but as time moved on, Nofret expected Teos's impending return and sensed an urgency to be away. She needed time to look more closely and study this one and, in hurrying to leave the room, she rolled it up and stuffed it inside the back of her belt where her robes hid it away. Returning the others to the box, she placed them back high and, without looking at where the scribe remained seated in his pool of light, she left the room.

The service to the triad in the Temple of *Isis* had indeed ended and meeting the returning retinue as it wound its way towards the high priest's home, Nofret stepped aside and bowed her head as the procession passed. Teos walked at the head and, remaining in the grip of the blue lotus, his eyes were wide and glazed as the words of the gods rang through his mind. Singing escorted him, and the raised voices of his priests and priestesses filled the surroundings of the island. But as the last passed, Nofret stopped a young ritual priest and asked where she could find Atsu, the *sem* priest.

She was told Atsu had not attended that morning's service and so could not, they thought, be on the island. Knowing the *sem* priest's jurisdiction included the banks of the Nile along with his service to the temples, Nofret thought he was about his business elsewhere. Thanking the young man for his answer, she hurried away. Feeling a need to examine the scroll in more detail, she returned to her rooms.

The cat was nowhere around but it had left the remains of a dead bird on the bed and, after removing the leavings through the window, the woman sat down. Retrieving the scroll, she unrolled it across the folded blanket. The architect had drawn the Temple of *Isis* in great detail and noted its dimensions in cubits, and in the margins, the profiles for each side of the structure received the same design. However, it was under the temple, its foundations and below, which Nofret looked at with interest.

These showed the layout of catacombs on two levels beneath the temple, the first drawn as ten irregular chambers with columns or walls separating them. These were the tunnels Essam had led her along with the rooms of sarcophagi leading off. But below this, further caverns could be seen. These sat way below the temple and although they did not appear to stretch as far as the burial chambers, they looked vast.

Nofret held the papyrus up. She was surprised at the immensity of the subterranean structures below the worshipper's feet, but whichever way she looked, the scroll gave no help in finding another way down. The architect had, however, drawn many shapes and diagrams in the margins and in the right-hand corner, a detail of the island sat with a small black arrow showing the side of the bank. This was where she and Essam had entered the catacombs.

Placing the scroll down, she wondered if she was looking for something that was not there, and a doubt rose in her mind. *Why am I even doing this?* True, she needed to know more about the island and its structures, and this certainly gave her more information. But this had no significance in the death of Safiya. She never even knew the woman and should leave well alone.

She sat for some time staring at the intricate lines, but the woman's death still unsettled her and with that, she felt it was her duty to find out more about Safiya herself.

***

Later, Nofret sat against the wall of the temple. The view here was pleasant and the shade of the palms guaranteed in the heat of the day. Sitting with the cool of the blocks at her back, she understood why Musa sat here to prepare their meals.

She had time to spare at that moment and, having decided to find out more about her predecessor, she waited to see if Atsu, the *sem* priest, would return. Seated in the warmth, her thoughts revolved around the visit to the catacombs. Having seen the painted face of the woman, her fate was beginning to be more on her mind and started to bother her. *She could have been injured from a fall from the island's edge,* Nofret reasoned, *but to have succumbed to it?* She thought it unlikely. *But if not, then how or where did she die?* Feeling the Island of Philae itself had little more to give in answer, Nofret needed to know more about the woman's passing.

An aging figure eventually appeared on the path and walking slowly up the dappled walkway, he leaned heavily on the man at his side. Nofret looked doubtful as they approached. *This was surely not the* sem *priest!*

"Atsu?" Nofret tentatively called out as the two came closer.

The man stopped, and raising his hand, he acknowledged the priestess. "*Em hotep*! Great peace to you."

Nofret dropped her head in recognition of the greeting

before rising and asking, "Can you spare me a moment?" She dropped her head again in respect to the older man with his position of power on the island, and settling her robe about her, she straightened her wig and pushed the ornate bracelets up her arms. Smiling, she ended, "Come and sit with me for a while."

The figures changed direction and, reaching the temple walls, Atsu gently lowered himself to the ground and lent his bowed back against the cool wall. He introduced his assistant as Garai.

The two welcomed the peace and relief from the wailing grief and sorrow they had just left behind. They had returned from beginning the drying out process of the body of a small boy found on the river bank. The way of his death had been unknown and the local physician could give no reason, but as Atsu gently washed him down and whispered his incantations, the almost invisible pinprick of a small snake bite could be seen on the child's right foot.

He passed his findings on to the family. And after saying he would return the following day to wrap the boy ready for his burial in the sand-enclosed burial plots on the far side of the Nile, the *sem* priest watched the men, mattocks in hand, move down to the river to exact their revenge.

Atsu shook away the memory of the bleached body of the young child and, lifting his bald head, he smiled at the pretty girl at his side.

"We're blessed to yet again have such an elegant priestess in the temple and we give thanks to the gods for your presence!" He patted her hand and stared questioningly up at her. "Now, was there something you wanted from me?"

Nofret came straight to the point. "I wish to give a

special service in the name of Priestess Safiya," she explained, and hoping to find out more about her predecessor, she added, "And in giving thanks for her service to *Hathor*, I would celebrate her life."

She watched the older man nod his head in recognition of the remembrance of the woman before asking, "Is there anything you could tell me about her?"

The old man seemed happy to be approached on the subject. In his line of work, he was most highly respected and, as keeper of the sacred words and spells which guaranteed the afterlife, often treated only one step behind the high priest. However, he had, surprisingly, known little about the last Priestess of *Hathor*. He had seen her around the island and spoken occasionally to her, but the woman seemed to keep within the bounds of her domain and rarely attended services in the other temples.

He explained this to Nofret before finishing, "She was lovely, and had been here for some time, as I'm sure you have been told." The smile increased on the old man's face as he recalled the slim figure walking beneath the palms around the Temple of *Hathor*. Finally, he added, "But of her character, I feel lacking in any knowledge of that."

"Well, thank you, Atsu," Nofret accepted, but in his telling, she was realising the woman would not be easy to get to know.

"But then what of her end?" she tentatively asked. "Surely you can enlighten me on that?"

"That came far too soon!" Atsu looked down at his hands.

The *sem* priest had been a young boy when he was first instructed in the art of mummification and, over the years, had perfected his skills to where he now stood in the island's community. He had seen it all, or so he thought, except for those brought off the battlefield. Yet on laying the young woman out, his heart had dropped as he saw her injury.

Her head was caved in on the left-hand side and the eye socket had collapsed, leaving the bloody orb dangling, squashed, and useless over her cheek. Dried blood plastered her shaved head and neck, and the left ear was missing as if torn away. Her ringed hands bore heavy scratch marks, and the nails at her fingertips were broken and torn. He had written all his findings down with a shaky hand, and his assistant had taken the papyrus to Teos.

"They found her body in the south," he eventually continued, and turning his head, he nodded in indication over his shoulder. Pushing away the vision of the woman, he brought his eyes to rest on the beautiful priestess who sat before him and finished, "She had succumbed to such grievous head injuries!"

"Such as?" Nofret let an alarm sound in her voice on hearing the words. This was the first time this had been mentioned. She had thought the woman more likely to have drowned. However, on hearing the report of the *sem* priest, it seemed doubtful.

"Injuries that are far too dreadful to be spoken of on such a glorious day!" Atsu would not be drawn further on the details, feeling the dead that had passed through his hands should rest in peace.

However, Nofret needed to know more. "Did the water kill her?"

"I think that is unlikely, given the injuries. But who knows?"

Rising suddenly with the help of Garai, the man

brought the conversation to an end with a flick of his white linen robe. "Now, I shall leave you to the work of *Hathor* and give my report of today's matters to the high priest." He looked in concern towards the water's edge and beyond to where the east bank rose sharply. "I feel Teos will want to send his condolences."

Holding out his hand, he wished Nofret *senebet*, and giving his farewell, he turned his back on the temple.

Nofret watched the figures leave, but she was not happy with the quick ending to their talk. She had further questions she would have liked answered. Yet as Atsu disappeared along the path, she thought they must wait for another time.

***

The evening light faded and Nofret joined her priests to sit at the back of the temple in the firelight. Watching the sparks fly into the overhanging palms, they spoke with soft voices as the bats flitted overhead. A senet board sat once more scratched between them in the sand, but the black and white counters remained gathered together and the throwing canes stood upright, their ends sticking out of the sand.

"I was thinking of having a commemoration in the temple for Safiya and giving tribute to her years in service of *Hathor*," Nofret tentatively began, as a sudden silence filled the camp. Wrapping her clothes around her shoulders, a slight chill was felt in the breeze and, in the light of the flames, she placed her hands towards the fire. "How do you feel about that?"

Musa and Abbas were eager to agree, but the other three seemed less so and Nofret quickly sensed a wish to move on and leave the past behind. She could not understand it and seemed surprised that Essam, especially, seemed disinclined. He shook his head at the suggestion and appeared loath to show his consent, but on seeing it, the priestess felt even more determined to see it done.

"Well, I feel it's something we must do." There was a certain authority in her voice as she finished, "And I'll be arranging it for the next Wag Festival."

The celebration of the dead, the Wag Festival, was many months off as yet, but the priestess felt in her heart that the Temple of *Hathor*, to whom Safiya had given her life, should commemorate her, if only this once. She looked around the gathering for acceptance and Lector Essam, seeing the determination around the young woman's face, could only concede. Yet, wishing to move the conversation on, he held out his hand towards the senet board and asked if she would play a game.

Nofret deftly picked up the stones and, sorting them out, set them alternating along the top line of ten spaces. Lifting the sticks, she threw them high in the air. They came down four black. It was the highest score, and after selecting to play the white stones, she again picked up the sticks and began her game. This time they came down two black and two white and, moving along two squares, she placed the sticks down and handed the game over. Essam eagerly picked them up and, throwing them high into the air, he smiled at his priestess. Nofret bowed her head to his challenge.

Time passed in the board's playing, but eventually, as the stars filled the night sky, the priestess, having won all her games, rose to leave. Letting the men continue in their play, she returned to her room and, throwing aside the wig, washed away her make-up. Kneeling on the bed, she let her arms rest on the window. Looking out, she could glimpse the Nile in the moonlight, and the cool breeze on her bare arms felt refreshing. Eventually, she lay down and closed her eyes.

The scratching started almost immediately and, on getting up to open the door, the cat sauntered into the room. She greeted Nofret with a soft cry. Receiving a quick stroke around the ears, she jumped on the bed and settled herself.

Nofret returned to lie down and stared wide-eyed into the greyness that filled the room. The moon was full and the shadowed shapes of the palm trees moved back and forth across the walls. The whisper of them came through the small window and, as Nofret strained her hearing, the constant and reassuring sound of the Nile played its tune in the distance.

***

In the early hours, as Nofret lay awake with her mind unable to stop, the cat jumped down and shot beneath the bed where it could be heard scratching. Leaning over the bed's edge and seeing the shape of the animal in the dark of the far corner, she wondered what it was doing. It kept pawing at something and Nofret thought it had caught a rat. However, watching its movement, it eventually blended into the dark and, as the scratching stopped, it disappeared.

Nofret immediately got up and, dragging the bed away, exposed the corner of the white wall. Dropping to her knees, the cat was nowhere around, but she could see where two pieces of the rough, hand-smoothed plaster fitted together and blended in seamlessly. As she prodded the place with her finger, a piece of it could easily be pushed aside and, angling her head to look along the floor, Nofret saw beyond to where the crumbling mud-brick hung together by its thin pieces of plasterwork. A hole sat within the foundations and, dipping down, it made a short tunnel to the outside. The cat's mysterious disappearance had, in Nofret's mind, at least, been solved.

CHAPTER SIX

The following morning, after the service to *Hathor* ended and her priestess had rejoiced in seeing further devotees, the temple returned to its peace. Nofret, seeing her *hem-netjer* about their work, took herself to the waterside to think. She had a lot going through her mind and her sleepless night had given no ease to her worries. Now aware that Safiya had received injuries that greatly upset the *sem* priest, she badly needed to find out more. Feeling she had been disturbed from inspecting the scene of her supposed death on her second day on the island, she headed in that direction.

As she passed the temples, the work of the island continued in its day-to-day routine and, in the sunlight, the cats darted between the pools of sunlight and played amongst the waving palms. Everything seemed serene in the island's setting, but in Nofret's mind there remained a doubt.

Reaching the craggy build-up at the southern tip, she paused briefly before kicking off her sandals and leaving them on the grass. She could see the darker shape of the rock picked out by Musa, as it balanced further out on the edge of the boulders. Stepping barefoot down onto the protruding ledge, she moved forwards onto the headland. Holding the grassy rim of the island, she carefully progressed along the boundary.

The limestone stonework on this southern extent had formed a wedge shape, leading back into the flow of the Nile. The rocks sloped gently on its western side and opposite, on the eastern edge, it seemed even steeper. However, on either side, the borders dropped away and the current of the river flowed lazily past on its journey north.

Nofret followed the shape of the rocks down and, letting go of her hold on the bankside, eventually reached the waterline. The Nile passed by sluggishly, but on bending and letting her fingers feel the refreshing coolness; she rose sharply as, passing by further out in the stream, a ripple worked its way against the flow. Stepping back instinctively in fear, she made her way back up the rocks before heading out from the island. It took some time to traverse the large boulders and, after carefully balancing on their hard, sharp edges, she let her bare feet find the grassy spaces formed between them.

The greenery spread wide around and, between the adjoining rocks, the wind-blown wild flowers had seeded and grown tall. As she carefully walked down towards the point picked out by Musa, Nofret saw the increase in the island's shape. She considered this area would, someday, become part of the mass of Philae and the soils washed down in the inundations would cloak the rubble with their silt and, over the years, build up this ground to the level of the land.

She finally reached the point picked out by her *wab* priest. This rock was darker than the rest, a rich black basalt boulder standing out from the irregular shapes of the pale limestone that lay scattered around. The softer stones appeared whiter and in some areas lay smashed and split apart. The hard black rock, however, stood perched on the edge of this misshapen mass and seemed out of place to Nofret's eyes.

She stared down. There was no evidence that Safiya had lain here but, in the woman's mind, the jagged surface of the boulder did not appear to be an easy place for a body to lie. It wavered along its top, leaving a hard, sharp ridge that fell away at its back and front. Yet, closer to the water where its southern side curved evenly and was washed by the river's inundation, it lay flatter and perhaps this was where her predecessor had been found. Finding no insight from it, she seated herself below its edge and, staring over the Nile, brushed her hands between the grasses.

She sat for some time, hoping for an understanding of why Safiya should be found here. But having only the company of the ibis birds which landed around and began their fishing, she reached no conclusion on the matter. Rising to make her way back, she left the ibises to haggle over the chosen spot.

Stepping onto a lush, green area between the white and black of the stones, she felt the grass like a soft cushion beneath her feet. Until, adding the full weight of her body, her foot slipped further between the rocks and she felt a sudden sharpness. Pulling back, Nofret rubbed her toes. There was a small cut to the edge of her foot and, bending to find the cause, she let her fingers carefully brush aside the grass. Looking down, she saw a glint of metal between the greenery.

Moving aside the tall strands, a silver anklet, carved delicately with two cow horns entwined together, eventually came into view. It was complete with a small bell made from a silver globe which contained a tiny stone. Lifting it, it jingled in the still air. It was dirty with the ingrain of soil and could so easily have gone unseen if not for her standing on it. Nofret immediately wondered, on noting the symbolism of *Hathor,* the Cow Goddess, if it once belonged to Safiya.

Holding it up to the bright blue sky, she rattled the bell and heard the faint tinkle of the stone, and curious about it being there, she pocketed it before returning directly across the tops of the boulders.

Collecting her sandals and walking along the western edge of Philae, she passed the Nilometer before arriving where the steep steps led down to the crypt. Pausing, she looked around before sitting on the bank and, looking across the river, she retrieved the anklet from her side. Twirling it about her finger as she wondered about it, she finally let it drop into her lap. However, on hearing approaching steps crunching across the ground behind her, she placed it around her leg and brought her clothing over to hide it away.

The voice of Teos disturbed the silence.

"Essam said you were about the island!"

Nofret turned, and raising her hand to shield her eyes, smiled up at the high priest.

"*Nene*, Teos. Greetings on this fine morning." She dropped her eyes and stared back at the water. "I'm enjoying my quiet time to reflect on the days since my arrival."

"Then I'll leave you to your contemplations."

The man stepped back and aimed to walk away but came to a stop as Nofret replied, "No, please join me."

The high priest reached the water and, following the woman's example, wrapped his cloak around and sat on the bank. The silence, punctuated by the cicadas in the palm trees that stood at their backs, grew between them until the roaring sound of the hippo's call disturbed the tranquillity.

"I hear you paid a visit to my library the other day." Teos's voice came lightly to Nofret's ears, but it held a certain interest as he added, "I hope you found it useful and it increased your knowledge of the island?"

"It did, thank you." Feeling she should give a reason

for her interest, Nofret explained, "I was looking for more information about the great temples that bless this sacred place."

"Any temple in particular?"

The Temple of *Isis* rose at their backs and, feeling its colossal presence, the priestess glanced its way and hoped to satisfy the man's curiosity.

"Well, I think the Temple of the Triad is certainly the most noted," she said, nodding her head to the vast shrine. "So I feel I should first start there in finding out its great history."

"It's certainly one of the most glorious buildings here which, as I'm sure you already know, began its construction in the reign of Pharaoh Nectanebo many, many years ago." The man recounted a little of the temple's history before abruptly coming to a stop. Standing and holding out his hand, he finished, "Come, I'll show you around. It will be easier for me to explain if we walk its walls."

Nofret briefly took the proffered hand and, rising from the waterside, let the man stalk off. Following him, the bell tinkled intermittently around her ankle as she walked and, on catching him up as he reached the outer wall, she stopped to stare at the building's magnificence.

"It must have taken years to build." Her eyes gazed at the great details that swept way above her head before, looking along the block work, the hieroglyphs and carvings led away on each side.

"Years uncounted," Teos replied, his eyes looking afresh at the enormous depictions of the ancestors. Knowing the multitude of great temples along the Nile were often overlooked in favour of this one, his pride in being its high priest suddenly knew no bounds and he revelled in the girl's enthusiasm. Taking the arm of the priestess, he directed her along the base of the western wall.

Later, after encircling the vast area with Teos preaching the history of the temple, the two found their way to the outer courtyard. Taking the slope into the hypostyle hall, they entered the cool realm of the gods.

"It's so good to have someone take an interest," Teos whispered, a smile fleetingly crossing his face. "Some find the sheer splendour too much to take in, but I can see instead of it overwhelming you, it brings fascination."

Nofret eagerly smiled back. The whole place was amazing in its structure and decoration, but in reality, it was below their feet in the temple underground that she was more interested. Yet, feeling she was learning more from the man than any papyrus, she let him continue his instruction.

Reaching the northern end, where the three great gods stood in their majesty, they stopped in awe and admired the magnificence of the altar that sat before them. The air within the massive building was chilly and Nofret, feeling a shiver run down her spine, dropped her head to the gods before walking to one side. Teos followed, his robes dragging across the hallowed ground.

"What about beneath the temple?" Nofret eventually risked asking the question. Her voice came as an echoed whisper in the space's vastness. "Is there anything down there?"

"Below us lie the catacombs of the dead. These sit directly beneath this temple." The man stared down. "The whole of the island is said to be riddled with caverns and I'm sure there may be some below these sacred places which possibly entwine their way under here."

Nofret did not let on about knowing of the catacombs. Yet her curiosity was aroused on hearing of other passageways. Her mind instinctively went to the papyrus that lay hidden in her room and, glancing at the tiled floor beneath her feet, she wondered if this was what she had seen drawn within its boundary.

Eventually, the tour came to a close and Teos, having finished his schooling, guided her away from the altar and back through the columned hall. Leaving the gods to their rest, he ended his instruction as he escorted the priestess out into the warmth of the courtyard. The warm smell of the Nile met them and the shrine's chilly enclosure instantly melted on the breeze.

"There are many scrolls in my library, as you have already seen," Teos lastly advised, as he guided Nofret through the opening in the eastern wall. "These, I'm sure, will help you with deciphering the hieroglyphs."

Turning away, they left the Temple of *Isis* at their backs and, walking the island in the heat of the day, he knowingly added, "But if it's the actual structure and design you look for, then you must consult the Papyrus of Meriiti. It is supposedly one of the most accurate held here."

***

Nofret entered her room from the open walkway and, leaving the door ajar to catch the breeze, she sat on the bed. After first pulling out the papyrus from beneath the mattress, she curled her long legs beneath her and spread the flattened design over her lap. In her first scrutiny, she had not looked for any name to the drawing, the intricate details of the buildings holding her attention. But this time, looking closer, the name of the architect Meriiti sat small and unassuming beneath the hieroglyphic title. His work, although faded over the millennia, was obviously in Teos's mind to be looked upon with merit, and the priestess hastily passed a fresh eye over it.

Nothing new came to her, apart from the realisation that the underground chambers which lay beneath could be connected somehow to the other island structures. If so, she needed to look further afield for the possibility of another entrance.

The cat arrived early and curled at Nofret's feet, its contented purr gradually lessened before coming to a stop as it nodded off. The two lay in the silence of the early afternoon and, as the shadows lengthened, the overwhelming heat lessened and the calm of the day fell through the window.

Nofret, her eyes tired of staring at the lines across the papyrus, eventually dozed. While beside her, the cat which she had recently named Aziza stretched out at her side. Aziza meant 'precious' and, as the company of the cat had been most welcome, the woman thought it appropriate.

Later, after the heat of the midday had passed, the Priestess of *Hathor* aimed to do as promised and seek further guidance from Teos's library. She was, however, reluctant to return the Papyrus of Meriiti. She needed to study it further, she thought, still unknowing of what she was really looking for. Pushing it back beneath the mattress, she let it lie flat against the boards, allowing the cat to stretch out further.

Leaving her room, as Aziza briefly lifted her head, Nofret turned left out of the walkway and headed north across the island.

She found Teos seated within the fusty library where, on seeing the priestess enter, he rose and gestured for her to join him. Around the tables, the scribes remained deep in concentration and, as Nofret passed by, their candles flickered in the disturbed air.

"Come and sit with me," Teos whispered. "I've something to show you."

The high priest sat with several unrolled papyri before him and, as the candle burned low, had obviously been there some time.

"I've not been able to find the Papyrus of Meriiti," he said quietly, pulling over a stool for the woman to sit. His voice held a disappointment, but then suddenly it lifted. "But look what I've found for you instead!"

Stretched across the desk, a brightly painted papyrus sat highlighted in the sultry flame.

"This is the Papyrus of Tentamun. She was Priestess to *Hathor* on the island many years ago." The man shifted the burial scroll to lie directly in the falling light. "I thought you may be interested in knowing another of your predecessors."

Nofret looked down over Teos's shoulder. The scroll showed the usual burial representation well known from her past schooling and the figures, highlighted by the stark whiteness, had kept their brilliance. It showed a typical scene noted for its artistry.

Anubis, the God of the Dead, stood tall behind the deceased, his arms wrapped protectively around the coffin as the *sem* priest, his leopard skin tied about his broad shoulders, performed the Opening of the Mouth ceremony. At the coffin's feet, three white-clad women sat upon the floor holding up their hands and, rattling their sistra, they bewailed the passing.

"It's beautiful." Nofret sat and admired the work before noting the smaller detail along the bottom where it showed Tentamun walking along an ornately tiled floor. It was a depiction which the priestess had not seen before, or at least not like this. The figure appeared in various stages of a tunnel, as if she moved along its length. But, in each portrayal, she was clothed differently.

"What's this bit along the bottom?" She placed her finger near the curled edge of the papyrus where it showed the priestess in her regalia, holding aloft a flame and walking beneath the overhang of a white-painted ceiling.

Teos dropped his head to stare intently at the pointed finger.

"I think it shows the priestess on her journey through the Duat!" He had not looked too closely at the surrounding pictures on the burial scroll, but seeing the cavern through which the priestess walked, he could see no other reason. "See, she carries the light of her profession with her to shed its warmth into the dark of the world and let the gift of the gods shine out."

The next figure also showed Tentamun in her finery. Yet further along the papyrus, it showed the subsequent figures on the left in various stages of undress until finally, in the last drawing, the form of the woman stood naked, a string of beads loosely tied around her hips. Her hand remained raised as the light shone around. She seemed to have reached the tunnel's end, and a dark archway stood before her.

Nofret was unsure of its meaning and wondered about its portrayal. However, pushing it aside she, continued to admire the overall skill and artistry of the ancient scribes before thinking of the recent passing of the young priestess.

"Was a scroll done for Safiya?"

"Of course!" Teos appeared to question the need to ask. "We would not have her enter the Duat without the spells to find her way! My men of the library worked diligently on it," he added, "and they ensured it contained the appropriate words from the Book of the Dead. With that, it blessed her time in this world and gave easy passing for her into the next where the eternity of the Field of Reeds awaits."

"Is it with her?"

"Naturally it is!" Teos again seemed surprised at the asking. "Where else should it be?"

Nofret had seen no scrolls around Safiya's coffin, but knowing these often lay enclosed within the sarcophagus, she thought that more likely the resting place.

Returning her attention to the papyrus spread before them, she suddenly wondered why this papyrus would not also be with its owner. However, as she listened to Teos and followed his hand across the hieroglyphs, she pushed that thought aside and concentrated on the richness of the wording set out before her.

Teos eagerly demonstrated his proficient skills in the ancient words, and as the time moved on in the ever-present scratch of the scribes, Nofret listened intently and added to her knowledge.

***

The Priestess of *Hathor* returned in haste to her temple to witness the evening ceremony and, after freshening herself and applying new make-up to her eyes, she straightened her wig and speedily walked the covered arch into the back of the temple. Around her foot, the anklet tinkled on each alternating step.

Her priests stood already gathered there, the coming ceremony only in wait for its priestess. Standing diligently before the statue of their goddess, the flickering flames lit their faces as the enclosed darkness and shadows moved gently in the ever-present breeze. Nofret shut the door behind her and, with some urgency, let the dimness of the interior surround her before she emerged out of the misty smoke of the candles.

Essam heard the tinkle of the bell through the gloom and stared wide-eyed as a sudden alarm filled his stomach. He watched the breeze of the closing door swirl the light of the candle flames around the feet of *Hathor*. Seeing a figure emerge, the priestess appeared through the smoke and the tinkling followed her through. Realising, however, that it was Nofret, the lector dropped his head and, as he controlled his breathing, his eyes stared fixedly at the detailed pattern of the tiled floor.

Stepping forwards, he lifted his head and greeted his priestess. "I thought for a moment you were the ghost of Safiya!" he whispered. The lector appeared shaken as, again looking to the floor, he saw the silvered anklet around the leg of the woman.

"Where did you get that?" His eyes stared up widely into the exquisitely painted face before nervously glancing back down.

"I found it," Nofret openly replied. But she noted the shock that fell across Essam's face. Realising the sound of the bell of the anklet must have caused the man's alarm, she wondered why its sound bothered him. Yet, moving to one side, she dismissed her concern and inclining her head in acknowledgment for him to begin the service, she let the sacred ritual of undressing the statue of *Hathor* begin.

The lector priest instantly took control of his nerves and, after straightening his robes, he walked sedately forwards, his head held high. He stood before his goddess and first bowing his head, he then, with shaking hands, gathered up the offerings and placed them in the waiting arms of Abbas. The ritual followed its usual course and after the white linen robe had been unwound, taken down and folded away, Nofret said her words to the heavens. The ceremony ended in the blowing out of the main candles.

At its end, Nofret let the men go their way. She did not wish to join them for their evening get-together and games, and so instead went to her room. She wanted to put more thought into the idea of a subterranean maze beneath the island.

However, after taking off her robe and wig and placing them on the bed, her thoughts took her along a different track. She now knew for certain that the anklet found on the rocks belonged to Safiya. With that, it firmly established in her mind that the dead woman had been there. Of course, she reasoned, the anklet could have been lost at any time, but she felt it more likely it had been with her body and that at least gave some confidence in Musa's words that she had lain there.

Taking off the silvered bangle, she twirled it in her fingers and let the soft sound of the bell fill the room. Outside, the voices of the men came and went until, as the darkness fell heavily over the island, the hush of night took its place and Nofret, placing the chain on the bedside table, settled to sleep.

Aziza eventually strolled through the open doorway, and jumping up, she joined Nofret. Purring loudly, she came to rest at her side.

CHAPTER SEVEN

The following days turned into weeks, and for Nofret, they passed in their constant ritual. However, try as she might, there was no further insight into the death of Safiya. Still, the feeling that something was not right in her ending would not rest in the priestess's imagination, and no matter how much she brought to mind her findings and asked around, it made no sense that Safiya's badly injured body was found on the rocks.

She felt sure the young woman had succumbed to something awful, but thinking herself foolish for being bothered about it when there appeared little concern by the rest of the island, she let it go. Instead, she concentrated her time on widening her knowledge and seeking the history of Philae.

With this, she was more fortunate. Spending uncounted hours in Teos's library, she found out more about the passages beneath the island where past reference was made to them in the old papyri of the temple priests. Yet, there was nothing written in any recent documents and on seeking some insight from the other priests and priestesses, they appeared to know nothing of their existence.

These older papyri, however, detailed them as being extensive below the island's structures and Nofret considered they should still exist somewhere, even if in a dilapidated state. They had, apparently, been used in many rituals of the past, especially regarding the dead and in giving easy access to the catacombs. However, the long-forgotten servants of the temples had also spoken of the labyrinth as being a way of communing with the gods.

Eventually, in her search, she found an old map of the

island, wrapped in an aged papyrus, and this showed the sites of the old temples worshipped here long ago. She felt, thankfully, she was getting somewhere and studying the faded document gave her more insight.

In her downtime from her service to her goddess, she visited the places of the various temples shown on the map, but most of these venerated structures had succumbed to a lack of upkeep. After the worshippers had moved on and the gods long forgotten, their temples had decayed and now lay enshrouded in sand and rubble.

The only one of any note was the ruins of the Temple of Augustus. This sat close to the northeastern edge of the island and, although the main part was derelict, the walls of the hypostyle hall still stood open to the sky and the enclosed area of the altar remained intact. Nofret walked through these ruins, hoping to receive some guidance, but the carved figures on the walls remained staring blankly across time. She did, on a couple of occasions, dig aside the sand that lay wind-blown against the foundations, but this revealed nothing further, apart from the line of hieroglyphs that sat beneath the carvings.

However, she was not put off, and in the evenings when the men played senet and their laughter and voices rose into the dark sky, she would often walk around the island's edge or look for further insight from the library documents.

***

The nomarch's daughter-in-law, Yara, did not attend several of the morning's services in the Temple of *Hathor*, and Nofret noted her absence. Finally, the young woman sent her sister Basma with her apologies, along with extra offerings to the temple. The young girl said Yara was suffering from a sickness of late and feared taking the crossing over the water.

Hearing the news, Nofret, on entering the sanctum of *Hathor*, gave added prayers. And, hoping she was not being overconfident in her assumption, let her words give glory and thanks to the Goddess of Abundance. Along with this, as the blue lotus added its haziness to the atmosphere of the enclosed shrine and the vapours made her head spin, she added her own prayer to ask for help in finding out more about the entrance to the labyrinth.

Later, after the temple had emptied and her priests were about their daily tasks, Nofret went and stood to watch the people leave and suddenly realised she had not left this place since her arrival. She felt she needed to rectify that and, after wrapping her cloak around her shoulders and making sure her wig sat straight, she took a brisk walk back to the eastern bank. A boat sat below, and stepping down, it took her swiftly over the water. It was her first time off the island, and the life governed by its rules and regulations lifted as she reached the eastern shore.

It had been night when she first reached here many months ago and then she had been given a room on the water's edge to rest. But now, in the light of day, she could see the village as it sat sprawled along the bankside. It spread up towards the edge of the desert and in its twist and turn of streets, its buildings of mud brick, a material found here so close to the Nile, sat side by side. However, they all seemed well presented and the tiny windows which pierced their dried out walls kept their rooms cool and ventilated. To Nofret, it immediately reminded her of her own home on the Red Sea.

Stopping the nearest villager who was passing by, with his donkey laden with reeds, she asked the direction of the nomarch's home. Receiving advice to go to the northern end of the town, she walked past the open-fronted buildings where the tradesmen worked. Here, men mended nets and dried the recent catch of fish. And while some women ground the wheat on their turning wheels, others placed the flatbread in clay pots and sat them within the open fires. Around their feet, the young children played with figurines of clay or wood and a feeling of constant daily demand fell about the place.

However, for those who had reached a certain age, they either sat to one side of their parents or else, further within the cool gloom of the rooms, sat with their heads bent forwards as they received schooling on the work that would soon rule their way of life.

Greetings were shouted as Nofret passed and, as heads turned, she gave out her well wishes for life, prosperity and health. The sound of a*nkh wedja seneb* rang through the streets for all those who took the time to listen. Eventually, the workshops were left behind, and keeping the Nile on her left, the bank slowly rose before her as the stillness of the upper town was reached.

Here, a continuous row of buildings on the right-hand side had been built for the more prosperous residents and for those who worked within the rooms of the master of the nome. These stood close by, for the scribes and their assistants to be always on hand if needed, and led up to the grand home of Mysis, which sat looking down the stretch of the road.

Reaching the top of the walkway, Nofret knocked on the ornate door and shouted her greeting. A young boy immediately met her and, bowing low on seeing the priestess, he opened the doorway wide to let her in.

"The nomarch is with his clerics at the moment, my lady," the boy advised, feeling no need to ask who the priestess sought. She was obviously there to see only one person. "But I'll tell him you are here."

The boy disappeared down the central passage, leaving Nofret standing at the doorway, but stepping over the threshold, she wandered around the hall and admired the sculptured statues that lined its walls. In between the ornate figures, she noted several fine tables stood adorned with statuettes, along with ivory and cedar wood chequered senet slabs.

On seeing the squares of the gaming board, Nofret picked up the throwing sticks that lay close to hand and, not knowing why, her thoughts returned to Safiya and the enclosure of the catacombs. She felt she was doing the woman a disservice to have so easily forgotten her. Yet, placing the sticks back against the oblong box, there appeared little else to learn about her death, and she needed to move on.

In time, footsteps echoed in the distance and, returning to stand in the doorway, Nofret waited to be received.

"Welcome to my home, priestess." The man eagerly came forward as he wrapped his cloak around himself and a broad smile crossed his face as he took the woman's hand. "My door's always open to the servants of Philae."

The nomarch gestured for her to join him and, shouting for wine to be served, he led Nofret through the building and out into the courtyard. The enclosing sides of the house gave shade at most times of the day, and the enormous pots of palms added their greenery to an otherwise stark environment. However, at its centre, a large pool of water sat within its raised ornate bowl and a small rock arose from its middle. Around its edge, several palm doves sat perched and, taking their turns, they enjoyed the cool splash of the water as it fell around them.

Mysis led the way into the back of the yard and, stopping at where a selection of cushions filled out a ledge, he gestured politely for the priestess to sit.

"I hope I've not disturbed you from important affairs?" Nofret began, and spreading her clothing about her long legs, she leant against the hard stone at her back. "I can call another time if you're busy."

"The affairs of the nome can wait!" The nomarch seated himself at her side. Placing his arm along the rear edge of the seating, he let the ends of Nofret's long wig drape over his hand. The woman shifted slightly but did not move aside.

The wine was swift to arrive, and after Mysis quickly sent away his servant, he took his time to pour the rich red liquid before handing the cup over.

"Now, what can I do for you?" Raising his drink, he took a sip, but his eyes never left the face of the beautiful woman at his side.

Nofret looked back and let her smile hold the man before explaining her visit.

"I feel you may be able to help, Governor Mysis, in my getting to know more of the island's history!"

She told of her interest in the Temple of *Hathor* and the recent talks with High Priest Teos on the island's structures before speaking of her findings on the underground labyrinth. She stated Essam had shown her the burial chambers of the past priests and priestesses. However, she added, she had found, on further research in Teos's library, that there were additional passageways even further down.

"Do you know anything of these tunnels?" she finally asked in ending. Raising her beaker, she let her dark eyes look over its top.

"I know about the catacombs," Mysis confirmed, his family having been aware of them way before Teos's time. "But of anything other than that, then I'm as much in the dark as you are!" He let his eyes linger on the woman's stare before glancing away. The water dripping from the pond filled the silence and, having emptied his cup, the nomarch reached forwards to refill it and again drank heavily.

"Is it important?" He wiped his mouth with the back of his hand. "I mean, it's not that they're used these days!"

"I feel, as Priestess to *Hathor*, I must embrace my position on the island," Nofret slowly replied, "and knowing its past, and that of the people who live in its surround, will give me an insight on that."

The man remained reluctant, but seeing the bright smile cross the woman's face, he stretched out his legs and, making himself comfortable, settled first into a tale of his own life.

"My family have lived here on the Nile's banks since records began, although it's only my father and myself who have been called nomarch." His voice held pride in the position, reached by the sweat of his father, which had so easily passed down to him.

"We were fishermen by trade, and for many here, that has changed little over time." He came forwards, and staring at his feet, suddenly realised the woman did not need to hear his life story and he changed the subject.

"Now, let me tell you a bit about the Island of Philae and its nome."

A plate of dates and watermelon appeared, along with more wine, and as the afternoon passed, the Priestess of *Hathor* listened as Mysis gave a chronicle of the surrounding lands. Thankfully, for Nofret, he did not go way back into the past, but it gave her an overview of the people of the Nile who lived and worked there. It was not really what she wanted, and the talk added little to her knowledge of the underground of the island, but the time spent in the cool courtyard with the soft cooing of the doves soothed her worries and let her have the time to think.

The day eventually moved on and, aware the sun was heading west, Nofret brought their conversation to an end. She had enjoyed the time away from the island and the reality of a normal life brought back memories of her childhood.

Rising reluctantly, as she sensed the need to catch the boat, the woman held out her hand. "Please give Yara my best wishes when you see her. Her absence has been noted these past days, and I've given extra prayers to *Hathor* for her continued protection."

The man took the hand but looked surprised at the words, as if unaware of the coming change to his family.

Seeing the bewilderment, Nofret added nothing further and, following Mysis back into the house, they passed through the rooms to where the senet boards sat near the doorway. Here the woman came to a stop.

"Do you play?" She picked up the nearest throwing sticks and rattled them around in her hand before placing them down, white side up.

"Of course." The man smiled at what he hoped was a forthcoming confrontation with the priestess. "It's a game many play, and I'd like to think I'm fairly good at it!"

Nofret lowered her head briefly in recognition of the man's supposed prowess.

"Then perhaps I'll come again and we can make a match of it!"

Mysis bowed his head in acceptance of the challenge and, smiling as he escorted the priestess down to the Nile's edge, he showed off his village, and the people stopped their work to shout greetings and give praise to the nomarch.

Reaching the water, he helped the young woman into the waiting boat and standing, hand raised, he shouted across that she was welcome to come at any time. Watching, as the crew fought their way against the current, the craft eventually grew small and blended into the mass of the island and the man turned away.

***

Hushed voices awoke Nofret in the heat of the night as she lay curled on her bed. They came from beneath the trees at the Nile's edge and, sitting up, she turned to kneel with her arms resting on the window where she could see out. The vague shadows of Essam and Ramy stood in the half-light beneath the palms and seemed in disagreement, the older Nubian flailing his arms as his agitation grew. The voices got louder, although Nofret could not hear what was being said, until, seeing Essam stalk off down the side of the temple, he disappeared from view and the argument ended.

Ramy stood for a moment. Before kicking at the sand, he sent a flurry of grains into the air, which blew back into his face as the scented Nile breeze gusted past. He hastily turned away and, following the line of waving palms, disappeared from Nofret's sight.

Wondering what the problem was, the priestess quickly dressed and pulled the hood over her bald head before stepping out. Aiming to follow Ramy, she walked to the right and, passing by her window, let the bank of palms lead her south.

The lector priest's shadow could just be seen in the moonlit distance crossing between the Temple of the Cow Goddess and Trajan's Kiosk, a temple building that once formed the entrance to the island's complex, and Nofret followed stealthily behind.

The shadow went no further and disappeared into the dark of the enclosed entrance. Nofret cautiously followed before finally reaching the corner of the kiosk, where she came to a stop. Not wanting to be observed, she let the wall of the building lead her down towards the Nile and, reaching the opposite doorway that opened to the river, she looked carefully around the stone-carved edge.

Ramy was nowhere within the building. Thinking he must have headed straight through and carried on down the bank to where the rocks clung to the island's boundary and the dark water flowed past, she stood in hiding against the weather-beaten stone and, letting the shadow of the wall conceal her, awaited his return.

She remained silent for many long moments, her eyes watching the path of the stars as they chased the moon of *Khonsu* steadily over the colossal temple structures of the island. But the lector priest did not reappear. Finally, she furtively moved away from the wall's protection and walked closer to the water's edge. Looking down through the palms, she noted the bare rocks that made the stepped slope of the bank. The glistening stretch of water which filled the gap between the island and the land of the eastern bank ran its forever course before her gaze, but the man was nowhere around. However, below her feet, the dark shapes of crocodiles lay submerged close to the reed-lined edge and Nofret came to a stop.

Feeling Ramy had not gone that way, she returned to stand in wait at the western doorway of the building. Yet, as tiredness slowly gripped her, she reasoned the lector must have returned to his rooms in the Temple of *Hathor*.

Wishing for the comfort of her own bed, she had just moved back to the path when the priest's shadowy figure appeared across the palm-ringed space. He was walking away from the Temple of *Isis* on the far side of the island, and the moon picked him out as he moved along the wall before he crossed the expanse of ground. In his hands he carried what looked like a flat platter on which sat an upright object and, singing softly to himself, he headed straight to the Temple of *Hathor*, unaware he was being watched.

Nofret knew the man had earlier entered the building which sat at her side and, surprised to see him returning from the opposite edge of the island, she wondered how that could be. Keeping to the shadow of the doorway, she let the man disappear, before turning to sneak into the enclosure. In the light of *Khonsu*, she could see no clear footprints on the sandy-tiled pavement, but Ramy's bare toes had, in places, briefly disturbed the overlay as he crept within the temple. They snaked across the floor as he walked towards the north side of the kiosk.

Staring down at the trail, Nofret followed alongside it before reaching the block work, where the prints came to a stop. A tall column rose before her and met the carved screen wall. Here, Ramy had obviously paused and

96

turned around. But on either side, the sandy floor appeared flat and undisturbed. It was as if the lector priest had stood there and just vanished.

Feeling at a loss, she looked to either end. In the east and west of the temple, the doorways connected the main channel through the building and the Nile, with its steeply inclined bank, could be easily seen in the dark at the eastern side.

Earlier that day, she had spent time around the unfinished kiosk, it being the nearest structure to the Temple of *Hathor*. But apart from admiring its carvings and standing at its eastern end to look across the Nile, she found nothing of great interest there. It had once been the resting place to shelter the barque of *Isis* on these eastern banks during its journey up the Nile, and hoops of hardened cow leather remained embedded in the floor to tie the celestial boat in place.

However, walking around this time, she concentrated on its structure. Counting the columns with their floral capitals, she noted that seven stood on both the northern and southern sides, each connected by a screen wall. And although the roof sat open to the night-time sky, she could see the unusual combination of timber and stone sat together within the sockets where roof trusses once sat.

Retracing her steps to where evidence of the lector priest's prints remained, she brushed her hands carefully over the carved scene that sat before her. It showed the usual depictions of the gods seated at their tables; the food piled high before them. And although it had once stood brightly painted, and the blues, reds and golds would have shone out in their glory, the carvings of the gods now sat bare of colour. Rubbing her hands across the deep lines, Nofret did not know what she was looking for, but her senses told her she was missing something.

Yet, after a few moments, the priestess lowered her hands. The Kiosk of Trajan was giving nothing away in the night's darkness and feeling she needed to clear her head on this, she left the building to the full moon and walked back to her room beneath the cover of the palms.

Returning to her bed, she lay wide-eyed for some time, wondering if she was being foolish. *There must be a simple explanation for the night-time activities*, she thought. But the sense of something not known, or for that matter, something being deliberately kept from her, would not be pushed aside. Letting it fill her mind, she briefly closed her eyes before opening them. For the moment she thought it best that Ramy, and, she reasoned, any of her other priests, did not think she was watching them.

Staring at the ceiling, she said her prayers to the goddess who governed her life and petitioned her for aid and guidance, if any would be forthcoming. Turning over to face the wall, she followed the delicately lined scratch marks that decorated the lime plaster before letting them merge. As she closed her eyes, the darkness took her.

In her dream, the Goddess Hathor *appeared as a bright light at her door, and rising, Nofret followed her down the open walkway and into the back of the temple. It was full of light and instead of the suffocating feeling of enclosure and the smell of blue lotus; the columned walls appeared pasted on the burnished veneer. A sense of vastness sped away to the boundary where the walls rose into the sky. She was standing on a flat plain and behind her, the altar of* Hathor *made its presence known. Turning to face her goddess, the statue looked down.*

"YOU HAVE AWOKEN SOMETHING, PRIESTESS,

AND YOU MUST PREPARE YOURSELF FOR THE CONSEQUENCES."

The goddess stepped down from her plinth and, taking hold of Nofret's hand, led her between the columns of the hypostyle hall and out into the courtyard.

Her priests stood in line before her. And with their arms at their backs and wrists tied firmly together, they stood sideways in her sight, as if part of the sculptured plasterwork.

"YOU MUST RELEASE THEM FROM THEIR TIES."

Hathor *handed down a curved blade, and its weight caught the girl by surprise. It slipped from her hand and fell with a dull heavy, thud at her feet.*

"YOU MUST USE THIS TO UNLOCK THEIR CHAINS!"

Stooping to pick up the knife with both hands, the images before her changed and instead of her priests, the figures of her mother and father stood in their place.

Waking slowly with an awareness of the growing light, Nofret lay for a while, recounting her dream. She often dreamed of her goddess, but in this one, there was a strange feeling of realism. It disturbed her and, along with the recent scene of Essam and Ramy disagreeing over something, she wondered about their argument and what was going on. Their night-time activity did certainly seem unusual, but thinking herself silly when there was possibly a simple explanation, she rose and moved busily around her room to distract her attention.

Finally, straightening her bed, she suddenly realised the usual dip where the cat slept was absent this morning. Aziza had not cared to join her this last night, and even that left Nofret feeling unsettled.

CHAPTER EIGHT

The cat Aziza did not visit the next few nights and at first, Nofret felt no cause for concern. There was plenty already on her mind and the cat was the least of her worries. She went about performing her services and witnessing the veneration of the goddess by the worshippers from the eastern bank of the Nile in some sort of an unconscious habit of ritual, but knowingly, her eyes remained watchful.

She kept alert for anything out of the ordinary from the ceremony of the temple, but her priests went about their days in the solemn worship of *Hathor* and as time passed in the constant formality to the gods, she relaxed. *It must all be in my mind*, she thought.

***

The morning service was long over and Nofret watched Essam slink off through the palms. Wondering why he was carrying a rushlight at this time of day, she wrapped her dress around her warm shoulders and, taking off the jingling anklet, she followed the twisted tree line along the bank. The palms gave some seclusion and relief from the sun as she darted from one to the other. Essam stopped once to look behind, but standing still in the shadows, he easily missed the priestess and hurriedly he scurried forwards.

Unknowingly, Nofret followed in the footsteps of Essam's partner, who had arrived on the island shortly after the services to the gods had ended. He, instead of following the well-worn road around to reach the top of the island's bank, had stepped to one side and headed into the undergrowth. Keeping the Nile to his left, he moved along the sloping bank. He was used to this walk along the water's edge and finally, Trajan's Kiosk came into view between the bushes, and he headed upwards.

He was first to arrive and, awaiting Essam, he stood in the shadow of the far corner and looked across the floor to the eastern door. He knew no one could see him, yet he kept still and counted the time in the slow progression of *Ra* across the sky.

The recognised figure of the lector priest eventually arrived as, feeling his temper rising, the man from the eastern shore came out of hiding.

"I was expecting you earlier!" he hissed, his face flushed from the heat. The desire for a cool drink had slowly risen as he stood, but he had brought none with him and he cursed himself for his lack of foresight.

"I came as quickly as possible!" The lector priest also seemed agitated. "I've had to check I've not been followed!" Taking the man by the sleeve, they walked through to the back of the building. Here they stood, completely out of sight, and the two relaxed.

"You know she's been taking an interest in the catacombs?" Essam did not need to mention the woman's name, and he saw instant recognition in the man's face that he knew who he spoke about. "And she made me take her down to see the resting place of Safiya!"

"Yes. I'd heard you'd shown her around the catacombs." He let the priest see the angry frustration on his face. "You should've been more spirited in declining this!"

"I know, but she's threatening to go to Teos!"

Essam felt a sudden fear and, looking out across the water, the ripples of the undercurrent swirled as a crocodile dropped its nose and disappeared beneath the dark surface.

"Perhaps we'd better leave it for a while," the lector priest suggested.

"No!" the reply came resolutely. "There's a boat coming from Thebes and I need something to send down the Nile!" The man had already received part payment in advance for the next relic and was loath to delay its despatch. "I need something now!"

"Very well." Essam had to concede to the man's request. "Then let's be quick about it!"

Entering the kiosk, the two headed to the right and reaching where the third tall pillar led out from the corner, they stopped. Essam bent to lift the strap at his feet and, tugging upwards, the stone slab gradually lifted and the wind-blown sand around its edge fell into the void beneath. A chilling darkness reached out, and standing back from it, the lector lit the rushlight. Taking the steps into the dark, he led the way down and they descended beneath the opened cover and disappeared as it gradually closed over their heads.

The enclosure of the tunnel surrounded them, and reaching the bottom, they naturally turned left. Knowing there was now no way back, as the door above only opened one way, they followed the well-known route of their ancestors and left the temple walls above to the rising heat of the afternoon.

***

Nofret arrived at the doorway of the kiosk, where hushed voices could be heard. But suddenly they became indistinct before stopping and the constant call of the cicadas took their place. The priestess waited for a long while before risking a furtive look around the smoothed edge of the column. There was no one there. The Kiosk of Trajan was empty and she could see clearly through to where the sprawling structures of the Temple of *Isis* sat opposite on the island's western edge.

Thinking the lector priest, and whoever it was he met with, had gone out that way, she cautiously walked through and stopped at the opposite door. Staring across the space, several figures stood off in the distance, but surprisingly, no one walked nearby. The men had simply vanished.

Perhaps, she foolishly thought, as her mind went back to the tales of her childhood, *there was a secret door*!

Looking around the tall circumference of the temple, she felt she was being silly in presuming such a thing, but it did not stop her from examining the walls. Strolling the perimeter, she stopped to rap at various places, hoping to hear anything out of the ordinary. All she heard was the reassuring thud of solid stone and eventually, her knuckles ached and felt sore. Holding them in her opposite hand, she cradled them to ease the pain and let her attention turn to the floor beneath her feet.

The walkway was not tiled in an ornate design like in the Temples of *Hathor* or *Isis*, but the large, grey, sand-covered slabs sat evenly in squares and rested closely together. Not a blade of grass was seen in the joins, yet the tiny grains of windblown sand highlighted their shape, giving a checkerboard pattern over the surface.

Looking more intently, the base of the temple seemed to be divided into two parts, an outer area of huge slabs that abutted the walls and encircled the entire space, while an inner one of smaller slabs covered the central part. Between these inner and outer slabs, straps of toughened cowhide lay inserted in carefully measured spaces and, flopping over to one side, they picked out the elongated shape of the royal barque. At certain times of the year, they were used for tying down the papyrus-made boat in its upright position, ready for the Nile festivals in the name of the Goddess *Isis*. Celebration and feasting went on around the temple when the barge rested on the island for its designated dates. However, outside of these times, this area was usually silent. And, since the daily dropping-off place for the ferrying of worshippers had moved slightly north, the steps leading up from the Nile and the welcome of the temple had become even more neglected.

Nofret bent to examine the straps. They had been soft and pliable in the past, but over time, the strapping had hardened in the heat of the strong sun and had become a toughened strip that lay across the slabs towards the walls. Tugging at each of them, she arrived at the one where, in the dust, she had previously noted Ramy's feet had come to a stop. This band seemed less rigid and surprisingly lay flipped over in the opposite direction to the others.

Placing her long fingers around it, it felt soft, and pulling upwards, she felt the slightest give in the strap. Pulling even harder, the small slab at her feet gradually moved up with some ease and a yawning blackness appeared before her. It was a slim hole, but easily big enough for a man. Leaning over, the priestess stared into the dark.

There was no sound to be heard from the gaping aperture, but the cool of the underground seeped out and crept its way over Nofret's warm skin. She shivered, and it was not just the touch of the air that caused it. Fear crawled across her neck, making the hairs stand, and its creep of coldness worked its way down her arms. But quickly, pushing it aside, the young woman wrapped her flimsy cloak around and sat down.

Leaving the trapdoor open, she cautiously dropped her legs and her sandalled feet found the first of the well-worn stone steps. A chilliness pulled her forwards and hanging on to the rim of the opening, she cautiously stepped down into the dark before realising she had no light with her. Coming back to sit at the top, she dangled her feet over the dark edge.

There was nothing she could do for the moment, she thought, as she did not know how far the tunnels might lead. But at least she had more knowledge of the temple's secrets. Looking around, she wondered what others might lurk below the Temples of Philae.

However, not knowing if others knew of this place, she reckoned she must keep her newfound knowledge to herself. Standing, she quickly closed over the dark hole. It immediately became part of the temple floor and any sign of its existence completely vanished.

Walking back along the water's edge, Nofret stopped to gaze across the Nile. It seemed idyllic as the water flowed on its constant journey north. Yet, as the hippos raised their heads and called out their bellowing cry, the eyes and noses of the crocodiles rose slowly near the far bank. Dragging their bulk out from the river, these fearsome beasts lay open-mouthed in full sight of the sun.

Leaving the scene, the Priestess of *Hathor* suddenly felt as if danger sat close by and it was not just in the creatures that slept along the riverside. But, turning away with some satisfaction, at least she now knew where Essam had gone.

Below the island, in the smoking dark of the tunnel, Essam and his partner wound their way confidently through the confines of the maze. Keeping to the main channel, it was a route they knew, and they followed its circuit deep beneath the surface.

The labyrinth, with its many twists and turns, was an old structure, formed originally as part of the geology of the land's past. However, it had, over countless years, become adapted to fit the needs of the old priests of the island as they came upon it, and they had used it in their services to their gods. They had added to it over time and now many man-made tunnels led further beneath the island. The underside of the great temples eventually became riddled by their excavation.

Yet, as the services to the gods saw the light of day, the maze of tunnels was gradually forgotten and their whereabouts consigned to the past. Even now, many dark entrances remained off the main passage, but not knowing where some of these led, the two figures quickly rushed on and left them at their backs.

Reaching the labyrinth's end, they passed by the first set of steps that led upwards, until, reaching the rough cut steps at the very far end, they finally climbed out into the catacombs. Coming out beneath a ledge that held the enormous sarcophagus of a high priest named Psusennes, they slid along the deeply chopped-out sill which hid the dark opening, and crawled out from beneath the overhang. The central walkway of the burial chambers became lit by the meagre light of the torch. To their left, they sensed the far-off doorway to the bank as an unseen flow of air caused the torch flame to stream in its passing, while, on their right, the catacombs spread beneath the island.

Essam headed naturally to his right, the torch held high above his head, and his associate closely followed the shadowy figure to the end of the corridor. Here, the lector priest kept a few necessary tools, along with more rushlights in a room which sat opposite the one he had recently shown Nofret around. Leaving his partner standing in the utter dark of the tunnel's end, he collected these and lit another torch to add its light to the realm of the dead.

"Are you looking for something special?" The whispered words floated between the two and the lights flickered at the rush of the priest's breath.

"Yes, something exceptional this time, Essam!" The light shone in the man's greedy eyes. "Something to placate the gods themselves!"

Essam nodded his head. He was sure he knew where he could find something. Over countless years, his many visits to the chambers of the dead had left large numbers of the ancient sarcophagi ransacked. Various trinkets, along with many of the shabtis that accompanied the bodies, had found themselves on sale in the markets in the north or else now graced the collections of the men of wealth. His associate, being the main contact on the banks of the river, had made the greatest profit from it, but Essam and Ramy had each received great reward over the years and never felt out of pocket.

However, in his time in the catacombs, the lector priest always ensured he placed the lids back and left no obvious evidence of his work. Therefore, he knew from his past explorations which ones would be profitable to reopen and, leaving the eager man standing alone in the torch's light, he headed back along the tunnel.

He knew instinctively where to go. Reaching the far end, where the oldest sarcophagi rested, he dropped on his knees to the tunnel floor and placed his tools at his side. Moving his hands over the lid of one of the ornate caskets, he found the notch he had previously made and, lifting his bar in place, easily levered the heavy stone top aside. A layer of rotting material covered the wrapped mummified body of the occupant, but pulling it apart, Essam found what he was looking for in the aged wrappings. He had overlooked this item in the past, having deemed it far too expensive a relic, but now he thought it right for the occasion and brought it out into the light.

Down the tunnel, where the unseen whispering wind gathered, the man from the village stood for a while. He took no part in robbing the aged mummies of the servants of the gods and left Essam to his work. Lifting his torch, he stepped through into the opposite chamber and, with no fear of the dead, seated himself beside the coffin of Safiya. He propped the light against the wall and let the flame scorch its chiselled stonework. Bringing before him the senet board that sat at the foot of the sarcophagus, he collected together the pieces and throwing sticks and placed them on the sandy floor before him. A brief smile crossed his face as he thought of his forthcoming good fortune.

He was hoping to make a profitable return from this visit, but first, he needed to ensure it was the right piece. He did not know or need to be told of the offence his customer had committed, but it must have been something terrible to have to satisfy the gods in such a way.

"The best you can get," Vizier Amethu, his contact from the north, had said. And implying there was no restriction on the cost, the vizier had made a down payment of two bags of gold. It was the most ever received as a deposit for grave goods and, greedily, he contemplated his gain. Essam and Ramy received a standard fee for their work, and knowing this, the remaining cost for this job would be all his own.

The senet board kept his gaze as he moved the flat tokens to sit upon their starting point before his concentration turned to the taller ones. Once set along the top of the board, he began his game. He always played the conical ones and, throwing the sticks into the air, he smiled as they landed four white.

Time passed in the chamber's silence and the only noise was the click of the tokens as they moved across the board.

The lector priest eventually returned, the raised torch adding its light to the darkness. He was holding a small golden figurine of the Crocodile God *Sobek*. It had, unusually, been cast as if the animal stood upright on its rear with its tail extended at the back as a support. Its mouth stood ajar and slivers of ivory picked out the pointed teeth. In its forepaws, it offered out a plate of fruit representing bounty and richness.

"Would this be sufficient for you?" Essam squatted at the man's side and held out his hand. The inlaid emerald eyes of *Sobek* sparkled in the light.

The man eagerly accepted the figurine, and turning it over in the light of the flame, he admired the work of the goldsmiths of the past. The statuette fitted perfectly in his palm and, moving it in the torchlight which Essam held, he noted the twinkle in the bright green eyes.

"I think this'll be more than satisfactory." A smile crossed his lips. "I'm sure my patron will be well pleased with it." He turned it over to check the reverse and, in the dim light of the crypt, saw the scaled pattern down the crocodile's back appeared enhanced by edges of pure silver while a spine of tiny emeralds went from nose to tail. It was a one-off and would certainly warrant the price asked.

"This'll do nicely, Essam." He smiled at the priest as his mind briefly wondered if he dared ask more for its worth. "My thanks to you for finding it."

Passing the figure back to the lector, he arose and kicked aside his game. "Now, let's get out of here!"

Essam neatly wrapped the statue in a grey linen cloth which he had wrapped around his waist and, knowing it was far too risky to take it away in the light of day, he placed it at the end of Safiya's coffin. Laying it down amongst the grave goods of the priestess, he knew Ramy would know where to find it.

"I'll leave it here to be collected," he advised his accomplice. Picking up the torch and handing it over, he added, "I'll be coming over tomorrow, so will you be ready to receive it?"

"The money's already paid, Essam, so I'll leave it to you!"

The two quickly left the dead to the dark of the catacombs and, with their greed rising in their hearts and no fear for their actions, they headed back into the maze of tunnels.

***

The labyrinth led one way in and one way out. And, after climbing the first lot of steps, Essam and his accomplice emerged from the tunnels into the Temple of *Isis*.

Stepping out from behind a figure of *Horus*, they left the underground chambers to the silence of the dead. The doorway closed behind them and, sealing itself to resemble the hieroglyph painted back of the statue, it disappeared into the backdrop of the temple's majesty.

There was, fortunately, no one about, but as the doorway shut tight and they stepped down, the birds above their heads took flight and fluttered noisily beneath the decorated ceiling. The two did not pause and, walking into the brilliance of the day, they headed left to reach the girdle wall. Here they went their separate ways.

The man from the village stalked along the towering wall and, letting the gods continue in their constant stride across the block work, he headed towards the home of Teos. Calling out to one of the young men as he entered the garden, he ensured he was seen entering the house and justified his presence on the island. Teos made him welcome, and although not expected, the remaining hours of the afternoon were spent in the discussion of village matters in the quiet of the high priest's home.

Essam, however, crossed the palm-fringed stretch between the temple walls of *Isis* and those which made the structure of the Temple of *Hathor* and, after washing his head and hands in cool water, he returned to his duties. Later, he knelt alone before his goddess and, asking for her forgiveness, he felt approval of his actions in her cold, silent stare.

He had been ransacking the catacombs for many years now and, at first, had felt great remorse. But that soon passed as the grateful recipients of his finds paid the price asked. He had thankfully not been caught, and with each prized possession came a feeling of greater approval from the gods. Now, it hardly bothered him and, after the evening service to *Hathor* reached its end, he sought Ramy, and gave instructions for that night's collection.

***

The evening service to *Hathor* seemed to be over in an instant, and Nofret joined her priests around the fire. She wanted to maintain the appearance of harmony in their presence, but kept her mind open to their talk and let her eyes be ever watchful. And although she smiled and sang, and clapped her hands as they ate their meal, she felt a distance forming between herself and the men.

The usual talk and games took up the evening, and after a short while, Nofret rose. Wishing the men a pleasant evening, she left them to their rest and retired to her rooms. Keeping her clothes in place, she first sat on the bed and, letting the evening hours pass, wondered about the madness of her actions. Eventually, she snuffed out the light and lay wide-eyed in the dark.

Hours passed, and she knew she had not fallen asleep, but slowly the voices from outside became silenced and the night stilled as the moon of *Khonsu* rose and its light fell over the night-time chill of the land.

Rising, she left her room and walked the eastern banks of the Nile. Positioning herself below the line of the bank at the foot of Trajan's Kiosk, she lay on her front with her head looking over the grassy lip. She expected Ramy, if he came that night, would enter by the western door as she had seen previously, but if for any reason he came along the bank, she should also be out of sight in the sloping land.

Nofret dozed, her tiredness overwhelming her before suddenly a sound brought her awake. Slowly lifting her head above ground level, she focused her eyes. The lector priest in the flood of moonlight stood above the open trapdoor. He was holding a torch at his side and its light fell around his feet. Hurriedly, he stepped down and, holding the flame aloft, disappeared into the hole in the floor and the slab of stone closed over his head, instantly shutting off the chamber.

Nofret was immediately alert and dashing across the distance, she stopped at the place where the man had stood. Kneeling, she saw in the moonlight the outline of the paving where the drifting sand had dropped and, running her finger around it, felt the slight lip of the stone. She knew how to open it, but knowing Ramy was below, she hesitated. Yet, she needed to know more of what was going on here. Standing, she stepped onto the slab and felt its smoothness beneath her bare feet. Knowing what lay below, she expected it to feel somehow different, but it appeared to be just the same as the others.

The moonlight gave no further insight, but remembering she had previously seen Ramy coming back from the Temple of *Isis*, she wondered if he would again return that way.

Leaving the kiosk, the moon guided her across the stretch of the shadowy land and brought her up against the girdle wall of the temple. There was nowhere to hide here, but instinctively she moved to the group of palms which sat in the centre of the island. These formed a circle of shade during the day, but in the moonlight, they threw their silhouettes across the ground as the wind whispered through their broad leaves. Hiding herself deep in its middle, Nofret made sure she could see both temples to her right and left while before her, the whole of Philae lay spread to the water's edge.

Ramy was not gone long and, creeping out of the shadows of the Temple of *Isis*, he crossed from the right and passed in front of Nofret. He was close enough to touch as he skirted the grove and the priestess instinctively held her breath. She could see he held a wrapped parcel, but what it contained, she could not guess.

He was instantly gone, but Nofret remained for many moments, not daring to move. Slowly, she inched her way through the grove and, emerging on the eastern side, hurried back across the sand to the safety of her room.

CHAPTER NINE

Nofret lay in the dark with her mind racing. She wondered about the tunnel beneath the island and where it led, and her thoughts immediately went to the catacombs that sat below the Temple of *Isis*. The suspicion that Essam and Ramy, her two lector priests, were entering the realm of the dead, crept into her mind. But what were they doing there? A suspicion that the two were robbing the crypts was eventually arrived at, but for whom, she could not guess.

She had heard whispers of this sort of thing done in the past in other temples and some of the great pharaohs had even gone to extreme measures to prevent it from happening to them. *But here on the island*, she reasoned, *the catacombs were mainly of simple priests and priestesses, and surely the grave goods they took with them on their final journey would likely be simple and personal to them rather than great riches?* Yet, all at once, she remembered the high recognition some of these people held on the island. Perhaps her assumption could be wrong for certain names and for those who held power in their position.

Also, thinking about the tunnel, she wondered if it passed beneath the island to the western temple or perhaps there was more than one. She was unaware of any tunnels leading off during her brief visit to the catacombs, but it was known that some of the grander temples along the banks of the Nile had widespread labyrinths beneath their walls. Even the great pyramids which sat on the plains of the river were said to contain many secret shafts and chambers within and below their shape. Where these led was lost in time, but some said it was written in the papyri of old and those with the knowledge could find these out.

Bringing her mind back to Essam and Ramy and their position as lector priests on the island, she wondered who else might be involved. Essam had been overheard speaking with a third person in the Kiosk of Trajan, but the voice had not been caught clearly enough, although it was obviously a man. *Yet*, Nofret reasoned, *if any stealing undercover in the dead of night went on and it was a clandestine activity, then there must be some on the island who remained unaware of it. Possibly someone above the lector priests?* She immediately thought of High Priest Teos.

However, thinking of her recent visit to the resting place of the priests and priestesses, she had seen no evidence of tampering with any of the sarcophagi on her pass through the tunnels. But then again, in the darkness of the crypts, she had not been looking for any. If Essam was involved in some purpose, then he would certainly have not wanted her to linger. He had appeared to want her visit to Safiya to be quick, but she had thought it more a fear of the place, rather than any trick on his part. *Also, thinking of that, why were these two entering the tunnels through the kiosk, if that was what they were doing? There was a key to the catacombs hanging in the high priest's office in the Temple of Isis and surely it would be easier to take this and enter that way. But then, perhaps, they would need permission from Teos.*

Seeing no reasoning to her thoughts, her mind went back and forth over these questions as the surrounding darkness faded to grey until, quickly sitting up, a final thought suddenly arose. *What if Safiya had found out about the lector priests' activities? If so, had her death come about to keep her quiet?* This question stayed in the forefront of Nofret's mind but, seated with her arms wrapped around her knees, the dawn light brought no answers apart from the need to keep her knowing to herself. She feared this went further on the island and, for the moment, dared not risk attracting any attention.

***

The dawn service in the Temple of *Hathor* saw Nofret taking her place below the statue of her goddess before stepping aside as her priests performed their daily ceremony. Watching as the incense rose into the tops of the columns, and the chanting filled her ears, her kohl-lined eyes flitted back and forth from Essam to Ramy. She saw nothing not witnessed before in their devotion to their goddess and her attention turned to the other men of the temple. They also went about their duties as seen previously, and their priestess quickly pushed aside any reason to suspect them.

An increasing number of supplicants had greeted the morning sun in the temple and it also saw the return of Yara and her husband. Both brought plates of gifts to place before the altar. The young woman's face was flushed and, recognising its cause, Nofret took her to one side after the service.

"The Goddess *Hathor* has answered your prayers?" She concentrated her eyes on the young woman as she noted the slight plumpness which filled the girl's cheeks.

"She has, priestess, and for that, I'm grateful beyond measure!" A smile lit Yara's face and, gently holding her hand over her belly, she stroked the swelling that finally gave her acceptance in her father-in-law's eyes. "I feel blessed by the gods in my fortune."

"Then from now on," Nofret warmly counselled, "you must ensure you shout the name of *Hathor* every morning to continue her watch over you." Her wise words fell around and, seeing the brief nod of the head, she knew they would be acted upon.

"I'll do that, priestess." The girl reached for her husband. "We'll both continue our praise for the Mistress of the Sky and call her name out loud!"

Nofret walked with them and the other supplicants to the edge of the island and, watching as their boat headed into the open water, she raised her hand in blessing. Seeing Abasi, the nomarch's son, wrap his arms protectively around his wife as the slight rise of the Nile lifted the boat, the Priestess of *Hathor* thanked her god that she had at least helped these two and her mind could rest from that worry.

***

Later, Nofret again strolled down to the landing. She felt a need to be away from the ritual of her everyday life as the unsettled feeling continued to bother her. Hoping the fresh breeze would calm her troubled mind, she followed the path along. Reaching the top where the steps led down, she came to a stop. There was no boat in wait below her feet, but over the Nile, a white sail was heading her way.

Nofret continued her gaze and, gradually, as the sun shone its constant glare across the rippling water, the craft edged closer. It took its time to traverse the space between the lands, but with each breeze filling the linen sail to its capacity, it gradually grew larger.

The Priestess of *Hathor* remained in place as the boat slid through the rocks and, seeing only Essam aboard, she waited as he stepped from the boat. He was carrying a small, heavy sack and, after first placing it on the ground at his feet, he glanced up and a look of surprise fleetingly crossed his face. Raising his hand, he addressed his priestess.

"Greetings to you, my lady. I've been buying fruit!" He held the woven bag open to show the small melons, dates and pomegranates that sat intermingled together.

"The food sellers were eager to give away their surplus to the temple for a cheap price, in exchange for our prayers to *Hathor*!" His voice rose up the side of the bank and he smiled eagerly at Nofret.

However, her only thought was that it seemed a demeaning chore for a lector priest to be undertaking. He could easily have sent Musa or Abbas to do this inferior errand, and immediately she felt suspicious.

"Can I help you with it?" She came closer to the bank's edge but remained standing above the man. "It looks heavy."

It was heavy and cumbersome, and Nofret watched him struggle to carry it up the steps. Reaching the top, she took the edge of the sack and together the two carried it between them along the path. It seemed to get heavier as they walked, but reaching the temple, they took it along the eastern wall and through to the back of the building. Here Essam gestured to leave it on the sands and the sack was dropped beneath the palms. Nofret was sweating and, wiping her brow, she sat beneath the shade and thankfully let the coolness wrap around her.

The lector priest also sat and, eagerly propping the sack up, he again opened it and lifted out a bright yellow melon. He held it out to his priestess.

"Would you like some? I'll get Musa to prepare us one." He looked hard at her. "Or perhaps you would like some later?"

"Later will be fine, thank you." Nofret remained wary and still doubted the reason for Essam's visit off the island.

The man let the melon drop to his lap and, covering over the remaining fruit from the gathering flies, he made himself comfortable beneath the shade as the sunlight played through the palms.

"You seem troubled today, my lady." He moved to sit alongside his priestess and staring ahead through the bushes, his eyes watched the passing of the Nile. "Is it something I might help with?"

The man seemed genuinely concerned, but Nofret quickly passed on his invitation and, rising to seek the shelter of her room, she left Essam holding the melon in his lap. Returning around the corner of the nearest building and taking the covered walkway, she opened the door to the shaded coolness that met her. Throwing off the wig, which was hot and sticky against her bald head, she let the breeze from the window cool her face as she stared out.

In the grove's quiet beside the temple, Essam placed the melon down before slowly standing and, looking around, he made sure he was alone. Upending the sack, the fruit fell to the floor, and picking through the various shapes, he threw them aside as he retrieved two small basketry bags. They were heavy and, after weighing them in his hand, he hid them in the long grass around the base of the tallest palm. Collecting together the food, he stacked the items one atop the other in their piles and, leaving the pyramids of fruit to the warmth of the day, he collected his fishing pole and headed across the island.

Nofret, from her room, watched him pass her window and hesitating for only a moment, she returned to stand beneath the palms. The tributes from the villagers sat in the shade, but their ripe smell hung heavy in the air as the island ants already crawled eagerly across their surface.

For no particular reason, Nofret looked around. Nothing seemed out of the ordinary, but her senses told her there was something wrong here. That sack was certainly heavier than imagined, she thought. Kicking aside the sand, she wondered if Essam had buried something before her eyes took in the palm-lined edge of the space. Reaching where the bases of the trees were ringed with grass, she began parting the surrounding greenery. Looking down, she eventually came upon the hidden packets.

The bags were elaborately woven, with a stripe of bright colour across their middle, and as Nofret weighed them in her hand, she hazarded a guess to their contents. Opening the cord which held them closed, the tiny nuggets of gold spilled out into her hand. There was a great deal there, and sparkling in the afternoon light, it weighed heavily as she thought of its worth. Now she could be certain of Essam's involvement. Returning the gold and lacing the bags back up, she placed them where she found them and let the long grasses hide them away. Leaving the spot, she hurried back to her room in fear of being found there, but in her heart, she knew she had been proven right.

***

There was an unsettling quietness around the evening fire when Nofret later sat down with her priests and, feeling her nerves already on edge, the overwhelming silence upset her further. The gold still sat close by and, as yet, none of the men had shown an interest. Her eyes kept flitting in its direction, but consciously, she dragged them away and fixed her mind on the moment.

Essam eventually broke the silence. He had cut up four of the ripe melons and adorned them with the dates, and the slices sat before him fanned out on a palm leaf. In the flames of the fire, they glistened with their juice against the green backdrop. The lector priest had also caught several Nile catfish, and these, cooked over the fire, added their pungent smell to the richness of the fruit.

"Let us celebrate the bounty of the banks and the rich waters of the great river Nile," he said in praise. "And let us place our prayers and grateful thanks for her everlasting protection and guidance at the feet of the Goddess *Hathor*." A smile lit his face as he shifted the leaves to lie in the centre of the gathering and, spreading his hands, he passed his blessing over them and invited them to dine off the valley's abundance.

Accepting the offered fruit, Nofret put a smile on her face as she forced herself to eat, but underneath felt she was deceiving no one. Later, the usual games of senet played out and, unusually, she did not win even one of her games. She appeared distracted throughout the time and her frustration at losing eventually showed. Yet on rising and straightening her clothing, she let the mantle of the Priestess of *Hathor* fall over her shoulders and the dignity of her position took over. Standing over her priests, she assumed her authority.

"I'd like us to begin preparations in the temple to mark

Hab Nefer en Sekhen."

She did not elaborate, feeling the priests of the temple should know the days of the year and not need to ask further about this forthcoming celebration in their calendar. But looking down at the fire-lit faces of the men as she spoke, she saw the questioning looks before the awareness of the event took its place.

"We'll make a start tomorrow!" she finished. Turning from the fire, she left the gathering and Musa, who had also played a bad game that night, rose and walked at her side through the palms.

"The gods are not with you tonight, my lady?"

"It seems not, Musa." She laughed, but there was a strain to her voice and the young man picked up on it.

"Perhaps they want you to trust in the throw of the sticks to find your way along the board?"

She came to a stop on hearing his words and looked into his boyish face. He was the least of her priests, but at that moment he seemed the only one who had noticed her anxiety.

"Take these, priestess." He handed across a slice of melon and two of the pomegranates. "Your appetite seems to have left you tonight."

Nofret gratefully accepted the offering and, leaving the youth standing in the shaded corner of the temple, she entered the open walkway and sought the sanctuary of her room.

Later, as the light of the moon lit the darkness, she stood to one side of her window. She could see the palm where the gold was hidden and, listening to the rustle of the wind through its leaves, she waited. The night went quiet, but hearing the croak of a disturbed heron on the bank, it alerted her and she ducked back into the safety of the room. A shape moved stealthily up the side of the island and reaching the palms, it paused beneath them. Nofret held her breath and, seeing the shadow turn, Ramy's face was picked out in the light.

***

After the next day's service, Nofret left her priests to begin their preparation of the Temple of *Hathor* for the upcoming services of *Hab Nefer en Sekhen*, The Beautiful Feast of the Reunion, which loomed large on the celestial calendar. This was when the Goddess *Hathor* was paraded in her finery and her union with the Sky God *Horus* was celebrated in drink and song.

Usually, this had only seen its performance at Dendera, the home of the goddess, where her statue was taken up the Nile in a sacred barque to the nearby Temple of *Horus* and the two joined in the ceremony of marriage. Nofret, however, in her first year on Philae, wished that this should be a special event that she oversaw on the island, if only on this one occasion. The great Temple of the Triad of *Osiris*, *Isis* and *Horus* sat nearby and, hoping to bring the holy orders together, she wished to celebrate the joining of the two houses.

She had slept little that night, the worry of what might be happening on the island keeping her awake. And seeing her priests about their work in the temple after the morning dedications to *Hathor* had ended, she briefly returned to her room. Staring into the polished mirror and being satisfied with the face that looked back, she closed the door and walked the stretch of the island.

Heading towards the home of Teos, Nofret found the high priest seated on the wall before his house. He had his back to her as he threw corn on the ground and watched the chickens scratch in the sand, so he appeared surprised when she came up behind him.

"Greetings on this fine morning, Teos." She saw the man jump before he turned to face her. Seeing the Priestess of *Hathor* standing on the sandy path, his dark face lifted from its thoughtful expression and a smile replaced it.

"Greetings, Nofret! Come and sit with me for a while."

The two exchanged the usual pleasantries between the hierarchies of the temples before the priestess joined the man to sit on the wall. It was warm in the sun and, as she lifted her face to feel its rays, she let the light covering of the sheer scarf fall away from her arms. The jet-black locks of her wig brushed her burnished shoulders, and the fringe sat heavy over her brow. Apart from the scratch of the fowl at their feet and the incessant call of the cicadas in the trees, silence fell around, and neither seemed to want to disturb their detachment from the day.

But eventually, Nofret lowered her head.

"I was thinking, Teos, of preparing a service for The Beautiful Feast of the Reunion. For *Horus* and *Hathor* to be joined in a celebration of their marriage."

She knew the man would know of which she spoke, and seeing the slight reserved nod, she quickly added that the smaller statues of the goddess which sat along the front of the main shrine were far too small for this occasion. However, she reasoned, the ones at either end of the altar, the two larger images of *Hathor* seated with her hands flat on her knees and the huge cow horns on each side of her head, might be sufficient for the event.

She added that if one of these representations of the goddess might be taken into the Temple of *Isis* and placed before the statue of *Horus*, it would unite the two deities in their marriage. She hastened to explain that it would be a special service performed just this once within the Temple of the Triad, if Teos thought it acceptable.

The high priest seemed happy to be asked but still gave it some thought before replying, "I can see no reason to say no, Nofret." It was an unusual request, one not heard before in his history as high priest, and he added, "But of course, it would have to be after the main services had finished. I wouldn't want *Isis* or *Osiris* to be offended!" His voice sounded serious, but a smile lifted the corners of his lips and Nofret relaxed on seeing it.

"Thank you, Teos." She smiled back and bowed her head in acknowledgment. "We are, as yet, a great number of days away, but I needed to know how you felt about it before I began preparation."

Relieved that her request was so quickly resolved, Nofret put it to the back of her mind and let her thoughts wander. And as the two sat in the morning sun, the discussion turned to the affairs of the island. The temperature rose uncomfortably in the warmth of the late morning and, in time, the palm trees' shade was welcomed in its place. They left the heat behind and soon beer and cakes appeared.

"Now, how are your temple studies going?" Teos sounded fatherly as he sat back, a cup of beer placed precariously on the wooden arm. "Any further in finding the Papyrus of Meriiti?"

"No, not yet. But I'll continue in looking." Nofret felt guilty for lying, but for the moment, she still wished to keep her recent findings to herself.

"Well, you must maintain your search." He seemed eager for her to increase her knowledge. "It's regarded as one of the best on the island."

"I'm sure I'll soon find it." Coming forwards in her chair, the cup held lightly in her hands, she finished, "But I visited the catacombs some days ago to pay my respects to Safiya, and that, in itself, was enlightening." Staring at Teos, she said the words slowly in order to witness his reaction. There was none, apart from the man taking an extra-long drink of his beer.

"Such a sad thing to have happened on the island!" He lowered his cup and seemed genuinely upset before he turned to look at the young woman at his side. "Although it has since brought you to us, and for that, we are thankful."

Nofret did not know what to say in reply, but inclining her head, she accepted the compliment of the man's words.

***

The Priestess of *Hathor* did not join her priests that night and instead kept to her room. She told Musa she had a headache and, after the *wab* priest returned with a piece of cloth soaked in the cooling waters of the Nile, she lay on her bed with it over her eyes. He had also brought a flask of water and a small plate of meat. Wishing his priestess a quick recovery, he left Nofret to her solitude.

The headache was not that bad, possibly brought on by too much sun, but wanting to keep to herself, she made more of it than its reality. The cool bandage, however, was refreshing, and slowly the throb in her temples turned to a bearable ache. The darkness covered her eyes and the sounds of the men outside as they played their games beneath the palms gradually faded.

She slept for hours, but on waking to the darkness, she lifted the cloth away and dropped it to the floor. Immediately, the fresh air took its place and the sound of cicadas filled her ears. Staying stretched upon the bed, Nofret let the buzz and hum fill her mind until its background noise became one with the silence.

The scratching began not long after, and on opening the door, Aziza shot through. Wrapping herself about the priestess's legs, she rolled around the floor and picked at the woven mat before jumping on the bed and settling.

Nofret shared the meat with her and, after taking a quick look outside where the stillness sat around the temple, she lay at Aziza's side. Her eyes remained open in the night's long stretch and, as she listened to the gentle purr, it slowly turned to a throb before eventually stopping.

She let her worries merge and gather in her mind, and unable to relax and let sleep reclaim her, she instead sat up, her bare back propped against the cool of the wall.

CHAPTER TEN

Nofret did not sit for long, her mind having decided to next day take a boat over the Nile and seek help from Mysis. Yet, feeling restless and with many hours of the night to pass, the nagging thought of her predecessor's death lingered on her mind. However, rising from her bed, she pushed that aside and instead concentrated on where her lector priests were going.

Retrieving the Papyrus of Meriiti from beneath her mattress, she lit a taper and, after lifting the cat to one side, stretched the parchment out flat. Holding it open with her sandals on either side, the faded lines appeared to move beneath her gaze in the shifting, wind-blown candle flame. *The answer to Safiya's death may also be here*, she thought, but keeping her intent on the tunnels and the activities of Essam and Ramy, she again pushed the thought away.

The main part of the temple drawing showed the underground chambers but gave no added insight. However, the scrawled sketches around the edge could give some enlightenment. Nofret had taken little notice of these on her first examination, thinking them the architect's jottings for his main drawing. But seeing some of them intermingled with each other, she looked more closely. In places, they were difficult to make out and the ageing scroll itself had frayed at the edges and, in some areas, the decay had eaten into the image.

Lifting it carefully, she held it to the flame for closer scrutiny and, seeing in one drawing many archways scrawled within the carefully etched lines, she concentrated on these. Beneath the curving forms, a small cloaked and schenti-clad stick figure walked through the tunnel with a torch held high and, like in the Papyrus of Tentamun, it disrobed as it stepped along the passage. At its end, though, the torch was lowered and cast to the floor. Stepping into the burning flame, the stick figure lifted its arms and was consumed by the fire.

Here, Nofret turned the papyrus on its side as the lines of the flame-filled tunnel rose perpendicular to the main passage. However, the arches continued and led onward and in this opposite scribble, the man slowly reappeared as the fires died down and played around his ankles. Having grown taller with a lightness radiating from his body, he seemed to be enclosed in the light. Nofret thought this might mean some sort of rebirth, but having never seen this before in her years of schooling at Dendera, she reasoned it must be something exclusive to the Island of Philae.

She felt the depiction was of some importance, but then her thoughts turned to the entrance and exit of the labyrinth. She knew where the entrance was, having seen Ramy enter at the Kiosk of Trajan, but on his return, he had appeared in the island's west, from the Temple of the Triad.

Nofret judged this needed further investigation. Rolling the scroll away, she hid it again beneath her mattress and slid in alongside the cat. Letting its sleek pointed head rest on her arm, she soon found sleep and woke the next day with the determination to get answers.

***

The gentle smoke of incense filled the Temple of *Isis* after the morning's service and, as the Priestess of *Hathor* entered, she brought her light scarf up from around her neck and covered her bare head. She had left her wig aside this morning, having endured its tight fit for the service to her goddess, and it felt so good to let the cool breeze play around her face. Her soul had been refreshed as she walked across the space between the buildings and the wind-blown sand at her feet brought back memories of her childhood. However, on reaching the steps into the temple's main hall, she brought herself back to the day and, in showing respect to the gods, hid away her features.

Around her, the *wab* priests were finishing their tidying of the foot-trodden sand, sweeping aside the defilement of the temple with their palm fronds. Seeing the industry as the men worked with bowed backs and heads bent forwards, Nofret passed them by and, walking the central column-filled aisle, she headed into the northern structure.

Looking around, the immensity of the building stretched in its glory around her. It was enormous and, wondering where to begin her investigation, she soon realised it was a lost cause. The exit from the tunnel could be anywhere and after wandering around for many moments and looking furtively behind the countless statues which lined the walls, she realised it was beyond her to even begin her search. She knew it was here somewhere, but the vastness of the temple was overwhelming.

Leaving the priests to their ever-present need to sweep away the sand and leave the stones of the temple pristine for the gods, she walked back into the brightness of the day. The scarf instantly dropped to her shoulders and her head felt the rays of *Ra* warming away the deep chill that had crept over her.

The temple rose at her back, but heading past the ring

of palm trees where she had previously stood in hiding, she left it behind in the risen sun. Skirting the trees, she startled several colourful birds and, flying out to take to the heavens, they noisily scolded her as they flew into the deep blue of the sky. She stopped and watched them for some time as they circled the cloudless vault before, as the priestess moved away and left the palms to the silence, they returned to settle within the safety of the fronds.

Walking past the Temple of *Hathor*, Nofret headed to the banks of the island and, not knowing how long she would have to wait for a boat, she sat beneath the palms. Lifting her scarf in place, she watched the lazy meander of the water.

***

Governor Mysis was surprised to see the Priestess of *Hathor*, yet in seeing the smile that filled her painted face, he felt a sudden rush fill his heart. Greeting her and, seeing the bow of the hooded head in recognition, he led the way from the entrance and they entered the main building. This lay open on one side of the garden courtyard, but the warm air that gathered beneath the overhang of the roof stopped at this invisible barrier and the shade of the room held a coolness.

The nomarch had been in a meeting with his clerks Nahket and Penthu, two brothers who had come to him from the north on the instruction of the pharaoh himself. Both were well known in royal circles and, having trained in the scribe's art, they came with excellent testimonials. Mysis felt favoured to have them in his service. They had been long in his employ and the brothers' adept hands had often embellished his monthly documents that took the boat up the Nile. However, hearing the priestess was visiting, he was quick to hand over the last of the reports and close the door on his civic responsibilities.

"Please sit down, priestess." The man extended his hand to the long couch and Nofret, letting her scarf slip to her shoulders, spread her dress around and sat squarely in its middle. There was no room on either side for the man to sit, so he sat opposite and let a small wooden table of carved ebony fill the space between them.

"You said you would come again." The man's voice held a note of surprise as he lifted his hand and called for drinks. Smiling pleasantly and sitting back in his chair, he added, "But I'd not expected it so soon!" The priests and priestesses of the island, in his eyes, seldom left its domain, instead leaving those of the lesser orders of the temples to cross the water and gather supplies and news from the village.

"I hope my timing is not inconvenient?" Nofret looked around as she asked the question. "Forgive me if you were about the business of the nome."

"I was, but my letters and messages regarding that are done for the day and are well in time to catch the boat heading downriver." He straightened the table between them and, as the drink appeared and was placed down, he poured the honey-laced wine and passed a beaker over to the priestess.

Lifting his own, he watched the woman over the rim and waited for her to speak. However, as silence filled the space between them, he noted her hesitancy. Feeling no need to rush the moment, the two drank silently until, placing his cup carefully down, the nomarch asked the reason for her visit and awaited a reply.

Knowing she had the full attention of the man, Nofret too placed her drink aside and came straight to the point.

"Something is troubling me, Mysis." She paused before continuing, "It concerns the island." She nodded her head in its direction. "And I would like to…" The sentence went unsaid for many moments as Nofret, repeating the words in her mind, went over the consequences of her action.

Deciding that she needed further guidance on her worries, she composed herself before finishing, "I need to seek your advice, nomarch." She spoke slowly as she stared at the man. "I don't know if you can help, but I need to speak with someone other than those from the temple!"

Mysis noted the urgency in the woman's voice.

"I'll help if I can," he politely replied, "but if it's anything to do with the island, then I'm afraid I'm not the right person to speak with." His jurisdiction of the nome was vast along this southern border and did not end at the edge of the river bank, for the waters of the Nile on either side of the valley also came under his domain. However, anything that sat within the middle of the river, along with the beautiful islands that were surrounded by its constant flow, was out of his hands.

"It is regarding the island," Nofret confirmed, before adding, "However, I fear it may go further and others may be involved."

The man noted the worry in her voice and, feeling a rise in his interest, he slowly sat forwards and held out his hands. "Please go on," he encouraged. "If anyone in my domain is under suspicion of anything, then I must be told about it."

Nofret cautiously began by telling of her concerns about the underground passageways which had come to her attention. She explained she thought they may spread web-like beneath the great temples and lead to many caves and caverns. Finally, she came to the anxiety that plagued her.

"I fear they may also lead to the crypts and tombs of past priests and priestesses, and Mysis, I think these are being robbed!"

"Well, it wouldn't be the first time!" the nomarch scoffed. Watching the anxious face of the young woman as she took in his words, he knowingly added, "Even the great pharaohs themselves take precautions for that likelihood."

"Yes, I know. But what if it's been going on for some time and Safiya found out about it?" Her voice held a concern. "What if that caused her death?"

"Have you any proof of this?"

As Mysis spoke, his attendant re-entered the room, and this time carrying a large tray of sweets to add to the drink, he lifted across another table and placed the delicacies down. Bowing to both the man and woman, he quickly left the two alone to their talk.

The nomarch waited for a reply to his question and, offering Nofret another drink, he picked up his own. Again staring over the rim, he took a long drain from the cup.

"Have you any proof, Nofret?" he repeated.

Nofret took her time to answer as she thought of her lector priests disappearing beneath Trajan's Kiosk, but seeing the intent stare of the man, she felt she must be honest.

"It's not anything that could be looked at as positive testimony, nomarch. It's only what I've seen. But it looks suspicious to me." She took a sip from the cup before letting her hands rest on her knee. Her head slowly dropped as she thought of the consequences of her action. Swirling the red liquid around in her agitation, she watched as it threatened to overflow.

The man opposite, after finishing his drink and picking up a sweet ring of dough from the tray, stared intently at the woman's bent head and watched her elegant hands tremble in her lap. On seeing the fingers eventually become still around the beaker, he spoke.

"Who do you think may be involved?"

Nofret stayed silent for a long time as she thought of betraying the men who had made her welcome in the temple. She could get Essam and Ramy killed for their actions. And what if she was wrong? She would lose the trust of her priests.

Knowing, however, that she must decide, she drew in a deep breath before realising she needed to explain her unease.

"I fear it may be priests from my own temple, Mysis."

Lifting her head, she stared directly back. Still, for the moment, she did not want to name Essam and Ramy directly, and realising she remained unaware of who the third person was, she added, "And who knows who else? But you can see why I can't go to anyone on the island regarding this?"

Mysis saw the worry etched in the girl's face and, hoping to raise her spirits, he reached across and reassuringly patted her hand.

"I can understand that, Nofret. And you must let me have some time to think before I can advise you on this." He said the words with some authority. "Leave your concern with me and I'll ask around in the village and see if I can find anything that may help."

Seeing the uncertainty lift slightly from the woman's shoulders, he changed the subject. "Shall we play a game?"

The nomarch rose, and placing aside the tray of sweets, he collected an exquisite marble and malachite senet board. Positioning it between them on the dark-topped table, he lay the throwing sticks at its side. Holding his hand open, he invited his guest to begin.

Nofret felt a great relief in telling of her concern and, thinking the man was trying to calm her unease with the distraction, she eagerly picked up the sticks and threw them high into the air. They landed in her favour and, concentrating her mind on the board before her, she let her anguish of the island slip away for the moment.

The afternoon passed over several games and, with the final one bringing the tally to three wins each, they had reached a stalemate and neither could claim an overall victory.

The two were left alone for the most part, their play only interrupted by Penthu, Mysis's scribe, who disturbed the game to require his signing of a last-minute document. In the company of each other, they enjoyed the afternoon until the sun began its stretch into the west. The shadows lengthened within the room and, noting the passing of time, Nofret reluctantly said her goodbye.

***

The torch-lit boat slipped through the waters from the far side of the Nile and reaching the island, a coin changed hands and the boatman was asked to await the passenger's return. The ghostly figure headed stealthily along the bank and arriving where the Temple of *Hathor* began its rise into the dark sky, it slowed down. The man did not want to be seen and, keeping in the shadows, he blended into the gloomy undergrowth beneath the palms.

Ahead, voices could be heard and, reaching where Nofret and her priests sat and ate their evening meal, he stopped and held his breath. Seeing the firelight in the grove of palms and hearing the voices, he slid down the bank and hid below its grass-edged ridge. Being in no hurry, he lay on the soft greenery and made himself comfortable. Staring up into the tops of the lush trees, he awaited his time.

The cool moonlight of *Khonsu* made its way across the heavens. Time slowly ticked by, before, as the stars sparkled in the deep of the night sky, the small group broke up to go their separate ways and use their free time as they saw fit. Essam and Ramy remained behind to ensure their campfire did not spread, and tidying away the empty palm leaves, they kept a watch as the servants of the Goddess *Hathor* disappeared into the dark.

Letting the moments pass in their activity and eventually feeling the coast was clear, Essam gave a low whistle. Waiting a moment, he repeated it over and over in a hurried chain of notes. It was supposed to sound like the call of a night-time bird, just in case others heard it. However, no bird on the island or in its reed-lined edge ever ended its call with a slight cough as the twisting smoke of the fire caught in Essam's throat.

The shape of the man slowly appeared beneath the palms. He had already sent a message across the water earlier that day, warning Essam of Nofret's interest in the labyrinth. Instructing the lector priest that they needed to act sooner rather than later, he had arranged this meeting.

The tall figure emerged out of the shadows alongside

the fire and the lector priest, handing across a drink of wine, sat beside the glowing embers and gestured for the man to sit.

"This won't go down well," Essam whispered. He felt he knew what was being asked and was unsure of his carrying it out. "It's far too close to Safiya's death." He drank heavily from the cup. "Far too close," he considered. Placing the drink down, he showed his rising concern. "You must realise the loss of two priestesses of the Temple of *Hathor* will bring the eyes of Teos once more in my direction."

"I know, but we need to do something!" The figure could not settle and rising, it paced the sand before stopping in the fire's light. The bright agitated eyes of the man looked directly at the lector before he added, "Well, it's her head or yours, Essam! So what do you want to do?"

He placed the question squarely at the feet of the priest before he finished, "I can probably get away with being looked on as a mere accessory, and the lash of the whip would be my punishment." He looked accusingly at his accomplice. "But you, Essam, have been robbing the sacred tombs for some time now, and that's looked on entirely differently!"

Essam stared into the glowing embers of the fire. He knew the punishment for grave robbing was at least the chopping off of the hands of the criminal, and that would be for a first offence. However, he had been doing it for so many years, and in this instance, the taking of the grave goods of the long gone from this world would be looked on with even greater punishment. It would either be the flames of the bonfire or the sharp stake of impalement that awaited him and Ramy. He shuddered at the thought.

Placing his hands flat down on the sand, he pushed himself up. Standing with the glow of the light shining into his face, he resigned himself to the coming action.

"Come on, then." He stepped out of the light and into the dark. "Let's get this done." Leading the way across the sand, he finished, "I've put extra essence of the blue lotus in her wine, so she should give us no trouble!"

***

Nofret had retired early to her room and found Aziza already curled on the bed. She felt overly tired and, thinking it was the effect of the strong wine, she swiftly removed her make-up and wig before undressing and lying down. The room spun as she closed her eyes. Feeling the rise of nausea, she quickly sat up and waited until the spinning stopped and the feeling of sickness passed.

However, sleep soon came, and with it, complete oblivion followed.

Essam, having crept in silently as the startled cat disappeared beneath the bed, held the blue-lotus-infused cloth over the face of his priestess and hearing her breathing become shallow and constant, it reassured him of her lethargy. Softly he called out, and Ramy and their accomplice entered the room. Swiftly wrapping the priestess in her blanket, they lifted her from the bed and left the room empty. With torches held high, they carried her along the banks of the Nile to the walled building of Trajan's Kiosk.

"I don't like this," Ramy whispered, as they laid the inert body of the woman down on the hard sandy slabs. Her bald head rolled to one side and, for a moment, her eyes opened and she stared blankly into the dark of the sky. Bending down, the lector priest quickly closed them and looked up. "There'll be trouble!"

"Yes, but we won't get found out, will we?" The man from the village glared at Ramy. "Not if you two keep to your story. The woman's already been nosing around and asking questions about the temple maze. If she takes things into her own hands and gets herself lost beneath these historic structures, then that's surely her own fault." The man looked decisively at the two before finishing, "Make your mind up!"

Ramy immediately bent down and, lifting the stone slab by its cow-hide strap, the darkness rose to meet them. Raising the torch, and letting its flickering flame light the entrance, he entered the labyrinth and turned around. Holding the wrapped legs of the woman, they fed her lifeless body down into the tunnel, and the two men followed its descent. As they came down the slope of the entranceway, the door above their heads quietly closed and the night sky disappeared from view.

Reaching the bottom, they lofted the torches and silently walked the upper passageways. Moving along its winding stretch of darkness, the woman's lifeless body slowly became heavy, and carrying her between them while holding aloft the torches was no easy task. The light of the flames whirled around as they attempted to hold both the woman and the light. They eventually placed her on the cold floor and, with Essam given both the torches to hold aloft, he led the way, while the other two carried the woman between them.

Her body hung slumped in the blanket as the tunnels went on and on in their twist. Finally, Essam came to a stop. Reaching where the gloom deepened, and the walls arched high above their heads, an angled sloping staircase led down to their right. The lector priest nodded his head in the flame's light and the steps were taken, leaving the main tunnel to its blackness. They now entered the smaller runs at the northern end of the deeper, convoluted subways.

Following the meandering contours of the clammy, airless corridors, they finally came to where several pitted chambers sat in a semicircle at the end of the maze.

These caverns yawned dark and wide in the sullen light of the torch and, choosing the middle one, Nofret was thrown down with no ceremony. The blanket flew open and, with her half-naked body sprawled within the light of the torch, her head came to land against the smoothness of the dank wall. Briefly, her eyes opened again, and she heard the voices of the men before being dragged to the centre of the cavern. The blue lotus held her in its grip and soon reclaimed her.

Essam, holding high the torch, checked again that the woman remained unconscious and, leaving her as she lay, the two lector priests left with no feeling or regret for deserting her, their minds only on safeguarding their own necks.

As the flickering light slowly receded along the walkway and the darkness closed in on the abandoned woman, the three men headed upwards and, reaching the Temple of the Triad, they let the doorway close at their backs and they each went their separate ways.

CHAPTER ELEVEN

Nofret slowly opened her eyes. Around her, the white flashes that filtered through her brain kept up their constant dance in her vision. Gradually they faded and a cold darkness took their place. She was lying flat out on the blanket, but the hard ground beneath her shoulders felt cold and stony. The silence was complete. Her head pounded and for a long time, she lay shivering before the sickening spinning in her mind gradually eased.

Edging to sit up, the stone of the floor bit into her bare hands and her bruised arms and legs felt heavy. She moved hesitantly to test for any injuries and found that, thankfully, nothing appeared to be broken.

Not knowing where she was, and unsure how long she had lain there, she called out and tentatively felt across the cold stone which surrounded her. It was sandy to the touch, and beneath that, the floor felt uneven to her fingertips. A silence only answered her echoing call.

Reaching out further, she let her hands find their way in a full circle about her. She could feel nothing close by, and eventually, knowing she must move, she wrapped the thin blanket around her shoulders and crawled uncertainly across the roughness. She was brought up sharply by the flatness of a wall, and coming to a stop, she came around to sit up and lean against its rocky surface. She at least felt some security in its solid presence.

Bringing her grazed knees up to her chest, she sat shaking as the darkness held her in its grip and, wrapping her arms around her scantily clad legs, she hung on desperately to warm her cold limbs. The blanket gave her some protection from the chill, but as the blue lotus remained in her system, her head slowly spun and a sickness came and went.

Eventually, as her thinking cleared, she could guess where she was and who had put her there. She had, in her subconscious, briefly heard the voice of Essam as he threw her down upon the ground and, in its knowing, felt the grip of fear tighten its hold. The slow rise of panic grew and, pinning her in place against the cold wall, her thoughts went back and forth.

She knew she was in the tunnels beneath the temples and, raising her head, she shouted out again. However, her voice went unanswered apart from the echo of the words, which rebounded instantly back to her ears and rolled around the confines of the cave.

Sitting still for uncounted time, the darkness continued its chilling embrace and, in it, she let her heavy head drop forwards as, in the last of the blue lotus's hold, she fell in and out of sleep.

In her dreams, she walked the Temple at Dendera and her floating steps took her along its familiar corridors and walkways and through the inner and outer hypostyle halls. She felt safe there and, even when the recognisable walls and statues led her into the dark, she had no fear. Following the paths, her feet walked the serpentine structures and followed the lead of the gods. Finally, she reached an arched doorway where the light shone brightly and, stepping out into the fragrance of the day, the blue of the Nile lay before her.

Suddenly waking, her position had not changed, and the blackness had grown no lighter. Blinking, she hoped to clear her vision, but it was no good. The utter darkness of the cave kept its hold. Her fear carried on its crawl through her mind and she hesitated to move, scared of the unknown, which lay unseen around her. Yet, aware that she could die here if she remained seated, she had to at least try to find a way out.

Rising to stand against the reassuring solidness of the wall, her breathing came shallow and fast. Wrapping the blanket securely about her cold body, she first pushed herself away from the wall and, making sure of her footing, she moved to her right. Her hands, flat against the support of the wall, followed the rough surface and, after uncounted moments of fumbling her way, her cold fingers reached the sharpness of an edge. She called out again and waited for some moments to get an answer before carefully stretching her arm out beyond the cave's limitations. Her searching hand could feel nothing, and the void before her appeared to show an opening.

She hesitated briefly, but not wishing to spend another moment in uncertainty, she placed her bare foot forwards. The floor continued on a level and she raised her left arm before her as she clung on with her right hand to the cavern's boundary. Stumbling out into the broader passageway, she unknowingly left her subterranean prison behind.

The wall was the only security that Nofret could feel and, keeping close beside it, she edged her way along until, unknowingly entering the walkway she had been carried down, her left hand felt the opposite wall as it closed in at her side.

The reach of her stretched-out arms now touched both sides of the tunnel and gave her some reassurance. Yet as time passed with each fumbling footfall, and the passage went on in its enclosure, she prayed to the gods for their help. In despair, she let her tears creep their way down her face. Her panic rose as the dark led her on until, after uncounted steps, her right hand came upon another opening that gaped unseen at her side.

She hesitated about which way to go, but on turning into the smooth passageway, she hoped she was going the right way. However, as she followed the sweep of the wall, she was, unfortunately, being fed further away from her attempt to escape and led deeper into the labyrinth.

Twice she came to a halt and wondered if she should turn back. But as time ceased its existence in this world, she continued to edge onwards, and the need to keep moving replaced that thought. Over and over in her mind, she wondered if she would die here, and no one, except the gods who heard her plea, would know where she was.

The darkness never let up but gradually around her, the stale smell of the tunnels was replaced by the sweet aroma of burning incense which punctuated the chill of the air as she blindly stepped into the west. The smell was instantly uplifting and, thinking the Temple of *Isis* must be above her, gave some certainty to her position.

Nevertheless, the dark remained, and she walked and stumbled her way within this underworld. Occasionally, she called out and waited for an answer. Nothing came back and, with the fear gripping her and churning its uncertainty in the emptiness of her stomach, it left her with a sickness that urged her on.

Suddenly, beneath her bare foot, she trod on something sharp and, instinctively kicking it aside, heard a tinkle as it spun off into the middle of the passage. Falling to her knees and letting her hands drop from the walls, she crawled ahead and followed its direction.

Cautiously grovelling on the floor, her cold fingers eventually came upon it, and she picked it up. It felt like a small metal chain and, as she held it, the faint ringing of the bell sounded reminiscent of something. She desperately tried to remember from where until, as its sound echoed through the dark, it came to her. It reminded her of the ankle bracelet found on the rocks in the south. The one belonging to Safiya!

Eagerly, feeling along its interwoven length, she found the two entwined cow horns and, letting the ringing sound fill the darkness, she now knew for certain that the last Priestess of *Hathor* had also been here. It gave her something to hang onto, but in finding it, her dread rose even higher.

Standing and reaching out again for the security of the rough wall, she stood for an uncounted time, the blanket her only source of warmth, before her imaginings took her on a journey of utter dismay and the surrounding passageways became filled with horrors. Safiya had also been down here. Yet, in knowing the fate of the woman, it was not a reassuring thought to hold.

She let her head drop to the side and her cheek felt the smooth coldness of the chiselled enclosure as her tears flowed in her anger and despair. Until, without warning, another far-off noise slowly invaded her consciousness. Wiping her face with her hand, she was sure she could hear something behind her and the breath of some terrifying monster filled her mind.

In her haste to flee, she scrambled away from the reassurance of the wall and blindly rushed on. But it continued to follow close behind until, having to stop as the exhaustion fell around, she held her breath and awaited her fate.

Nothing happened, and the vibrations of the sound slowly disappeared. Yet, as soon as she moved and breathed, the sound returned and, with some relief, she reasoned it was an echo of her own fearful breathing that dogged her steps.

Still, even given that knowledge, she remained lost beneath the island and turn after turn made in the darkness brought her no closer to escape. Drained of energy and cold from the labyrinth's chilly air, her collapse finally caught up with her and she could walk no further.

Letting her hands drop from the wall, she fell to the ground. In her grasp, she hung on in desperation to the anklet as if it were her only link to the world above. Her childhood fears held her in place and, hoping to dispel them, she tried to imagine herself on the sands beside the Red Sea as the waves washed up the beach. It worked for a while, but as the cold horrors of the dark came flooding back, freezing her mind, she felt she was already dead.

***

As Nofret stumbled about in the dark, and the horrifying realisation fell chillingly over her that she was trapped by the island's hold, above her in the Temple of *Isis*, Teos began his morning service to the ancient triad and his voice joined the smoke and chants of the supplicants as they filled the vaulted ceilings.

While across on the far side of the island, in the Temple of *Hathor*, Essam dutifully stood in wait for his priestess as the morning sun began its rise. He knew for sure she would not come, but putting on his usually calm and grandiose face, he waited patiently and let the time move on.

Yet, as the temple filled up with an increasing amount of petitioners from the far shore and Nofret had still not appeared, his demeanour changed. Putting on a look of growing annoyance, he sent Musa to check for the priestess. The *wab* priest was quick to return and, whispering to Essam that she was not in her room, he stepped back and let his senior decide the course of the moment.

Essam looked concerned for some time and, counting out the minutes, he paced the floor before the altar. Until, knowing the service could not delay any longer as the sun began its rise in the east, he was given approval by the other Priests of *Hathor*, and raising his arms, he turned his face to stare up at his goddess.

He began the service the same as when Safiya had disappeared and took charge of the morning's observance while Ramy dutifully assisted him. The priests looked on as the Goddess of the Sky received her due reverence, and prayers and supplications were said in her name. The ceremony strictly followed its progression in the goddess's eyes and ended with the retinue of worshippers placing their gifts at the feet of the central statue before, turning away from the fixed gaze of *Hathor*, they received the blessing of Essam. Filing out into the courtyard, the worshippers from the east bank then left the essence of the temple behind.

After the last of the supplicants had left, and the sun was thankfully risen high in the sky, Essam went himself to look for Nofret. He needed to show his eagerness to find her. But knowing where her body lay, he instead spent many moments seated on her bed thinking of the previous night's work. He relived the walk through the passages of the labyrinth as they carried the woman's heavy body, and the sickening thud, as her head hit the ground, played itself in his memory. He was not sorry for his actions, for his own neck was more important than hers.

Still, wanting to banish these thoughts, he began looking around at the meagre possessions that made up the woman's life. Picking up one of the alabaster jars that sat beside her bed, he lifted the stopper and took a sniff at the contents before carefully placing it down. Between the jars, her beads, bracelets, and necklaces lay strewn about.

Staring around the confines of the room, her clothing appeared to have been carelessly tossed aside in some disarray. But letting the urge to clear these up and tidy away the disorder of the woman's life slowly fade, he remained seated and let the thought of Nofret evaporate on the rising heat.

He did not want to linger on the night's activity and would rather let the time pass by in contemplating the service to *Hathor* he had just performed. He had seemingly, with the gratitude of the gathered crowd, stepped into the priestess's shoes with little difficulty. He had done his best, but tomorrow he would be better prepared. His memory played back to him the look of thanks that filled the supplicants' faces as he gave them pardon for their everyday actions and sins. His feeling of superiority over them rose. Filling his mind, he knew he stood above those who knelt before him.

Eventually, he returned to the present and, thinking he had given enough time in the room's search, he stood and left behind the remains of the woman's life. Closing the door carefully on the clutter, he walked across the open aisle and returned to the temple.

The Priests of *Hathor* were awaiting him before the statues of their goddess. All of them, except Ramy, carried on their faces a look of increasing concern. The priestess's absence especially bothered the *wab* priest, Musa, knowing she had recently seemed troubled by something. Lifting his head as Essam returned, he asked, "Has she left us?"

"She's not taken any clothes," Essam replied on hearing the uncertainty in the man's voice. Hoping to reassure the worried priests, he finished, "So it would seem she hasn't gone far!"

"Then she must be somewhere on the island."

"It would appear so. But who knows?" Essam stood at the base of the statue of *Hathor*, and not knowing why, he added, "Perhaps she took a walk in the dark and fell? Or she could be lying somewhere on the island's edge, unable to shout for help…" A fleeting image of Priestess Safiya sprawled across the boulders rose in his mind. Swiftly pushing it away, he cynically ended, "We all know the banks of the Nile can be hazardous to those who may stray along its boundary."

His words did not ease the priests and, sensing the growing concern for Nofret's whereabouts, Essam appointed each of them to look for her on different sides of the island. The men were quick to hurry away to the task. Ramy, however, after watching the others leave, remained behind.

"No point in wasting my energy!" He sat down at the foot of *Hathor* and after helping himself to a slice of coconut, which sat cut up and decorated on its woven palm leaf, he stared up at Essam. "We both know they won't find her!" He turned away from the harsh glare of the lector and, picking up the donations closest to him, he tidied away the gifts from around the feet of the goddess.

Not long after, when the silence had grown around the

temple, the priests returned one at a time, and reported that no sign of Nofret had been found in their search. Each had walked the island down to where the water met its ring of stones, but they discovered nothing to say that she had even been there.

The worry of her whereabouts was growing and, hoping to ease the fears for just that bit longer, the lector priest tried to calm their concern.

"Let's not get too worried." He patted Musa on the arm and smiled fatherly into the young man's eyes. "Perhaps she's just off the island at this moment, and doing the work of *Hathor* elsewhere."

His words sounded hollow in the hall's vastness, but, instructing his men to continue their service to the gods, they each went their way to start the everyday duties that came with their position.

***

Essam waited patiently until the sun was heading into the west before he went to seek the advice of High Priest Teos. He did not want to appear overly eager to report the missing priestess, but seeing the anxiety gathering in the minds of the temple priests, as Nofret still failed to appear, he dared not leave it any longer.

Teos sat at the back of the building under the overhang of the roof and, greeting Essam as he came through from the front, he let the lector priest take the seat opposite where the dying sun lit the underside of the palms. The cicadas sang out loudly at this time of day and over their incessant noise, Essam told of Nofret's absence.

"She did not attend the service this morning, Teos, and I've had the servants of *Hathor* scouring the island. She's not to be found anywhere!" He let his voice fill with uncertainty as he carefully watched the reaction of the man opposite.

Teos immediately became agitated, and standing, he paced the covered area before stopping at where the lector priest sat with his head upturned in the last rays of *Ra*.

"You should have let me know this sooner!" the high priest shouted. "With Safiya going missing and then being found dead on the rocks, surely you felt the need to alert me straight away?" He turned from the troubling stare of the man and attempted to control his anger.

"I had the morning service to *Hathor* to perform in Nofret's absence, Teos."

Essam's voice cut through the rising tension and as he addressed the man as an equal, the high priest spun around in resentment.

"Remember your place, lector!"

Essam reluctantly nodded in acceptance of Teos's superiority before adding, "But I had to ensure the goddess received her due attention. At that moment, it seemed more important than worrying overly about where the priestess had gone, don't you think?" He let his eyes hold the watch of the high priest as if daring him to say he had done wrong.

Teos eventually glanced away. He could understand the reasoning, knowing that the service to the gods always came first. Yet, he felt the lector had been more than lax in showing concern for the priestess.

His fear gathered in his thinking and centred on the recent death of Safiya and the finding of her battered body on the island's rocky surroundings. *It surely could not happen twice*, he thought. Sitting down, he came to the edge of the seat and haughtily asked, "So where do you think she may have gone?"

"I don't know," Essam arrogantly replied, "but word is that she has recently been seen taking the boat over to the village." He let the suggestion form in the high priest's mind. "She has, I understand, twice been to visit the nomarch and perhaps she may have spent the night there?" He left the sentence to hang in the air with its implication of misconduct on the woman's part. Letting this seed of thought grow in Teos's mind, he hoped it would take the search away from the island.

"Then we must send word over the water." The high priest knew that for some, life on the island was restrictive. But the Priestess Nofret, in her short while of service, had not given him any concern in that regard.

"She must be found immediately!" he finished.

***

Meow, meow. Meow, meow.

The unexpected sound came from Nofret's left and after the frightening quietness of the passage, it startled her and made her jump. It echoed in the cavern-like space of the tunnel and, magnified by the constraint of the walls, it sounded like a chorus of cats. She initially froze on hearing it, but realising that these runs beneath the island could be the homes of the temple cats and the dark underground passageways known to them, she stopped and let the noise come to her.

The invisible cat rubbed against her cold bare legs as Nofret sat up and leaned against the wall. She tentatively reached down, and the cat stretched to receive her touch.

"Aziza?"

The cat meowed its greeting in response to her voice and, rubbing against the cold bare leg of the woman, it chirruped its comfort. Nofret stretched further and, touching the softness of its back, she felt a sudden rush of relief.

"Where did you come from?" The sound of her voice echoed along the black tunnel.

The cat jumped on her lap and, settling itself across her knees, she let her warmth give some ease from the creeping chill. Nofret held on tightly. She was more than grateful for the comfort. But it was the overwhelming relief that she was not alone which was welcomed even more. The cat stayed in place and, as the time passed in the pitch-black, the Priestess of *Hathor* eventually hung her head and let the extreme tiredness take her into oblivion.

Later, waking to the cold dark, Aziza had dropped from her lap and left her knees feeling chilled. However, the cat had not gone far. She was curled up at Nofret's feet and, sensing the woman waking, she stretched and rubbed against her legs.

Meow, meow, meow.

Nofret let out a sob of thanks to the gods. Knowing the cat had found its way in, she realised it would know its way out. Holding on to that fact, she let hope rise in her heart. The feeling pushed her to stand and ignore the biting cramp that coursed hard up her legs.

"Come on Aziza, show me the way out!"

The cat shot off down the tunnel, meowing loudly, and Nofret, moving with purpose in her soul, followed its call. With the cat at her feet leading the way, the darkness seemed just that less daunting. Yet, as she stumbled within the labyrinth and the increasing hunger and thirst made itself known, she doubted ever getting out.

Outside, the day was passing into another night, and the concern for the absent priestess was growing. The Priests of *Hathor* kept up their devotion to their goddess and, after her shrine was disrobed of its finery and left for the night, Musa kept a lonely vigil in the temple's candlelit gloom.

***

The next morning, after spending a restless night after hearing the priestess was missing, Teos joined the search for her. Taking the boat over the water after his service to the gods, he bypassed the workshops where the tradesmen were opening their shutters and the children were busily displaying the wares at the front of the buildings. Walking quickly to the large house at the top of the street, he banged on the door of the nomarch's home and waited impatiently while Mysis was fetched from his breakfast.

The nomarch was surprised to see the high priest. It was usual in the status of both men that they met on the island and to see the man standing before him in his hallway put him on his guard. Something must be wrong, he immediately thought.

"Welcome, Teos." He let a smile cross his face and wiping his hands on the cloth which sat tied at his side, he finished, "I hope I find you well this morning?"

Teos immediately dismissed the usual niceties given to his status and, with a quick wave of his hand, he came straight to the point. "Is the Priestess Nofret with you?"

"No, she's not here!" Mysis was genuinely taken aback at the suggestion and wondered why Teos was even asking. "Do you think she should be?" he slowly added. Indicating for the high priest to follow him through to the garden and take a seat, they left the cool hallway behind and sat in the sun's warmth. There, the nomarch continued his questioning.

"Is there some worry about the priestess's whereabouts, Teos?"

"She's been missing from her temple since yesterday morning!"

"Since yesterday!" The man shot forwards in his seat, sensing a familiarity in the words. The conversation had a likeness to one spoken not so long ago. "Why then have you left it so long to come over?"

"We've been searching the island, and although Essam has had his priests scouring the banks and the ruins of the buildings, she's not to be found anywhere."

"Did they ask the ferrymen?"

"I asked on the way over, but they too have not seen her." Teos looked down at his hands. They were moving agitated within his lap and, bringing his focus on them to cease their shiver, he purposely moved them aside and gripped his knees. The past years had left their mark on the man's whole demeanour and with the recent situation with Safiya in his mind, the worry on his face heightened. Looking up, he finished, "I don't want a repetition, Mysis!"

"I'll ask around in the streets for you, Teos." The nomarch too suddenly felt the unease filling his mind. "But you have my word that I've not seen her."

"Then she must still be on the island!"

**

Nofret came to a dead end after following the guidance of the cat. And Aziza, leaving behind a cry that filled the air, suddenly disappeared, leaving her alone in the dark. She could still be heard calling, but it sounded now as if it was way, way above Nofret's head and as if a wall stood between them. The priestess shouted, but there was no reply. Suddenly, it felt as if she had been abandoned.

A wall stretched on both her left and right, but following it to her left where she had last heard the cry of the cat, her cold toes eventually stubbed themselves on the bottom rung of a stairway. Reaching down, the sharply cut ledge led up in a series of steps. Thinking this may be the way out, Nofret began a cautious climb.

Moving upwards, small landings curved against the face of the wall and interspersed the stairs and here Nofret ran her hands along its enclosure. There was still no escape, but as she climbed, the sound of the cat's voice gradually grew closer.

Eventually, she unknowingly reached the top, where a small upper area sat in the dark. Feeling the bow of the wall as it enclosed around and no further steps led off, there appeared no way out from here and the labyrinth still held her.

In desperation, as the cry of the cat sounded so near, she dropped to the ground, and letting her hands search the lower walls, she scratched around in the dust before coming upon the smallest of holes into which Aziza must have disappeared. It was hardly big enough for the cat, let alone anyone else. With a growing panic, as she pushed her hand through and sensed the touch of a breeze as it played around her fingertips, she realised she remained trapped, even though the outside was so close.

It appeared there was no leaving the labyrinth that way

for her. Yet, on continuing her feel around the bottom of the wall where it joined the gritty floor, she found a wooden peg that seemed out of place in the tunnel. It felt well-worn and smooth to the touch and desperately she hung on to it.

It moved beneath her hand, and Nofret eagerly tugged at it, wondering on its purpose. She pressed it down, but it did nothing and in her rising frustration, she twisted and turned it around. It still achieved nothing. However, on pushing it in and lifting it, a grating sound came on her right and the sudden inrush of air took her breath away.

An opening widened as the doorway was released from its tight hold, and beyond, the darkness of the Temple of *Isis* met the fearful enclosure of the labyrinth. The sweet-smelling freshness of the scent-filled air permeated Nofret's lungs. Stepping through with such great relief falling around her shoulders, she came out from behind a statue of *Horus*.

She was met by the cry of the cat as it scuttled back and forth across the temple floor, before pausing only briefly, it shot off to hunt the rats that scurried around the home of the gods.

CHAPTER TWELVE

Nofret sat at the foot of *Horus* and hung her bare head. Her prayers and thanks to all the gods she knew came whispered on her breath and, hearing the scrape of the door as it closed fast behind her, she let the tears stream down her cheeks. For some time, she could only sit and send her prayers out into the temple. At her feet, the cat Aziza returned and played on the polished floor before, hearing the far-off scratch and patter of feet, it ran off into the columned hall.

Eventually, the Priestess of *Hathor* raised her eyes and, wiping her face, stared into the dark. She wondered about her next step. She feared returning to her rooms would only alert Essam and Ramy that she remained alive and, wanting them to continue believing her lost beneath the island, she did not want to change that thought. However, she was exhausted and badly in need of food and water.

Feeling a sudden chill fall over her, she rose and, wrapping the blanket closely about her shivering body, she walked the silent temple corridors. Knowing the day's offerings would have already been removed from the altar and enjoyed by the priests and servants to the gods, she eventually headed towards the doorway. Leaving the cat behind to continue its chase, she took the sloping walkway down into the freshness of the open courtyard.

Above her, the sky was black and pock-marked with stars, but to Nofret, it felt like a rebirth as the cool wind touched her bruised skin. Leaving behind the temple complex of the gods, she hurriedly followed the wall around its western edge. Letting the Nile keep its forever flow on her left, its dark waters glistened in the light of the crescent moon. She trod cautiously and looked warily out for the huge, dark shapes of the crocodiles as they dozed on the banks. She feared them, but her greater fear was returning to the Temple of *Hathor*.

Knowing that avenue of thought was closed to her, her only option remained to seek the help of High Priest Teos. Yet, she was uncertain of even doing that, her mind still wondering if he played a part in Safiya's death. But there was nowhere else to go. She thought only of finding safety.

The sand-lined edge took her along the western side of the island, where she kept alert and wary of the lower banks. Further out, the hippos occasionally called and the Nile valley filled with the roar of their chorus as it escorted her to the north.

Finally, on reaching the darkness of the shadow of the building, a single light remained in the high priest's house and, following the route to the back of the low-lying structure, Nofret tried the door. It was thankfully open. Stepping through, she hesitated a moment, cautiously listening for voices. Hearing only silence and the unmistakable sound of her own anxious breathing, she quietly closed the entrance at her back and followed the snaking walk of the hallway.

She knew the high priest's private quarters sat at the front of the building, but on reaching there, she hesitated. A soft glimmer of light shone beneath the closed doorway and, hoping she was not wrong in her thinking, she paused a moment before knocking gently and pushing it open.

She stood beneath the arch, her tear-stained face lit by the lights placed about the room. Hearing the door open, Teos immediately turned.

"Nofret!"

He was expecting to see one of his servants bringing in refreshments and was completely astonished to see the priestess standing before him. He had been unable to find sleep since hearing of her disappearance and, for the last few hours, had sat repeatedly sending out a plea for her safety to whichever god he thought was listening.

He was also, just in case his appeal went unheard, composing a letter in his head to be sent down the Nile to the powers at the Temple of Dendera, saying that once again the Island of Philae needed a Priestess of *Hathor* to give honour in her temple. He had just put the words into some sort of order when the door opened and Nofret had appeared. Raising his hands to the heavens in grateful praise, he thanked the gods for an answer to his prayers.

Rushing to the woman's aid as he saw her near collapse, he wrapped his arms around her cold body and, pulling a blanket from off the nearest chair, he guided her to the seating beneath the window. Wrapping the warmth of the cover about her frozen shoulders, he poured wine for her and let her drink.

"Thank the gods, Nofret!" He looked with genuine concern into her eyes. "Where have you been? We have been so worried about you."

The words were said with honesty, the anxiety in the tone unmistaken, and hearing it, Nofret felt secure in his presence. Her worry that Teos was involved in the robbing of the crypts immediately evaporated and the fear that once gripped her rose from around her heart. Holding onto the man, and letting the feel of the warm wine permeate her chilled limbs, she sat still for some moments.

"Where have you been, priestess?" the high priest asked again after topping up the beaker. Sitting beside the woman, he held her cold hand until he felt the shivering lessen.

Nofret, however, held on gratefully to the warmth and eventually explained her waking in the labyrinth below the island. She had expected a look of surprise in her telling of the unknown passageways, but Teos only nodded his head.

"So you know about the tunnels?" She let go of the man's hand and, bringing the blanket up to cover her bald head, she wrapped the tasselled ends over her slim shoulders.

"I do," he immediately answered. "This whole island is supposedly riddled with them."

He explained that the once-used ceremonial passageways had long stood abandoned by the priests of the ancient gods and not used for many, many years. He added they went on in their run of the labyrinth and the stretch of the tunnels in the past had resounded to the sound of many feet.

"The voices of the priests once echoed loud in chant and song beneath this island," he made clear. "But the services held there, over the uncounted years, were brought into the light of the Sun God and here in these temples worshipped not only by their priests."

Nofret sat in silence as he ended and in her imaginings, she heard the tramp of feet as they echoed along the blackness. "So they're not used now?"

"Not for many years, even before my time." The high priest stood and walking the room, his hands brushed the back of the chairs that sat around the space. Suddenly, he came to a stop and asked, "But how did you get down there?"

"I don't know." The effects of the blue lotus had long

left the woman's body, but the bitter residue which remained in her mouth was recognised. She took another sip of the wine to dispel the taste. "I think I must have been drugged!"

"Drugged?" Teos appeared genuinely shocked at the suggestion. "By whom?"

A fleeting image of Essam, smiling as he passed over the cup of wine, played itself in Nofret's mind. "It was Lector Essam!"

"Your own priest!" Teos came back to where the woman sat and after refilling her cup, he took one himself and drank deeply. "I feel that to be most surprising."

"But that's not the least, Teos." The Priestess of *Hathor* felt supported by Teos's words and continued, "I think the crypts are being robbed, and the grave goods of the past priests and priestesses are being sold for profit." She took another sip of the warming liquid. "I think Essam and Ramy are involved."

The high priest knew of this sort of thing happening elsewhere, but the audacity of it being done under his own nose was hard to take. He continued his walk of the space between the chairs and let his anger build.

"Have you any proof?" he demanded, returning to stand before the woman. "You can't just make these accusations, Nofret!"

"Not proof as such." She realised she had no real evidence apart from what she had seen. "However," she added, "I think there's someone in the village who moves the artefacts on fairly quickly."

The high priest let his shoulders sag, and he sat down. Stretching forwards, he patted the woman on the hand. "Well, at least you are safe, and that's one less worry."

A silence fell around the room and, in it, the two sat

with differing thoughts filling their minds. Eventually, the priestess broke the quiet.

"Teos, I also found this in the tunnels." Bringing out her hand, she showed the anklet found in the labyrinth. It sat in her palm like a small jewelled snake, the entwined cow horns lying flat within the shape. "I think this belonged to Safiya!"

"How do you know that?" The reply came sharply and, reaching out, Teos took the jingling chain from Nofret's palm and held it up to the candlelight. The tiny bell tinkled as the mirrored flame flickered on its surface. "Most of the priestesses wear these." He handed the anklet back.

"But note the cow horns, Teos. It's identical to the one I found on the rocks!"

The high priest sat back and let his head hang. His mind went over the possibilities and implications of what the woman was saying and, bringing the image of Essam to mind, he now wondered about the man. The stealing of grave goods, yes he could understand the temptation there. But the possibility of murder was a different thing.

"I never would have thought it," he whispered. "Someone on this island being involved with such a crime!"

Nofret suddenly felt sorry for the man, and taking a hold of his hand she hoped to comfort him. She had brought all this anxiety down upon his house by heading there to seek safety, but she had nowhere else to go.

However, another even more troubling thought came clear to her mind. She did not want the other anklet falling into Essam's hands.

"Teos, you must get the first anklet from my room." She remembered taking it off and wrapping it around her scented jars on the tabletop. "These are evidence and mean nothing if kept apart. However, together, they add up to something completely different."

The high priest understood her thinking and resolved to do as asked, but as he rose and opened the shutters to the grey of the morning, a more important thought filled Nofret's mind as she thought of the approaching day.

"No one must know I'm alive, Teos, you understand that?" Her voice held a note of definite authority. "You must carry on as though I'm still missing. Don't let anyone know I'm safe!" A sudden thought flashed through her mind. "You know we must get Essam to admit to his crimes and we need time to think about how to achieve this."

The two sat in an uneasy silence as the darkness beyond the room lifted and, on hearing the cockerel's crow close by the window, Teos knew he must soon ready himself for the morning's service to the gods. His head ached and his tiredness seemed overwhelming, but looking across at the woman, he saw the extreme weariness that sat about her shoulders.

"Now, Nofret, what about my sending a dispatch up the river in your absence?" The man had pushed this thought aside, but once more it rose in his mind. "I shouldn't be delaying in doing this or it may arouse suspicion."

"Then you must do exactly as you did when Safiya went missing," Nofret reasoned.

Knowing they needed to keep Essam and Ramy in the dark, she added, "You must act as though I'm missing, presumed dead, and my body lost to the Nile."

"That I can easily do, Nofret. But what about you? What will you do?"

"I shall continue to play the part given to me by Essam and remain dead to his eyes."

"But where will you hide?" The high priest looked at her with growing interest. The woman desperately needed his help and he would give it. But he would not jeopardise his long-held position on the island, not even for her. "You can't stay here, Nofret. My staff have a complete run of these rooms and would be watchful if I kept them out."

Nofret had already given some thought to this and, well aware she could not return to her temple, she had come to only one conclusion.

"Then the Temple of *Isis* must give me sanctuary."

"The Temple of the Goddess is there for everyone, as I'm sure you know. But as befitting the house of the great gods, my priests come and go as they please. It would be hard for you to hide there for long."

Nofret could see his thinking and, knowing the exit of the passageways came out within the temple, she realised that anyone leaving the labyrinth could find her if she hid in the temple building itself. The only place that would give her sanctuary and keep her safe was the inner sanctum.

"Then I will seek the sanctuary of the gods and hope they, in their goodness, will hide me." She looked across at Teos and, seeing the suggestion of her words recognised in his eyes, she finished, "I'll place myself in the hands of the gods."

***

The light was growing on the eastern horizon when Nofret returned along the bank. She felt enlivened by the food and drink and carrying with her a reed mat and blanket, along with a small flask of water and some bread and fruit, she headed immediately to the Temple of *Isis*.

The coolness of the growing dawn followed her as she walked the slope of the outer gateway, yet on entering the hypostyle hall, the darkness gathered and held her in its embrace. Passing the imposing figure of *Horus,* where she had left behind the terror of the labyrinth, she hurried past and continued down the temple's stretch before entering the domain of the high priest.

No one else ever came here, these three interlocking rooms being the private realm of Teos and his gods. With that, the Priestess of *Hathor* felt some safety from the eyes of the world. As she carefully closed the door behind her and leaned against the cool back of the carved wood, the feeling of security fell around in the quietness and she could finally relax.

She was used to being alone in *Hathor*'s inner sanctum, but looking around and seeing the darkened room stretch away from her, she was impressed. Over on the far side of the island, her own domain had been small and simple, a room of prayer befitting the priestess. Here, though, the sacred place of *Isis*, *Osiris* and *Horus* was lavish in its grandeur to the triad.

Instead of one small statue with its shrine and kneeling place where the high priest communed with his god, three distinct altars sat within each space. One in the west, one in the east and one in the north. The three were simple in their design. No great grandeur was needed here to impress the worshippers who knelt in awe within the main temple. But the rooms themselves gave out a feeling of everlasting glory to the gods, and their surrounding presence was immediately felt.

Standing in the dimness before the altar of the Goddess *Isis*, Nofret placed a piece of fruit at the foot of the small statue and, bowing her head, gave her thanks for her survival. Her whispered words echoed around the chamber before rising and heading out through the open roof.

The goddess was sculpted in fine pink alabaster and the paleness of its delicate colouring added to her ethereal presence. Her raised head, crowned with an ornate throne that denoted her position in the realm of the gods, looked out over the space, but her eyes appeared to stare down upon Nofret as she stood bare-headed before the altar.

At each side of the main chamber, the statues of *Osiris* and his son *Horus* stood looking at each other across the span of the room. These were both sculpted in solid granite, the stone glistening in the increasing morning light that lit Nofret from above.

The Priestess of *Hathor* gave both their due reverence before placing the reed mat on the western side beneath the gaze of *Osiris*, the God of the Underworld. Feeling the presence of the great god's statue as it looked across time, she made herself as comfortable as she could in the confines of the room's sanctuary.

Seated on the mat, she stared across the smoothness of the foot-polished floor and let her mind become calm. Picking up a piece of bread, she nibbled the edge and, letting her shoulders drop and clear of all the tension that gripped her, she pushed aside her fear of the labyrinth and gathered her thoughts. Now she had time to think.

***

On the opposite side of the island, Essam, having taken control in the temple of the Goddess *Hathor*, continued with the plans Nofret had put in place regarding the upcoming *Hab Nefer en Sekhen* ceremony. He thought, as the realisation that Nofret was gone grew in the community and they awaited a new priestess, this would be a distraction and take away the worry about her disappearance.

In the coming days, he put into place the priestess's wishes and, with ones of his own, the service for the joining in marriage of *Horus* and *Hathor* took shape. Essam would often repeat that it would have been what Nofret wanted, and the Priests of *Hathor*, wanting to do what was right, were happy to be doing the will of their priestess. With that, they pushed aside the constant worry of what could have happened to her and instead focused on something to celebrate Nofret's name.

Her body had still not been found and – as the slow realisation that she never would be – took over, some calm came to the temple.

Musa, however, could not fully settle his worries, knowing his priestess had been concerned about something. And, in his downtime from his worship and menial duties in the temple, he was forever searching the banks of the Nile. Walking out over the rocky peninsula in the south, he would often stop, unknowing of the reason why, by the place where Safiya's body had lain. Occasionally, as he stood watching the water sweep past, the head of a crocodile would rise, its long, flat snout pushing through the water. Each time, on seeing the deadly beasts, Musa would pick up the smaller stones that lay about his feet and hurl them in his frustration at the passing danger.

***

Over time, Nofret lost touch with the outside world, and her life became one likened to that of a prisoner. The days were easy enough, spent in the brilliance and light of the room, but the nights were dark and chilly. Teos had offered to bring lamps, but Nofret thought it unwise. It was not usual for a light to be seen in the sanctuary and would be looked on suspiciously. She could easily open the door and leave, but her fear kept her in place.

Her only contact with the world outside came when Teos sought the seclusion of his sanctum in his ritual of daily prayers. He brought with him, layered beneath his robes, extra clothing and the chill of the night for Nofret was eased. Food was always present in the gifts given by the supplicants, and she ate well from the benevolence of the townsfolk. Yet, the silence in between these times was a trial, and she was more than grateful for the high priest's presence, for it gave her a chance to talk.

However, to those who stood excluded from the stare of *Osiris*, *Isis* and *Horus*, the actions of their high priest gave a cause for concern. On entering the realm of the gods, his voice appeared changed and the rise and fall of his words as he took the petitions before the triad became one filled with whispers and hidden words.

More often, of late, they had noticed the moments spent in contemplation with the gods took up more of his time. He often hid away for long stretches and, believing him to be affected by the loss of another priestess on the island, they let him deal with it in his own way.

Within the sacred temple, Nofret counted the days by the passing of the sun and moon in their constant trail above her head. Yet the spirits of tedium and boredom filled her day and her impatience grew. Time spent in the confinement of the four walls let her thoughts come and go, but her dreams, whether god-given or not, were insightful. Still, on hearing from Teos that Essam was going to hold the Beautiful Feast of the Reunion ceremony in her honour within the Temple of the Triad, an idea began forming in her mind. She saw a plan coming together and the next morning she reminded Teos of the need to retrieve the anklet of Safiya from her room.

***

Teos waited for his moment and in the guise of seeking news on the upcoming festivity, he walked the island pathway and entered the courtyard of the Temple of *Hathor*. Not finding anyone about the walls of the building, he walked the length of the cool, shaded house and, briefly looking to see if he was being tailed, left behind the silence of the empty shrine and headed down the open walkway in the south. Pushing open Nofret's door, he was quick in his search.

The anklet lay where Nofret said it would, entwined around her scented jars along with her other beads and baubles. Teos untangled it and, wrapping a piece of cloth around it to silence the tiny bell, he slipped it into his pocket.

"Can I assist you with anything, high priest?" Ramy had been standing beneath the palm-lined edge of the island and, seeing the shadow of Teos pass along the walkway, a sudden fear gripped him. Instantly, he followed.

Teos stood by the small bedside table, his back to the door. Turning in surprise, he saw the lector standing in the doorway's shadow.

"I was just looking to see if we had missed anything as to why Nofret would have left us!" He walked away from the bed and stared at where the plastered wall was subtly indented with the handprints of the artisan.

"So you think that's what's happened?" Ramy opened the door wider with a creak and stepped through. "You think she's left the island and may still be alive?"

The high priest shrugged his shoulders and turned back. "Who knows, Ramy, but something here feels so unlike the loss of Safiya." His voice held an intense note. "I can't explain it, but in not having found Nofret's body, I fear we may never know where she is!"

Picking through the clothing that lay across the end of the bed, the high priest moved each one aside before reaching a decision.

"Can we get these things tidied away?" He let the sheer robes fall through his fingers. "Perhaps you'll let Essam know that I've given the order."

Turning his back on the Priest of *Hathor*, he left and, stepping to the right as he came out into the open corridor, he headed towards Trajan's Kiosk. After a stop in the temple enclosure where he stared at the ground for uncounted time, he walked the island's edge along its southern strip and, following in Nofret's footsteps, returned past the Temple of the Triad and reached his home.

***

Ramy went in immediate search of Essam and, finding him strolling across the island's eastern stretch with his fishing pole over his shoulder, he waited for him to reach his position before falling in at his side. Accepting the catch of the day, he kept his silence until arriving at the fire pit at the back of the temple.

"Teos has made us a visit." He carefully laid the catch down.

"A visit?" The senior lector threw down his pole to one side and, looking up, he asked, "To the temple?" His voice sounded cautious. "Or has he been elsewhere?"

"Elsewhere, Essam. I found him in Nofret's room!"

The lector priest became still as his thoughts went from one thing to another. There was no way Teos could suspect anything about the priestess's disappearance on the part of her priests, but he was obviously suspicious.

"What was he doing there?" He stared hard at Ramy.

"Going through her things."

"Was he looking for something?" He said the words slowly, a note of attention heard in his voice.

"I don't know. But he's advised we need to tidy up her room."

Essam heaved a sigh of relief. He too wanted the woman's things cleared away, but had hesitated on making the decision. Yet, with the words coming from the high priest himself, it passed the settlement out of the lector's hands. Thankfully nodding his head, he reasoned Teos must think the woman was dead and lost to the great Nile River.

"Very well, if that is what Teos has instructed." A smile spread across his face. "You can get Musa to start tomorrow."

***

Musa was tasked to fold away the sparse items that made up his priestess's life. They remained as she had left them, apart from where Teos had briefly moved them around, and the linen robes lay scattered about the bed. Picking up each item, he folded the sheer garments neatly to one side and, after moving around the scented jars,

174

unwound the jewellery of the woman and laid the beads atop her clothing. Finally, he planted the black wig, pyramid-like, on the top. He left them at the bottom of the bed, not wanting, as yet, to leave the room empty of her essence.

He still wondered what had happened to her and, making the job last that bit longer, he sat down on the bed. Letting his mind wander, his hands rubbed along the edge of the mattress. Suddenly, the tips of his fingers met a difference to the smoothness of the pallet and, lifting the bedding, he found the hidden parchment tucked beneath.

Pulling the papyrus out, he stretched it fully across the bed and looked down on the Temple of *Isis*.

CHAPTER THIRTEEN

Musa stared at the intricate lines that stretched over the woven papyrus and wondered why his priestess would have concealed the scroll. Perhaps this was what had been bothering her recently. He looked intently at the straight lines and hand-traced columns in their black ink.

They were illustrated expertly, but to Musa's inexperienced eyes, they meant little. However, he recognised what it depicted and his head came up to stare across to the opposite side of the island. Why would his priestess have a drawing of the Temple of *Isis*?

He wondered about leaving it atop the bed and letting Essam deal with it, but remained unsure if he was doing right. The idea that Nofret had hidden it gave him cause to consider his action and, rolling it up, he placed it back beneath the bed. Looking around the room, it seemed tidy enough to his eye and, feeling there was little else to do, he closed the door and headed into the temple. He had the floors to sweep after the morning's service and did not want the wrath of Essam to fall again around his shoulders.

While the constant swish of the broom filled his ears as it moved the gritty sand across the foot-polished floors, his mind could not rest regarding the papyrus and, after the last of the grains was neatly brushed aside, he returned to retrieve it. It must have some importance, he thought, and tucking it into the back of his schenti, he threw a blanket around his shoulders and headed out along the western side of the building.

His feet carried him towards the ruined Temple of Augustus and on reaching it, he looked around to ensure he was not being followed. Sure of his solitude, he stepped to his right and, walking to the far end of the fallen wall, he ducked beneath the overhang. Here he had a secret place known only to himself, where he kept a few personal items out of sight of the other men. Pushing aside an ornately carved slab, he lifted away a mouldering piece of wood. Beneath, the oddments that gave a memory to his young life lay enclosed by the ever-seeping sand. Reaching down, he placed the scroll alongside the wooden beads, which once belonged to his mother, and closing over the slab, he hid it away.

Later, after the priests had eaten well from the offerings given to their goddess and games had been played, which mostly Ramy had won, the men went their separate ways. Musa lay awake for some time beneath the tree-lined edge of the Nile and let the sound of the cicadas become part of the backdrop. The thought that the Temple of the Triad might hold something that explained Nofret's disappearance grew in his young mind and took him along differing paths with many scenarios that gave no apparent end.

Until, with his thinking becoming muddled and making no sense, he stared into the underside of the greenery and could rest no longer. Needing to know if the temple held answers to the questions that filled his mind, he rose and, lifting a small torch that blazed at the side of the temple, crept his way across the island.

***

The sound of the sanctum door quietly opening woke Nofret from her bored slumber, and seeing a dark figure slip into the room, she slid beneath the altar to *Osiris*. Coming up against the cold stone, she clasped her hand over her mouth to calm her breathing. It was still night, but of a time when the greyness was growing in the centre of the room. However, it was not the hour for Teos to be performing his rituals. The man had never come outside of the hours that governed his position and Nofret felt a sudden fear run through her heart.

Whoever it was carried a flaming torch and from her position at ground level, as the light flickered around in the gusts of air, she could see the intruder's feet and lower legs. She could not tell who it was, but could easily guess it was a man, not a woman. The sandalled feet strode slowly around the room as if unsure of where they stood, before coming to a stop at the stone altar of the Goddess *Isis*. A voice then whispered its appeal.

"Forgive me for entering your house, Lady of the Moon," it declared before the frozen image of the goddess. "I am here to seek your advice."

Nofret recognised the voice immediately. It was Musa.

Sliding out thankfully from beneath her shelter, she came up softly behind the man where he stood before the goddess and placed her cool hand on his shoulder.

"Put the light out, Musa," she breathed.

The young *wab* priest jumped with fright and immediately spun around. The light of the torch flared and reflected in his startled eyes. But, on seeing his priestess before him, he was overjoyed. Letting the feeling of dread instantly evaporate, he lowered the light and let it fall to the floor at his feet.

"May all the gods be praised!" Tears filled his eyes and holding on to the woman with no thought of what he was doing, he let his emotion overwhelm him. "I thought you were dead!"

Nofret, however, was angry at being found. If any of

the other priests knew she was here, it put her plan in jeopardy and she was still unsure who to trust.

"What are you doing here, Musa?" she furiously whispered.

"I found the temple map hidden beneath your bed," the young man replied, his voice rising. "I thought it must have some importance for you to have put it there."

Nofret pulled the man down to sit on the smooth ground and the darkness surrounded them as the flame of the fire slowly died on the chilled tiles. Silence crept in, and over their heads, the three gods stared out into the gloom.

"Do you still have it?" Nofret eventually asked. She had forgotten about the Papyrus of Meriiti and hoping it had not fallen into the wrong hands, she finished, "The map, Musa. Is it safe?"

"Yes, it's safe and out of sight."

"Good." She let out a sigh of relief before asking, "And what about the others of the temple? Have you told them anything about the map?"

"No, priestess."

Nofret sat back on her heels. *Thank the gods*, she thought, before realising she must get the man's word to keep her hiding place a secret.

"Musa, I must have your guarantee that I'll remain dead to everyone on the island!" Her words came slowly as the man seated opposite nodded his head. But then, in thinking of the third voice she heard at the Kiosk of Trajan, it suddenly gave her some doubt. Unseeing who it was, yet suspecting he came from the village on the Nile, she quickly added, "And that goes for those who live on the banks of the river. You must tell no one I am alive! You understand that?"

The man meekly carried on nodding his head, and the many questions that filled his mind went unasked as Nofret changed the subject. She was in her heart glad to get some news from the Temple of *Hathor* and, wanting to know how the forthcoming celebration was progressing, she asked, "Now, how's it going with the ceremony for the marriage of *Horus* and *Hathor*?"

She knew that in Dendera, at the capital where *Hathor* was worshipped in her glory, the preparation was long in its planning and the festival could go on for many weeks with its feasting and dancing. Here, though, on the island that sat dedicated to the Goddess *Isis*, she had envisioned it being a one-day celebration and thought it unlikely that would change.

"It goes well, priestess." A smile briefly crossed the man's face. "But I sense Lector Essam wants it over and done with as soon as possible. I think he feels it'll draw a line under your disappearance."

"So, no date has yet been set?" Nofret had lost all sense of time as she sat in the confines of the temple and was unaware the festivities would begin in the coming days.

Musa, however, enlightened her, as he explained, "We'll be bringing the goddess over tomorrow and establishing her at the feet of *Horus*."

Hearing the words, the Priestess of *Hathor* imagined herself walking before the retinue as it carried her goddess across the Island of Philae for the ceremony. In her mind's eye, she was holding aloft her staff of office and the songs and tributes once heard at Dendera rang in her ears. Smiling, she let the memory carry her further in its splendour and, picturing herself entering the Temple of *Isis* at *Hathor*'s command, the retinue of devotees slowly followed. Standing at the feet of the gods, she felt at one with them as her years of observance and worship held her enthralled in the ritual, until Musa, his whispered voice breaking into her thought, brought her out of her daydream.

"Essam will conduct the service, Nofret." He stated the fact before realising what he said was obvious to his priestess. "He's been preparing for days."

The priestess was not happy knowing that Essam would take her position in the commemoration. But then she held some satisfaction that it was happening in the first place. There was little else she could do about its performance, and she, too, wanted it over quickly, but for a very different reason.

She sat for a long time thinking of her plan, and the young man's company was welcomed as he chatted away at her side. He filled the time in bringing the recent news to Nofret and added those who worshipped in the temple greatly missed her. He said her disappearance had especially saddened Yara and her husband. Yara had cried, he added, and become so distressed on hearing the news. Fearful of her losing the baby, her husband had taken her away and since then, they had not returned.

His chatter softly subsided. However, the gloom of the night slowly turned from a darkness to a lighter grey and as the Great God *Ra* left behind the underworld and began his lift onto the horizon, Nofret felt an urgency to end the conversation.

"You must go, Musa. It's not good for you to be found here." She looked around the sacred space of the gods, aware that the punishment for stepping foot here could see the young man thrown out from the temple and barred from the island. That would be the least of the punishments, and Nofret knew they could be worse. Stressing the urgency, she added, "You must leave quickly and quietly."

"Has Essam done wrong in your eyes, priestess?" The words came unexpectedly as the man rose to his feet. "I've always looked up to him, even when he's shown me the error in my mistakes."

"Yes, he's done wrong, Musa, but not in the way you may think. It's in the eyes of the gods that he has fallen, and that brings its own punishment."

Nofret did not go into any greater detail and after wishing her priest a good night and hearing again his thanksgiving that she was alive, she watched as he left and saw the door close behind him. Alone once more, she knelt in the growing light before the Goddess *Isis* and, lifting her hands to the heavens, she prayed he would keep his word.

***

Sleep did not come again for the Priestess of *Hathor* and she lay awake beneath the stare of the triad as their figures emerged out of the dark. She counted on her *wab* priest staying silent, but if Essam suspected anything, then having received recent treatment at the man's hands, she was well aware of what he was capable. He had left her to die in the labyrinth with no care or concern for her fate and with that, she felt, it would take little more for him to stain his hands with blood if need be. He would save his skin on this, she had no doubt, so her plan must be played to perfection.

Teos and his retinue eventually arrived with the usual fanfare and the service to the gods began as the sun rose in the east and ended as the light flooded the island with its rays. Within the sanctuary, Nofret listened to the song and chant of the priests and sat patiently, waiting for the door to open.

Finally, as the singing and rattling of sistra continued in the main hall, the high priest finished conducting his service. Leaving the crowd of worshippers standing before the triad, he came alone to bring their pleas and speak with the gods.

The door opened and Teos walked sedately through. The essence of the blue lotus hung around his robed body, and his eyes stared widely around the sanctuary. For a moment, he paused before turning and closing the door.

Nofret was immediately on her feet and bowed her head in respect of the man who stood before her. Seeing the measured response, she whispered her usual greeting.

"Welcome in peace, Teos. The light of *Ra* has risen and, in joy and celebration, we greet this beautiful day."

"Praise to the gods and let us be thankful for their blessings," the high priest replied.

Stepping aside, he continued in his service and knelt in his usual place on the cold floor. He had one last duty yet to perform within the temple and, for the gathering who stood in silence before the altars, this was the most important. He was there to pass on the pleas and petitions, along with the words of thanks, from the people. And for uncounted moments, his lips moved as he communicated with the ancients.

In the time that Teos conversed with his gods, Nofret waited patiently. She knew the importance of this part of their service. This was the reason for their very being in the eyes of those who collected before the statues and brought their offerings. In their eyes, the higher authorities in the temples had a direct link to the gods and should be seen to play their part. That was the rule of the temple, and those who had risen high in its surroundings must know how to play the game and do their duty.

After a while, Teos spoke his last words and, imploring the gods to look kindly on his people, he rose stiffly. Straightening his robes, he pulled them around his shoulders and turned to face Nofret. She too rose from her sitting and, walking across the stone floor, they met at the western side of the room. The two came together beneath the stare of the gods, and Teos passed on his news.

Whispering and keeping his voice low, he repeated the words spoken by Musa and explained the service for the joining of *Horus* and *Hathor* would take place the following morning after the service to the triad. He added Essam would bring the chosen statue of the goddess over to its position in the temple later that day and, if Nofret was aware of the noise of singing and the accompanying fanfare at an unexpected time, then this is what would be occurring. She should not be alarmed, he added, but should remain hidden from sight.

Nofret did not reveal she already knew of this happening, not wanting Teos to know of Musa's visit and, hoping the surprised look on her face appeared genuine, she accepted the word of the high priest and expressed her gratitude.

Again, she imagined the chosen representation of her goddess being lifted from beneath the feet of *Hathor* and carried with dignity across the width of the island.

Teos, though, aware that his time with her was limited, brought her back to reality and, taking out a bag that hung unseen at his waist, he held it out. He had found make-up for Nofret this time, as she had asked. And, handing the folded cloth over, he watched as she sat and opened it on the floor. The small alabaster jars of red carmine and crushed malachite spilled out and a kohl stick along with some brushes of reeds sat alongside. Smiling, she was satisfied it was all she needed apart from one crucial element in her plan.

Placing the items alongside the set-aside clothing the high priest had already brought to her, along with the second anklet of Safiya's, the Priestess of *Hathor* eventually repositioned the jars to sit on the top and reminded him she now only needed a wig.

Teos smiled and nodded, knowing this would be easy to achieve. However, regarding Nofret's plan, his expression changed, and he revealed the doubts which had recently risen in his mind.

"Essam will never confess to Safiya's death, Nofret, you know that."

"Then I must make him admit it." The woman looked up, her eyes showing determination. "He must be punished, Teos, if only for the desecration of the tombs. He must admit to that in the least."

"He'll never do that, either," Teos scoffed.

"He will if he stands accused before his gods!"

Nofret's voice rang out and, carrying upwards through the sanctuary, her words thundered in the heavens. Inside the temple, it was heard as a reverberation from on high and the supplicants, lifting their eyes to the sky, dropped to their knees before their gods.

***

The Priests of *Hathor* carried their chosen statue across the island in some ceremony, the image of the goddess supported on a stretcher of slats with strong bamboo poles running through the folded edges. Raised high, she sat like a heavy grey monolith between the men, her horns glinting in the morning sun. Essam led the way, his staff of office clutched proudly at his side and his head held high. Behind him, the eyes of the goddess were seeing the light of day for the first time since the roof of the hall had closed over them and the dark of the interior had made its claim.

Ramy and Abbas walked at its front, the poles carried on their shoulders, while Musa and Kheti, being the younger Priests of *Hathor*, walked behind their goddess and carried her great weight with an honour that was becoming of their position.

The official ceremony for the Beautiful Feast of the Reunion was not until the following morning, but Essam needed to ensure the correct positioning of the statue for his observance of the ritual. He had already inspected the site in the temple's enclosure and, after pacing out the steps between the two statues, he knew where his goddess should be placed.

The island had turned out for the start of the formality and stood lining the ceremonial path. Palm fronds waved high in the sky's blueness and the voices of the priestesses rang out in shouts and ululation. All were dressed in their fine white clothing, and following the course of the goddess, they formed a retinue that danced beneath the risen sun.

Inside the temple, Teos waited in a blaze of torches before the statue of *Horus*, where the great god stood at the northern end of the hypostyle hall. He'd had an area, with the agreement of Essam, cleared at the front, and all the recent offerings had been moved aside. The polished slabs of granite gleamed in the flickering light.

Hathor entered the temple with a crash of cymbals, rattles and bells, and the priestesses, having placed their palm leaves down, let their voices fill the void. They followed, dancing and clapping their hands as the litter passed beneath the heavily engraved roof. Filing down the columned hall, the echoes joined and rebounded around the goddess.

The stretcher bearers eventually reached the front of the hypostyle hall, and Essam fussed around to ensure the distance between the statues was correct in his mind. He needed five paces on either side to be walked in his joining of the two. Stepping from one side to the other, he was finally satisfied, and lowering his staff, the litter with its statue seated atop was placed down.

The poles were silently slid out, and the smaller image of *Hathor* came to rest upon the greenery of the woven mat. She seemed out of proportion with the image of the hawk-headed *Horus*, who looked down upon her in his piercing gaze. Yet in their forthcoming marriage, the two ancient gods would be equally revered in their unity.

Lector Essam, a smile on his face, appreciated the moment deeply within his soul and, dropping his head ingratiatingly to Teos, he wished the high priest "*Senebty*" and farewelled him for the moment. Escorting his priests out, he let the eyes of the colossal statues of *Osiris*, *Isis* and *Horus* fall heavy at his back and, reaching the step down into the south of the temple, where the fresh air of the late afternoon met him, he stopped and turned. The small figure of the high priest remained standing in the gloom at the feet of his gods.

Essam knew the man had no authority in the coming service and, seeing him belittled by the statues, he felt his superiority rise. Tomorrow, when the ancient ritual began in the Temple of *Isis*, it would be he, not Teos, who would stand before the people and command the celebration.

CHAPTER FOURTEEN

Nofret heard the excitement and song as the statue of *Hathor* entered the temple. She desperately wanted to be there to see her goddess receive her due reverence on this historic coming together, but could only sit with her resentment rising and, impatiently, she let the time move on. Thankfully, the noise died down and the silence beyond her prison stretched away until the door softly opened and Teos appeared. He had waited until the Priests of *Hathor* had left and the quiet of the hypostyle hall returned to its usual cool hush of the afternoon.

"The God and Goddess of the Sky sit awaiting their reunion," he greeted her, a hint of a smile filling his eyes. "And let me say they look glorious in their coming together."

The priestess dropped her head in thankful recognition.

"Then the Beautiful Feast of the Reunion has begun," she replied. "And we look ahead to their marriage in the morning and our celebration of their union." She smiled back, but her anger at being denied her rightful place in the ritual of the gods showed in her eyes.

The Priestess of *Hathor* had, however, fixed the following day firmly in her mind and having discussed at length the ceremony with Teos, they both knew they had a part to perform. Teos's was the easier of the two, yet in his providing Nofret with her costume and makeup, he knew he had played a supporting role and done his best to help.

He had brought the last item she had asked for and, removing it from beneath his robes, he shook it out to straighten the dark curls. Draping it over his fist, he held it out for her scrutiny.

"Will this one do?" It was the only one he could find in his house and, after hiding it for some days and hearing no word of it being misplaced, nor any demand for its search, he was now sure it was not missed.

The wig was longer than Nofret usually wore and looked out of proportion on the man's large hand. But it would have to do. And after shaking it out to remove the bunched-up edging, the twisted, tasselled fringe, once pulled across her head, came well down over her eyes. She could still see through and possibly, she reasoned, it would help with the disguise. Turning to Teos, her head held high as she peered beneath the beads, she asked, "What do you think?"

The dark curls surrounded the girl's face and brought to her slim features the similarity shown in many of the temple's wall decorations. *She could easily be mistaken for any of my priestesses*, he thought.

"I wouldn't know you if you passed me in the temple," he declared with a satisfied grin.

Nofret thankfully smiled back. She hoped the idea would work, but could only do her best with the things provided.

Beneath the stare of the great triad, Nofret went once more over her plan. Teos listened and, having already made his arrangements for the following day, he reassured the woman he would not let her down.

Leaving her with a wish for a restful night, he closed the door at his back, and after giving his praise to the triad, along with the extra statue of the goddess who now sat in the temple's north, he left the four deities to the darkness and stalked down the hall. He disappeared into the lingering sunlight at the southern edge of the building and the temple returned to silence.

Nofret sat with the wig in her lap. She was unsure of what she was doing but had to make Essam admit his part in the robbing of the crypts. She was absolutely sure of his involvement in that. But what about the death of Safiya? She knew in her heart that could also be placed at his feet and that her predecessor's unnatural death had occurred to keep her quiet.

She must ensure he admitted his guilt on both parts, she thought, and he must pay for his actions. However, she knew it had to be done before the assembly of people and more, in her reasoning, before the gods themselves.

Later, seeing the rise of the silvered moonlight colouring the sky above her head, she knew the hour would be safe to leave her confinement in the temple's sanctuary. Cautiously opening the door, a brief thought that Essam may have left a guard to keep the statue of *Hathor*, company in the Temple of *Isis*, ran through her mind and brought her to a stop.

Yet, peering carefully around the door, she saw only the flicker of small candles that decorated the altars and, beyond their glare, the stretch of the columned darkness led away. *There could be someone out there*, she briefly considered, *seated within the gloom of the majestic hall*, but her desperation to leave the sanctum gripped her and eagerly she moved forwards.

It was the first time she had stepped back for any great time into the main temple since escaping the labyrinth and, as the decorated columns and richly carved walls of the hypostyle hall marched down its darkened length, it gave her a feeling of space and freedom not recently felt and immediately it uplifted her spirit.

There was no challenge as she took in a deep inhalation of old incense, and only the softness of her breathing sounded magnified in the columned loftiness. Sensing the splendour of where she stood, she approached the front of the long altar. Here her goddess sat before it, positioned between two of the exquisitely carved and painted columns. Pausing to give her praise to *Hathor*, she eventually looked up. The sharp-beaked head of *Horus* stared down and, lowering her head in observance, she gave the statue its due formality. On his right, the mighty statues of *Osiris* and *Isis* stood together in their domination of the altars, and the Priestess of *Hathor* gave them equal veneration.

However, it was her own goddess that required her attention. *Hathor* sat naked and uncovered beneath the temple roof, her headdress topped by the sun disk enclosed by the two sharp cow horns. The image seemed stark in its undressed state, but this was as Nofret would have expected. Tomorrow, in the service of her marriage to *Horus*, she would be decorated and dressed for the occasion, and all honour given to the two in their union.

She seated herself before her goddess, and the Priestess of *Hathor* looked up as the flickering candlelight bled her elongated shadow across the foot of the statue. The head of the goddess, however, was lit fully by the light and Nofret, thankful for being given the time together, whispered her appeal that the next day would be as effective as she hoped.

As she prayed, around her, the cats of the island, knowing the temple belonged to them for the night, skittered about and chased each other in the building's vastness. The cooler air suited them and the lift of the afternoon lethargy had given way to their playful side as they stalked the hall for their dinner.

Aziza, after finishing her chase of the vermin and

taking her fill of the catch, joined Nofret at the front of the hall and wrapped herself around the feet of the woman. Adding her warmth to the chill of the cool flooring, she kept her company as the Priestess of *Hathor* performed her lonely vigil.

The grey of the morning soon faded to the colour of cornflowers, and Nofret hastily retreated to the confines of the inner chamber as Aziza padded along at her side. She wanted to be ready for the opportune moment, and dressing in the clothes Teos had brought for her, she then applied the makeup thickly to her face. She decorated her eyes in the emerald green powder and outlined them lavishly with the kohl stick and let its dark line run towards the edge of her face. A sense of pent-up expectation filled the mind of the young woman and, wishing for the quick passing of time, she sat cross-legged on the polished floor and turned her thoughts to the coming event. For the moment, the wig remained at her side and the dark trails of its beaded curls lay with a dullness surrounded by the coming brightness of the morning.

***

On the far eastern side of the Island of Philae, Essam prepared himself for the day with extra care. He felt honoured in his position as overseer of the forthcoming ritual and his superiority over others in the temple knew no bounds. Still, knowing he had the everyday service to perform before the grand event at the Temple of *Isis*, he set aside the rich robes he had chosen for the marriage service. Instead, he placed the simple attire of a priest around his frame. Ramy, as ever, escorted him into the Temple of *Hathor*.

The chamber was fuller than usual, the mass gathering of villagers wearing their traditional gowns and costumes. Silence filled the hall, and the lector noticed and valued its hush as he came through. In a growing feeling of self-importance, he raised his head. They were all there to witness his celebration of their goddess and, smiling at those who looked his way, he delighted in his newfound status.

At the front of the gathered group, the nomarch stood with his son, Abasi, and alongside him, Yara held a small bunch of flowers over her swollen stomach. There was a feverishness that sat about the young woman's features, and she looked nervously around at the gathering as they met for the coming festivity. Her lips moved as her unheard words of devotion and thanks filled her mind and, spilling out into the smoky surroundings of the temple, her whispering to the goddess who had finally answered her prayers, knew no bounds.

Essam led the service to *Hathor* over its usual course of prayers, and after anointing and dressing the main statue, many offerings were brought forwards and placed at her feet. Further words and appeals were taken in to the sanctuary's seclusion and, on the lector's return to the hall, the daily service came to a close.

However, as the assembly broke up, and the crowd left to await the coming ceremony, Essam held up his hand and Ramy shouted for the people to remain.

"Today we shall mark the union of *Hathor* to *Horus*," Essam declared, staring at the assembly as they paused in their leaving. "But let us not forget the priestess who brought this splendid festival to the island, even if only for this one time."

His eyes took in the sad expressions of those who had

come to a stop as the silence filled the hall. Before looking away, he turned to stare up into the features of his goddess.

"Let us remember the Priestess Nofret and hope our goddess is with her wherever she may be." His words faded at the end as his memory of the labyrinth filled his mind and the torch-lit image of the woman, her body sprawled across the cavern floor, briefly flashed through his recall. Shaking it away, he awoke from his inertia and, pulling the mantel of a priest of the temple around his shoulders, he finished, "Now let us prepare ourselves for the marriage of the goddess."

He waved his hand in dismissal of the gathering, and the crowd appeared to come out of their trance. Their leaving of the hypostyle hall rose noisily until the last supplicant had left and the echoing sound of their departure turned to a silence.

Essam walked along the open passage to Nofret's room, where he had left the ceremonial clothing he had sent for from Dendera. He had taken over the room of late, feeling that his position in the temple deserved some privacy.

Quickly changing out of his lector robes, he threw round his shoulders a robe of the finest white linen, which he tied about his waist with a golden band of interlocking metal chain. At his wrists, he placed several rich bejewelled bangles which he pushed up his arms, while around his neck he wore a *wesekh*, a broad collar of rainbow-coloured beads. Over this, he placed an amulet dedicated to his goddess. It showed the face of *Hathor* surmounted by the large horns of a cow and in between the curved antlers, the golden disk of the Sun God *Ra* sat firmly on her head.

Essam felt the rise of his supremacy in his very being and, walking the length of the hall, he came out into the morning light. He stood in his finery, and heading to the front of the crowd which opened in his passing, he swiftly chose four of the younger men to hold aloft the flames to light their journey to the temple. Then, followed by his priests, who carried the light linen wraps that would unite the two gods, he set off across the island.

The crowd of followers had earlier left extra gifts along the temple walls especially for the coming celebration, and having collected these in readiness for the procession, they held them out before them or else carried them at their sides as they fell in behind Essam.

***

Teos had performed his morning ceremony in his usual glory and deference to the triad and, letting the blue lotus fill his mind, he finally took the prayers of those gathered before the altar into the hallowed presence of the gods. Nofret was eagerly waiting, but knowing the high priest had his service to perform, she sat patiently as he knelt before the shrine.

In time, Teos arose, having done his duty in leaving the varied appeals of the many to the generosity of the gods. Nodding his head in final homage, he turned away from the ever-present stare of the statues.

His attention focused on the woman who remained in stillness, his eyes wide with expectation, and Nofret could not tell if it was the blue lotus that lingered there or if the coming event held him. Yet, she, too, had an anticipation that all would go as planned.

"Are you prepared for what you must do, Nofret?" The

man's voice came high-pitched, obviously influenced by the lotus vapour, yet as he stood tall before the priestess, his look of concern was unmistakable.

Nofret rose slowly to her feet and placed the wig upon her head. Pulling it down tightly around her ears, she stood before the high priest.

"Yes, Teos, I'm ready."

"Then let me prepare the stage for you!" He grabbed her cool hand and, not wanting to hold up the coming performance, briefly kissed it before letting it drop. Turning away, he left and closed the door.

Straightening his attire, he emerged out of the smoky mist of the candles and walked sedately back to the assembly. Here on his return, the worshippers, instead of readying themselves to leave the temple of the gods and return to the sameness of their everyday, remained in place before the altars for the upcoming festival.

The high priest looked at them with what he hoped was a smile of joy for the coming ceremony, but deep down, he knew it might turn into an even more memorable occasion. However, not able to wait any longer, he looked along the stretch of the hall and, seeing the gathering at the door where Essam stood in wait, he raised his hand.

A fanfare of copper trumpets made the announcement, and at the southern outer edge of the hypostyle hall, the senior lector arrogantly led the way in. The four Priests of *Hathor* followed, carrying the rich white robes which would clothe the god and goddess.

The entourage walked with heads held high, picked out by the flaming torches that lit the darkness of the columned hall. Behind these, the supplicants stretched out in a convoluted line. At the head of this procession of villagers, Nomarch Mysis walked with his family following in his wake and in his hands he carried a large woven tray of cooked chicken legs surrounded by a ring of dates seated upon white flower petals. The occasion called for extra donations to be given and was seen in all the offerings.

The music of the temple accompanied the slow, steady tramp of their feet while the joyous singing rang out and added to the parade. As they reached the front, High Priest Teos stepped aside and, blending into the shadowed columns, he made way for the followers of *Hathor* and gave the temple over to Essam.

The lector priest arrived with a sense of expectation at the front of the building and, stepping left, he came before the triad and paid his respects with a sedate bow of his head to each statue. That done, the Priests of *Hathor*, their arms holding the linen which would wrap and unite the two gods, took up their positions on either side of their goddess. As the torches blazed, they lit the front of the magnificent altar and the flames sparkled in the eyes of the gathering.

***

Lector Essam stood exactly between the two carved figures. And, in the flickering light, his wavering shadow seemed out of proportion to the statues that surrounded him. He held his long staff in his hands, but placing it at his feet, it left his hands free.

Turning first to the altar of the triad, he took his five paces before reaching the statue of *Horus*. Here he fell to his knees and his lips moved as if in prayer to the gods. Yet in reality, he had never in his long term as senior lector to the Temple of *Hathor* ever seen or taken part in this ceremony before; it having been reserved for those who worshipped at the Temple of Dendera. Therefore, not knowing the appropriate words to say at this special moment, he hoped the gods accepted his invocations. Still, he knelt for some time and, in his mind, said something suitable, hoping that *Horus* would take it in the spirit given.

Eventually rising, he stepped across the space and fell to the woven mat upon which *Hathor* sat. Again, he was ignorant of the occasion and could only repeat what he had said before the hawk-headed god. That done, he rose to his feet. Returning to the middle, he clapped his hands smartly, and the echo rang out in the hall's silence.

"Bring forth the ties that will bind the Gods of the Sky and let us rejoice and celebrate this day in their reunion."

Ramy and Abbas stepped forwards and, slowly and carefully wrapping their goddess around and around with the linen swathes, they left the long ends to dangle at her feet.

Musa and Kheti then did the same to the imposing figure of *Horus* and enclosed him in the wrap before returning to stand at their goddess's side.

Lector Essam first stepped towards the hawk-headed god and, bowing low, he picked up the drooping ends of the ribbons of white and carried them to the middle of the floor, there laying them down. He placed his heavy staff over them to hold them in position before, with great reverence, he collected those from around *Hathor* and placed them also beneath the staff.

Raising his hands, he blessed the two gods in sight of the assembly and then, reaching down to pull up the white ends of the cloth, he held them out before him.

Stretching the linen out on his left and right, the full extent of the wraps on either side was reached and held tightly in his hands. Tying the ends of the pure white wraps together, he united the two deities in their reunion.

"*Horus* and *Hathor* have come together on this beautiful day and are reunited in our presence." His voice filled the hall and, in the temple's canopy, the roosting birds flew up in a confusion of wings.

"Come, let us celebrate! Bring your gifts to place at their feet and let all present give praise and hold this joyful moment in our hearts!"

***

The celebration of *Hab Nefer en Sekhen* was reaching its end and Essam, receiving the offerings of the people as they sang and danced their jubilation, placed the last basket of bread and fruit down before the royal couple, who sat bound in their festooned linen wraps. A silence fell as the smoke of the flames gathered around the gods and in its hush, the occasion seemed overwhelming to those who looked on.

Suddenly, the loud banging of cymbals rang out and filled the air above the festivities. Teos, his arms held high, emerged from the back of the columns, and holding the silvered cymbals he had left hidden in place behind a statue of *Osiris*, he banged them together with a crash before letting the silence fall back.

"Let the gods also give their blessing on the ceremony," he declared in the stillness. Looking towards the doorway to the sanctum, he brought the cymbals together in one almighty thunderclap, and added, "And let them bestow their gifts upon all who stand in witness to this occasion."

Expectation fell on the assembly as the echoing ring of the gong disappeared into the heavens and in it, the door to the sanctum of the triad slowly opened. The gap to the sanctuary grew wider and, unseen by those who stood frozen before the gods, Nofret stepped through. She was dressed simply, shoulder to foot, in a sheer cloak of fine white linen bound by a purple sash and with her face made up and, wearing the dark curled wig securely over her head, she looked like any priestess of the temple.

About her legs, the cat Aziza, head held high, prowled at her side and let its voice rise in the shocked silence. Around the ankles of the ghostly spirit, the cow horn embellished anklets belonging to Safiya jingled with each step and, in the smoky silence, the sound of their tinkling bells filled the air and became a constant as Nofret walked forwards.

Nomarch Mysis felt his daughter-in-law stiffen at his side as she grabbed a hold of her husband's arm. Tightening her grip on Abasi's wrist, she looked in terror as the smoke of the candles swirled before her eyes and the choking incense caught firmly about her throat.

A voice thundered around the front of the altar and sounded loud in the shocked stillness that descended on the gathering.

"Before the eyes of the gods," the figure declared as it came to a stop, "I am here to give judgement on those who have committed the cardinal sin of robbing the dead and violating their sacred catacombs." The words hung in the air before Nofret angrily finished, "And I have arisen to seek vengeance on those guilty of my murder!"

Emerging out of the smokiness, the clothed white figure stepped into the light and the ringing of the anklets about her legs magnified in the quiet.

Within the stilled crowd, Yara witnessed the hazy figure slowly appear from out of the shadows. And with her senses heightened by the ceremony and the essence of the blue lotus, she heard the soft tinkle of the bells. Seeing only the figure of Safiya, the dead priestess, she let out a terrifying scream. Falling to her knees, she covered her head with her arms and, cowering on the temple floor, hid her eyes from the fearful apparition.

CHAPTER FIFTEEN

Mysis glared at where his daughter-in-law lay on the ground and, not wanting to draw attention to her or himself, he hoisted her off the floor and pulled her close to his side.

"What are you doing?" he furiously whispered. Holding her roughly, he glanced around to see who was looking. "You're making yourself and the name of my family look foolish!"

"But it's Safiya!" The girl screamed, and glancing with outright fear towards the spectre, she stood in shock. "She's come back!"

The young woman was beside herself in utter dismay and, as her voice rose high, the assembly of priests, priestesses and villagers all heard her words. In the nomarch's vicinity, the gathered supplicants looked around and, unknowing the reason for the outcry and fearing some difficulty had arisen, they moved aside, leaving Mysis and his family standing alone.

Nofret saw the commotion within the assembly from the far side of the hypostyle hall and, thinking it was something to do with Essam, she rushed forwards to play her last card. Teos also stepped down and, brushing aside the crowd which had thickened before him, he eventually arrived in front of Mysis.

"What's going on, nomarch?"

The high priest saw the man holding the young pregnant woman about the waist and thought there must be some concern for her well-being. Yet, it was the expression on Yara's face that held him. She was staring at where Nofret was heading towards them and, as the candle-lit ghostly vision of the priestess drew near, a look of horrified dismay showed in her eyes.

Nofret eventually reached the high priest's side but stopped on seeing Mysis holding his daughter-in-law. She was astonished at the terrified reaction of the young woman. This was not what she had hoped for.

"Has something happened?" she asked. The words filled the surroundings of the gathering and, as they met the stunned silence, her voice banished the ghost of Safiya.

***

Before the shrines of the triad, Essam too had stopped, frozen in shock as the spirit of the priestess appeared. Hearing the jangle of the bells around the woman's feet as the words of accusation filled the temple, he felt them directed at him and realised the actions of his past had caught him up. He had to make a choice. He knew he could face the charge of his many wrongdoings and fall on the sympathy of High Priest Teos, or he could flee and save his skin.

He chose to make his escape and, grabbing a hold of Ramy, the two hurried along the front of the altars as fast as their cumbersome clothing would let them. Kicking aside the countless offerings that lay scattered about the feet of the gods, they dipped beneath the white drapes that united *Horus* and *Hathor*. Escaping along the western side of the hall as the vacant eyes of the statues followed their flight, they reached the doorway and stepped out into the light of the day.

The sun was rising high in the sky's blueness and, in its brilliance, the heat and light caught the men unexpectedly after the candle-lit gloom of the temple.

They stood dazzled for a moment, until, hearing running feet in the hall of the gods, they sped off over the island.

Racing towards Trajan's Kiosk, there was only one thought in Essam's mind. They must escape and hide.

***

Behind them, Teos had seen their quick departure and instantly he instructed his younger priests to seize them. He watched as the men disappeared into the candlelight of the temple before his eyes came back to the spectacle before him.

Mysis had let go his grip on his daughter-in-law and Nofret, seeing the distress of the young woman, had taken her to one side. She was trying to comfort her in her anguish, but all the girl could say as she held her in her collapse and walked to the side of the hall was, "She promised me! She promised me!"

"Who promised you?" Nofret sat down beneath a statue of *Osiris* and, holding the distraught girl away, she looked deep into her eyes. "Who promised you, Yara?"

"She promised me so many times," the woman repeated, sobbing as she clutched at Nofret's arm. "She promised me."

Nofret heard the words of despair and, suddenly feeling the woman had more to tell in the death of Safiya, she felt a different approach was called for.

"What happened, Yara?" Her voice came calm and kindly as she took hold of the girl's hand.

"It was me, Nofret! I killed Safiya!"

The words filled the temple and along the front of the shrines, the milling mass of bystanders drew closer in expectation as the hush of their chatter died away.

Yara hung her head at making the admission, but felt an unforeseen relief that the words had been said. She explained to Nofret that Safiya had reassured her so many times that her prayers would be answered and the stigma of her perceived failing swept aside.

Looking down at her hands, the young woman told of her many visits to the temple for the blessing of the goddess to give her a child. She had brought countless gifts and donations to place at *Hathor*'s feet, but each month there had been a disappointment. She only asked for one child and did not feel she was being greedy about doing so.

Seated at the distraught woman's side, Nofret knew the Priestesses of *Hathor*, the goddess of motherhood and fertility, were often called upon in these circumstances, having received their training at Dendera. And in her own time there, she too had learned about the herbs and potions which could be called upon in times of such desperation. However, having never come across this before in her short service to the temple until she met Yara, she had felt it best to first see if the gods granted the wish, rather than relying on the alternative. She had been more than thankful and given extra blessings at *Hathor*'s altar when Yara had finally confirmed the blessing of the goddess.

Yara sat silent for a moment as her words played back and forth in her mind. Before bringing herself back to the moment, she continued her telling. She explained that around her, her friends and family had added to their offspring year on year and after the false smile of pleasure on their announcements could no longer be endured, she had slowly withdrawn into herself. Over time, her anger and resentment had grown before finally, on hearing her sister-in-law was once more pregnant with her third child, the rage had taken over. In her anger and despair, she had taken the boat across the Nile and, in the guise of bringing offerings, had entered the Temple of *Hathor* to seek something more from the goddess.

Safiya was not there, but Essam, seeing a relative of the nomarch standing before the altar, had quickly rushed off to fetch her. The priestess arrived with great haste and had listened to the hopelessness heard in the woman's words. She had instinctively reassured her that her time would come and that she must be patient and wait. Together they had knelt before the statue of *Hathor* and Yara had placed her offerings at its feet.

"But then." The young woman lifted her head and sarcastically added, "After all this time of my prayers, Safiya suddenly declared that the goddess had spoken that it may be my destiny to remain barren! She said I must strengthen myself for this outcome and look to the blessing of the gods in other ways!" Yara said the words softly, but she could not disguise the rage that sat beneath them at the injustice of the Goddess of the Sky.

"She went back on her promise," she spat out in frustration. "She said it was my fate to be childless!"

The moment as the two knelt before the statue of *Hathor* suddenly flashed through the woman's mind. She had been consumed by so much rage that she had suddenly reacted. Reaching forwards, she picked up the closest thing to hand.

"I think it was one of the small statues that sat along the front." Her memory played its recall as the feel and satisfying thud of the stone sculpture smacking against the woman's head echoed in her mind. "It was the most wonderful feeling of pleasure as I hit her!"

Nofret looked shocked as a smile spread across the young woman's face. There was definite jubilation there. But she could see that Priestess Safiya may have possibly been trying to ease the difficult situation that completely controlled the life of the troubled girl. She was trying to ease the suffering she saw and give recognition to the fact that motherhood was not for everyone.

Yet Yara had seen it differently. There was more than a hint of satisfaction in her upturned lips as she became still and replayed the images in her mind.

Nofret waited a moment before gently breaking the silence. "I know you didn't mean it, Yara." Her words came whispered. "It was done in the moment, and after such a long time of despair, your action must have felt like a release."

"It did, Nofret. It felt so wonderful!"

The words of guilt rose into the air as the onlookers of the temple stood in witness to her admission.

The Priestess of *Hathor* raised her eyes in dismay to look into the smoke-filled chamber of the gods. She had been praying for an answer to Safiya's death, but the reality of it was hard to bear. However, knowing Safiya's body had not been found in the temple, she knew there must be more to the story.

"What happened afterwards?" she calmly asked.

Yara brushed away the tears and explained rationally that the cry of Safiya had brought Essam back into the temple. Seeing his priestess on the ground, he had come to her aid. The head wound was deep, the sharp edge of the statue driven into the soft temple, and after inspecting it, Essam had said that Safiya was dead.

Yara added that she panicked on realising what she had done and, having dropped the weapon, she had stared in horror as the lector priest turned the woman over. Safiya lay across the floor of the temple chamber, her blood seeping across the tiles.

Essam said that he would take care of everything, Yara further explained, and ordering the distressed girl to leave the island, he ensured she must say nothing of what had happened there.

She had returned home via the ferry and remained in her room for many days, not wanting to see anyone. But unable to sleep or eat, she paced the floor in growing panic as news of Safiya's disappearance went around the village. Finally, flinging herself on the bed, she cried the time away until sleep eventually gave its refuge and blurred the horrifying reality of her conduct.

The thoughts of her actions held the young woman in the past until slowly she came back to the here and now and her behaviour seemed to change.

"But you saw my sadness, Nofret. And you kept your word to me." The girl looked down with great joy at her swollen belly. "The Goddess of Fertility has, at last, answered my prayers."

Yara smiled as she gently stroked the bump, which finally gave her recognition in her father-in-law's eyes. However, above her, the gods of the triad looked down and, feeling their heavy stare on the back of her neck, the realisation of her actions slowly crept back into the woman's heart and the smile of delight turned to a look of frozen fear.

***

The darkness at the bottom of the ladder met the two lector priests, but Ramy, having a map of the labyrinth in his head, sped off into the maze as the panic held him and coursed through his body. Essam followed the noise of his hasty flight, but after some time had passed, he felt the cramp bite deep around his ankles. He stopped, and leaning against the cold wall of the tunnel, shouted ahead. Ramy came to an abrupt halt and, feeling his way back along the smooth walls, he stumbled across the man in the dark. Both were out of breath, and the panic at their escape was slowly subsiding, taken over instead by the need to ensure their survival.

"I think we're safe for the moment." The gasping echo of Essam's voice held some certainty, and the two stood for uncounted minutes as they brought their breathing under control. In the pitch-dark, neither could see the other, but in their perceived presence, they felt some thankfulness in the companionship.

"What do we do now, Essam?" Ramy eventually asked. A total despair was heard in the man's voice.

The blackout surrounded them and the cool walls of the labyrinth seemed to close in further. The rebound of their harsh breathing gathered as the senior lector thought through his options. They were, in a way, trapped beneath the island's surface. Yet, in knowing they could escape at any time through the door into the Temple of the Triad, there was at least some hope for their eventual freedom if they kept their heads down. However, the darkness was a growing concern. Still, in Essam's mind, that could easily be dealt with.

"First, let's get some light." The lector knew that torches still sat within the caverns of the catacombs. "We must get to the crypts and make ourselves comfortable and wait out our time."

"And then what? We can't stay down here forever!"

"No, we can't. But we must hide within the labyrinth until the festivities are over and then leave by the temple door."

Essam knew that would be the easy part and that getting off the island would prove more of a challenge. Teos would certainly have the island's edge patrolled to stop their escape. But, knowing he had paid the ferrymen well over the years, he prayed that at least one of the many feluccas would remain this side of the water and they would be cooperative in their escape. After that, they would need to have faith in the third man. He was just as guilty as the two of them and, Essam reasoned, would be equally eager to get away and save his neck.

Feeling less worried at his situation, Essam relaxed slightly and feeling the stricture of the cramp ease in his lower legs, he shifted away from the wall.

"Come on, you lead."

He pushed the man away and, following the heavy noise of his breathing, the two worked their way slowly beneath the island.

The cold silence of the labyrinth wrapped around them, but following the remembered tunnels, they soon reached the place where, upwards on their left, the exit led from the caverns into the Temple of *Isis*. Here, the two stopped.

Escape was so close and, straining to hear anything that might mean the temple remained filled with the sound of the supplicants, the two stood in silence. However, they could hear nothing from this position below the temple wall. Feeling they needed to stay hidden for much longer, they decided for the moment they dared not leave that way.

Knowing the crypts were in the opposite direction and

sat close by, Ramy headed deeper into the labyrinth and Essam swiftly followed.

***

The Beautiful Feast of the Reunion had come to an abrupt halt and Teos had declared the temple to be cleared. The supplicants left behind the shrines and the festooned figures of *Hathor* and *Horus* and headed out into the southern courtyard before leaving to cross the island.

The celebration had been glorious, but their talk was only of the appearance of the ghost of Safiya and, in the telling, the story grew. The words of Yara became twisted and added to, and accusations of murder were heard in their whispering. Those who stood at the back of the assembly had seen little of Nofret's performance, but the ones who remained alongside the nomarch had seen it all and were eagerly sought by those wanting to hear more.

Nofret sat for some time with the nomarch's daughter-in-law in her arms. But on seeing the temple empty, she led the young woman out into the light of the day. Yara seemed to have withdrawn into herself as the realisation of her actions played before her and she seemed not to have a care for the implication of murder attached to them. Humming softly, the girl's mind had taken her away from all the trouble and she had retreated to the safety of her innermost self.

The outer courtyard was slowly clearing as the crowds thinned. Yet, many of the villagers stopped to look at the priestess as she stood with her arms wrapped around the girl. Further along the temple structure, Mysis and his son had paused on the right side of the doorway while the Priests of *Hathor* had gathered in a shocked silence at the far corner nearest the river.

Nofret did not see any of the stares of bewilderment that came their way. Her concern was only for Yara and raising her hand and beckoning the young husband over, she said, "Take her home, Abasi, and make sure she's looked after."

The young man nodded his head, and the couple left, the husband holding his wife's hand at his side as he guided her across the courtyard. As they walked away, Mysis came to stand beside Nofret. Watching his son, his arm now wrapped protectively around his wife's waist, the nomarch suddenly realised the dilemma he was in.

As overseer of the nome, it was for him to supervise the governance of the area and deal out justice to all within his realm. But it was his daughter-in-law, one of his own family that he would eventually preside over, and she had admitted in public to the killing of Safiya. He was in a quandary of what to do. However, aware society would judge him on the ruling of this trial, he knew he had to be fair.

The nomarch eventually left the Priestess of *Hathor* standing by herself in the doorway to the temple and High Priest Teos took his place. The blue lotus had long left his system and his eyes, instead of holding a look of fervour, now held a sadness.

"That didn't go as I thought it would, Nofret."

"No," the woman replied sadly. "But then it's usually the same for most things in life. We spend our time searching for answers, but sometimes they don't turn out to be the ones we want." She smiled wistfully at the high priest as he looked out over the island. "We'll just have to accept, Teos, that at least the gods have given an answer to our prayers."

The last of the supplicants were heading out through

the enclosing wall and Teos, seeing their backward glances, raised his hand in blessing, before letting it fall heavily at his side. He stared up into the blueness of the sky. The morning was moving on as the rays of *Ra* fell upon his face and in that moment he felt the last hours weigh heavy on his soul. Nevertheless, on seeing the returning men who he had sent out in the chase and hopeful capture of Essam and Ramy, he prayed for the good news of their arrest.

***

Teos's men were quick to report back that the two priests had simply disappeared off the island. They had been seen heading towards Trajan's Kiosk, but after that, no trace of their departure could be found. The river ferries had been stopped and checked, and no one had apparently left that way. So, they reasoned, the two must still be around somewhere.

On hearing this, Nofret thought she knew exactly where they had gone and, not wanting them to escape justice so easily, she hurriedly left the brightness of the day and walked through the gloom of the hypostyle hall. She stopped before the statue of *Horus* that guarded the doorway out of the labyrinth and, remembering the door opened outwards, she returned to the statuette-lined front of the shrines. She chose a small marble figurine from the foot of *Osiris* which showed him standing tall and bound by the robes of death. Thanking the God of the Underworld for his benevolence, she strode back down the statue-lined aisle.

The little god fitted between the wall and the heavily hieroglyph-etched legs of *Horus*. Wedging it into the tight space, and ensuring it would not slip, she said a quick prayer and hoped it would hold the doorway out of the tunnels closed.

**

Satisfied with the placing of the sculpture, Nofret's attention returned to the wide-open entrance into the temple. The Priests of *Hathor* stood silhouetted in the brightness as, at their backs, the day moved on. They awaited their priestess and, seeing her walking the columns of the hypostyle hall, they became vocal in their jubilation at her return. Musa especially let the tears fall as he showed his joy, and clapping his hands together, he gave his thanks to all the gods he could think of.

The men led their priestess across the island with much singing and dancing and, on entering the Temple of *Hathor*, their celebration was brought before their goddess. Nofret felt she had been a long time away as she walked the columns of the large hall, but seeing the offerings remaining at the feet of *Hathor*, she thought Essam had, at least, kept his word as senior lector and done his duty to their goddess.

On reaching the statue-lined front, the priestess fell to the tiled floor. Lifting her eyes the stony stare of *Hathor* looked blankly back. Dropping her head, Nofret sang out her praise to the gods for the answers to her prayers, yet at that moment, after the performance in the Temple of *Isis*, all she wanted was the oblivion of sleep to take her away from the overwhelming sadness of the day.

CHAPTER SIXTEEN

Nofret lay on her bed. It felt so comfortable to be back in her room after the cold of the floor in the great temple's sanctum. But despite the utter feeling of collapse, sleep would not come. Her unsettled mind went hurriedly from one thing to another, first revisiting the scene at the Beautiful Feast of the Reunion, before she remembered the long lonely days spent in silence planning the appearance of the spirit of Safiya. Last, her concentration settled on the murder of the priestess committed at the feet of the goddess in the Temple of *Hathor*.

She was thankful for at least an answer to that. But on thinking more clearly about it, she wondered if Yara could have actually killed the priestess with one blow. The nomarch's daughter-in-law was slightly built, similar to her own figure, and she could never imagine herself being able to inflict the force to kill someone. *Still, the heat of the moment may have played its part, and who knows what a person is then capable of?*

Sitting up, the light from the small flickering lamp that sat on the side table reflected on her troubled face as she ran the words of the woman through her mind.

"It was me, Nofret! I killed Safiya!" echoed in her ears. She conjured up the image of the woman as she impulsively lifted the statue before bringing it down heavily on Safiya's head.

However, in her saying, Nofret recalled, Yara had stated she only struck once. Yet Atsu, the *sem* priest, had said the woman's head was bashed in. He was a man used to documenting and detailing unfortunate calamities that so often filled the world of the villagers as they made their living on the river, and she felt he could be trusted in his reporting of the incident. But that was not how Yara had described it. One blow was what she said, not the many that would have caved in the side of Safiya's head.

Nofret could see no reasoning for it apart from suddenly wondering if Essam, having said he would deal with the situation, had made more of a job of it. His was the only other name mentioned.

But why should he want to kill Safiya?

She lay back against the cool of the wall as the question rolled around her mind. Until recalling bitterly the treatment she had received from the lector priest, she wondered if the same had fallen on her predecessor. *What if Essam thought Safiya had found out, like I had, about the stealing of the precious grave goods from the tombs? If so, then perhaps he had seen the opportunity and seized it with both hands. However, he would have needed help to dispose of the body. He could not have carried the woman alone but,* Nofret pondered, *with the help of Ramy, his assistant, it would be so easy to dispose of Safiya in the labyrinth.*

Thinking of the tunnels, her mind spontaneously took her back to the pitch-black passageways and the horror and fear of waking to the utter dark unknowing of where she was. She had been tossed aside and left to die there and possibly Safiya had received the same fate.

Pulling up her knees, she held her breath and hung on tightly as the cool of the early morning chilled her bones. She remembered the overwhelming feeling of such terror and dismay as she shuffled blindly along the tunnels and the hopelessness that had grown with each stumble and faltering step. *But then, thank the gods, Aziza had appeared.* She knew the cat had been her saviour and that she would have died without its help.

Pushing away the panic that gripped her, she looked around the safety of the room and let her breathing return, before another thought slowly grew as she stared into the light. *If Safiya had been left to die in the labyrinth, then why was her body found on the rocks in the south? If she had been presumed dead in the tunnels, then surely her body should have remained there, and her bones left to desiccate in the dryness of the caves.*

Nofret thought of her own body, slowly decaying in the labyrinth's dark enclosure, and a fearful shiver ran through her soul. Quickly, she pushed the vision aside.

Returning to the dilemma of Safiya, the only reason that came to mind and the one that seemed the most probable was that Essam had removed the body of the priestess from the labyrinth so that she could be found. Then, she supposed, a line could be drawn under her disappearance and the search called off. Perhaps he hoped it would look like a crocodile or hippo had taken her and she had escaped to climb up the side of the rocks. Or else the poor woman had initially fallen in the dark and lain injured and hidden beneath the reed-lined edge of the island. Either way, the finding of her body would have brought the search to an end and, in the long term, had caused Nofret to be now sitting there in the morning's chill.

The hope of finding any sleep was at last left behind and, rising from the comfort of her bed, she picked up the lamp. Pushing open the door, she left the room. The currents of wind swept across the island and played around her bare legs as she walked along the open tunnel that led to the temple. Reaching the doorway, she paused briefly to look around. The darkness of the early morning remained around the island's palm-lined edge and the whisper of wind was all that could be heard. There was no other noise; even the cicadas had ceased their constant call.

Entering the Temple of *Hathor*, Nofret's echoing steps filled the vastness. As usual, a simple light sat in a dish at the foot of the main statue, but the lamp the priestess carried added to the illumination and, as she approached the altar, the shadows were chased into the dark.

Stopping before the image of the Mistress of the Sky, she placed the light down. The silence and smell of where she stood filled her senses and, closing her eyes in prayer, the dark fell heavily over her. On instinct, she quickly opened them and hastily looked around to ensure her safety. Once satisfied she was alone, she dropped her head and, keeping her eyes open, she brought her hands up to rest lightly at the feet of her goddess.

"Tell me I've not done wrong, *Hathor*, in leaving Essam and Ramy to their fate!"

The prayer came whispered as she thought of her trial beneath the island. It would not be an easy way to die. They could spend days wandering the labyrinth and find no way out or else, realise their destiny and wait for the inevitable.

"Guarantee to me, Lady of the Stars," she continued her appeal, "that on the day of my judgement in the Hall of the Two Truths, when I stand in front of the great gods and the feather of Ma'at is placed upon the scales, my heart will not weigh heavy and the deaths of these men go against me!"

The hush of the temple fell around and, staring into the flame of the candle, Nofret finished in a whisper, "Please give me a sign!"

A silence fell as the words echoed into the temple's roof and Nofret, looking hard into the face of *Hathor*, hung onto the cold stone of the ledge. Knowing the gods, if agreeable to the request, could give their approval in various ways, she waited out the time.

Eventually, a sound came on the edge of her hearing, likened to that of a low growl of a dog and knowing there were none on the island, Nofret turned her head cautiously towards it. Out of the corner of her eye, she saw the serpentine form of the snake emerge. A huge cobra appeared from beneath the bottom ledge of the altar, where it had been watching the priestess from the shadows. It slid soundlessly across the tiles and, reaching the woman's side, it lifted its head and reared up, its hiss sounding loud in the quietness.

Nofret froze.

The enormous asp took up the position of the uraeus worn by the pharaohs, its hooded neck spread wide as its tiny black eyes took in the stilled figure. With its fanned-out head moving slightly from side to side, its tongue tasted the air and Nofret felt the flicker brush past her cheek.

She knew the goddess could take on the form of the cobra, but was also aware that in the lives of the local Egyptians, the bite of these deadly creatures meant certain death. Fearful in the moment, she kept still and held her breath. The snake, too, held its ground and did not move, its eyes holding the woman in its stare. Time seemed to stand still before slowly, the cobra lowered its head and rested on the floor. However, it remained at the woman's side and, bringing its hooded shape back up, it again displayed before the priestess. Three times it did this before, on the last, the serpent lay still.

Tentatively, Nofret stretched out her hand and, placing her fingers lightly on top of the serpent's ring-engraved crown, she nervously dropped her head in thanks for the reply to her prayers. The snake let out a long, slow hiss before, leaving behind a sense of divine guidance, it slid off into the darkened columns of the hall.

Nofret heaved a sigh of relief as the creature disappeared and let her head rest on the front of the altar. She was sweating heavily and her mind was again in turmoil. But having seen the response of the snake, she felt *Hathor* had answered her plea and given her blessing.

***

Leaving the temple, the priestess quickly took the route behind her room and, following the path along the bank, she reached the walls of Trajan's Kiosk. In the growing light of the eastern edge of the valley, it stood stark and drab in the shadows and as Nofret stepped through, leaving the sluggish flow of the Nile behind, she walked purposefully down the right-hand side before coming to a stop. The dust-covered trapdoor lay firmly shut at her feet.

She knew Essam and Ramy, by her placing the statue across the exit in the Temple of *Isis*, had now been trapped within the labyrinth for the whole day. Yet she felt no grief for having imprisoned them in the tunnels, knowing they had felt none for her. However, the fate of both men lay in her hands. She could remove the statue, and let the door out of the crypts be open to the men, or else she could easily lift this door which lay at her feet. Propping it open with one of the smaller boulders which lined the river's edge, it could be left clear for the two to escape. But she hesitated in doing either of these. The Goddess of the Sky had given her blessing on her actions and instead of opening the entrance, she scraped the dust of the temple floor into the edges and made the slab of stone blend in with the rest of the tiled decoration. Doing so, she hoped to hide away the portal into the labyrinth and, in her mind, she drew a line beneath her concern for the men.

Stepping back, with no care left in her heart, she sat against the temple wall and let the day begin over the Nile. Above her head, the grey sky lightened to blue, and her thoughts turned to Yara. Here was where she was needed. The young woman had taken full responsibility for Safiya's death, believing in her confused mind that she was responsible, and the days to come for her would be a trial.

Yet suddenly, seated in the growing light, a thought occurred that if the two lector priests remained undiscovered within the island's hold, it could be thought likely they had escaped and possibly headed north. If so, and evidence could be presented to show their part in the killing of Safiya with a link to the ransacking of the tombs, it could, she reasoned, possibly minimise the punishment of Yara.

**

In the tunnels below the island's enclosure, Essam and Ramy had swiftly moved upwards into the crypts and, leaving behind the darkness of the labyrinth, they came out as usual, beneath the casket of Psusennes. It was equally dark here, but the unmistakable musty smell of the dead-filled chambers could not be confused with the labyrinth. An eerie foreboding wrapped around the two priests and Ramy automatically held his breath and briefly placed his hand across his nose.

Pausing for a moment, they pushed aside their fears and, straightening up, they instinctively held out their hands to touch either side of the painted walls. Moving slowly in the pitch-black of the catacombs, they made their way down the sloping tunnel.

Finally, they came to a sudden halt as they reached the wall at the end. Turning right, Essam whispered to Ramy to remain outside the room. The senior lector stumbled into the far corner and said a quick prayer of thanks to the gods as he came upon his stash of torches. There were only a few left, but picking up what was there, he attempted to make his way out.

After losing his direction in the darkness and clumsily walking into a wall, he shouted to Ramy and followed the man's voice back. Returning carrying the rushlights, flints and tinder he had thankfully found, the two blindly crossed the aisle and entered the last of the crypts.

Essam was quick to light a taper. In its sudden light, the two glanced around. There remained only the two sarcophagi here, but the perpetually dusty floor was filled with traces of past footprints, their own included. The dark shadows gathered in the corners and cast their elongated shapes over the carved ceiling of the vault. The place was silent and only the breathing of the two came clear in the hush.

The lector priests were glad of the meagre light which cast its glow around their feet but, as they stood and stared at each other, they both held fear in their eyes. Yet thinking themselves at least out of danger of being caught, they soon relaxed.

"We're safe here for the moment." Essam's eyes were filled with the reflection of the close flame. He was hot in the cumbersome clothing that still held him in its grip, and tearing off the head cloth and unwrapping the cloak from his upper body, he let the reek of sweat add its odour to the chamber.

Ramy glanced at the casket of the Priestess of *Hathor* which sat at their feet, before asking the question that played through his mind.

"Was that really the spirit of Safiya?" His voice came as a whisper in the tomb's stillness. He had seen the image as it appeared out of the smoky gloom and, aware of his involvement in the woman's disposal, he felt retribution had found him.

"Of course it wasn't!" Essam angrily answered, kicking aside the finery he had discarded. Knowing the body of Safiya lay at their side, he reasoned it was probably some ploy on Teos's part to enliven the celebrations.

But then, who was the woman dressed as Safiya?

In his mind, he recognised the voice but the name of who it belonged to evaded him for the moment. He thought hard to grasp it and was just on the edge of remembering when Ramy's voice interrupted his reflection.

"How long must we wait?" Looking around the chamber, Ramy's eyes took in the enclosure of the four walls before he brought them back to rest on the sarcophagus of Safiya.

Essam chose not to answer and instead stared angrily at the casket which held the priestess's remains. He felt all their misfortune came back to his dealing with her death. It had seemed auspicious at the time and a fitting way to be rid of the priestess who he knew had been asking around regarding certain night-time activities on the island. Her questioning would have soon reached the ears of Teos.

Furiously, he rose. She had been the start of all the heartache that had brought them to where they now sat. In his anger, he kicked aside the senet board which sat at the foot of the funerary box and its pieces flew across the chamber, rattling against the wall as they hit hard.

Time passed and was measured in the lighting of the tapers as each one burnt down. The men had usually been brisk about their dealings in the catacombs, not wanting to linger in the realm of the dead. However, as the feeling of entrapment and agitation slowly grew, Ramy could sit no longer. He was used to the feel of the catacomb walls surrounding him, but this time, feeling it more like a prison, he could not rest.

"I think I'll check to see if the temple is empty." His voice echoed into the low-lying roof and his breath made the torch flicker as he lifted it out from the sand.

Essam, not wanting to be left alone in the dark, followed as they made their way back into the labyrinth, but this time the light of the torch lit their way.

Reaching the stairway that led up to the hidden door, Ramy handed Essam the light and let him lead. Climbing the steep steps, they unknowingly followed Nofret's path as she escaped the labyrinth's hold. Reaching the highest landing, the senior lector's fingers found the lever, and pushing in and lifting it, the usual sound of the door clicking open sounded reassuring in the tunnel's silence.

"Wait there a moment, Ramy," Essam whispered. "I'll make sure the way is clear." Eagerly, he pushed against the solid block. It had always been smooth and light in its opening, but this time, it would not move. Ramy joined him, bringing the flame overhead to light the doorway, and the two pushed harder in desperation.

"Why won't it open?" Ramy madly asked. The nearness of their freedom sat tantalisingly close behind the wall.

"I don't know. Push harder!"

The statue of *Osiris* pinned the doorway closed and the more the men pushed, the more it wedged against the legs of the colossal image of *Horus* and held their exit from the labyrinth shut.

The priests tried desperately to escape as freedom sat easily within reach, before, finally overcome with exhaustion, they stopped and sank to the floor. Gradually, as their breathing returned to normal, the slow realisation crept over them that the door would never be opened. They were trapped, sealed within the labyrinth. But knowing there was another way out through the catacombs that lay beneath the temple, Essam started back to the coffin-lined crypts.

Returning to the walkway below the shelving of the sarcophagi, he lifted the light and headed up the sloping tunnel towards the doorway. Yet, as he passed by the resting places of the long-gone and Ramy followed the flickering flame, they both knew in their minds it would be locked. It had been kept locked all the long time they had been servants to the gods on this island, and it was unlikely that had changed. Still, in their growing fear, they desperately needed to check. Both held on to a prayer they might find it open.

The door came into view at the top of the long slope and, holding the light over the lock, Essam pushed against the wood. There was no give in its tight blockade and, in despair, the lectors heaved against the barrier. Time after time, their shoulders hit hard against the solidness before their strength gave out and they stood back, breathless in their exhaustion. Staring at the barrier to the outside, the slow understanding of the situation crept its way over the prisoners.

"It's hopeless! We're stuck down here, Essam." Ramy's voice echoed down the tunnel and held such dismay in his misery. "Now what do we do?"

"We must wait and see if the gods are good to us and answer our prayers."

Essam leaned his head against the barricade that blocked their escape, and his words sounded muffled. "But, of course," he added, turning his head to one side and glaring at Ramy, "you must realise that if we are rescued, then we'll inevitably be tried by man for our misconduct."

The two priests knew the punishment for the robbing and violation of the tombs would be brutal and in the end, a death here, surrounded by all those gone from this world along with the riches they took with them, might not be so bad. It would take its time to come, of course, but in the meantime, they could send their prayers into the heavens and hope the gods looked kindly on them.

However, the senior lector held on to one last hope. Someone knew they had entered the labyrinth and whoever that was had barred the door to their exit into the temple. Someone knew they were down here and perhaps he or she would come to their rescue. But then again, perhaps not.

The figure of the robed woman standing before the altar kept playing in Essam's mind. *Who was she? And was she the person who had blocked our escape?*

She had emerged from out of the smoke of the candles and, with the anklets jingling at her feet, appeared dressed as Safiya. His mind knew that could not be the case, but the voice sounded so familiar. He remembered the tone as being similar to that of Nofret, the last Priestess of *Hathor*. Yet aware her body lay somewhere deep within the labyrinth he knew in his heart it could not be her.

Pushing these thoughts aside, his mind returned to their dilemma. The two had nowhere to go, apart from returning to the crypt at the end of the tunnel.

Reaching the safety of its enclosure, they gathered together the lights. Seated against the far wall of the tomb, time passed, but to the men, it was noted only by the flare of the torch and the dwindling of their supplies.

The last torch, over time, slowly burnt down and its illumination went from a comforting brightness to a dull, blood-red glow before disappearing in a puff of smoke. The dark, which had gathered as the light died, fell completely over the two men. At first, the afterimages of brightness remained sparkling in their eyes, but within moments, these disappeared and the blackness closed in. The silence collected in the corners of the room as the breathing of the two became the only sound in the stillness.

There would be no escape from here, Essam realised, and stretching out his legs along the sandy expanse, the remaining clothing of the lector priest caught about his legs and held him down. *All of this is no use to me now*, he bitterly thought and, disrobing out of the finery, he cast it aside. Instead, he let the enclosing chill crawl its way across his bare skin and, not wanting to think of the coming listlessness, he took his mind back to happier times.

Ramy eventually left Essam alone and, moving

hesitantly on his hands and knees in the pitch-dark, he felt his way cautiously across the crypt floor. Reaching the edge of the casket that held their priestess, he came to a stop. Feeling some security in its solid reality, he propped himself up against the smooth painted wood and let his head fall to his chest. Seated at the foot of the sarcophagus that held Safiya, he softly wept at his misfortune.

CHAPTER SEVENTEEN

On the Island of Philae, the ever-constant daily observations in its grand temples went on with the timely rising of the sun ushering in each new day. The gods were given their due reverence. Yet outside the formalities, a feeling of disquiet wound its way around the palm-fringed island. Sadness and disbelief were seen in the faces of the priests and priestesses who knew Essam and Ramy from their long service to *Hathor*. Amazement at what had happened in the temple was first mentioned, before a rising doubt took its place and the whispered voices gathered.

The event before the statues of *Osiris*, *Isis* and *Horus* on the Beautiful Feast of the Reunion had unsettled many of the priesthood, and Teos, wishing for a return to the balance of a life spent in ritual and prayer, was quick to strip the statues of *Horus* and *Hathor* from their wedding ties. The personification of the cow-headed goddess was removed with little fuss and returned across the island and the altar swept clean of the event.

The northern end of the hypostyle hall returned to the worship of the triad and in Teos's heart, he thanked the gods for an end to the ceremony. Thankfully though, the question of the death of Safiya had been answered, but that, too, opened up other worries.

***

On the eastern edge of the island, the statue of *Hathor* returned to the hall where she had stood for countless years and was placed back alongside the imposing figure which dominated the altar.

Nofret was eager to return to her duties, even though

Abbas reassured her that in her absence, the services to the Goddess of the Sky would be performed while she recuperated. However, she gave herself no leave and straightaway took back her position as Priestess of *Hathor*. She was down by two priests, but the remaining three covered all the duties and the goddess was given her due rights.

The ritual of the temple once more became Nofret's life and her reason for being there. Yet, on her strolls around the island, she could not walk past Trajan's Kiosk without pausing at the point where she knew the steps led down. She wondered what had happened within the confines of the tunnels and, unable to think of anything that lightened her fears, her overwhelming dread would again return her to the dark.

It was even worse at the great temple that sat on the western edge of the island. Her ceremonial duties sometimes took her in that direction and often she would stop in front of the concealed doorway.

Standing before the statue of *Horus*, with the statuette of *Osiris* remaining firmly in place blocking any escape, she imagined Essam and Ramy realising their plight and the slow panic that would have overwhelmed their souls. She felt the rise of the terror gripping them, as it did her in her own solitude within the labyrinth. They would die a lingering death, their thirst and hunger growing in each desperate moment of the darkness until a lethargy would wrap around them and the cares of the world would, in the last, be cast off.

She knew she could easily remove the statuette, yet could not bring herself to do so. Instead, she simply distracted herself during the day from thinking of what was happening beneath her feet and let her temple duties fill the time as the worries of others were placed before her. But at night, when the dark filled her room and her dreams and nightmares left her troubled, she was often led back to her time spent lost within the shadows of the island tunnels.

***

Opposite the Island of Philae, with its great temples and everyday rituals, the village on the Nile's eastern bank also returned to its routine after the spectacle in the house of the gods. Here, though, among the backstreets, the story was retold with greater relish over the market stalls and in the open shop doorways. And along the pathways at the side of the river, it grew and heightened in each telling.

The accusations against the nomarch's daughter-in-law became more than just her connection with Safiya's death and soon she, too, was being linked with the robbing of the tombs and the supposed violation of the dead. The allegations seemed wildly out of place and far-fetched, some stories having her stealing across the river in the dead of night to rob the catacombs. But, however fanciful, they did not go away.

Governor Mysis, hearing from his staff the news off the streets, knew he would have to deal with this. Whispers followed his feet down the alleyways and streets, but closing his ears to the gossip, he first aimed to find out who had been helping Essam and Ramy. To him, that seemed more important.

Knowing Nofret suspected someone in the village was involved in robbing the catacombs, he discreetly asked around regarding any information. Most seemed unaware of this activity and those who did kept closed lips to the nomarch. But on speaking with the men who took the boats down the Nile, he heard that now and then his scribe Penthu sent extra parcels along with the usual reports. And when Basim, the ferryman, added that the scribe occasionally took a boat over to the island at night, Mysis's suspicion became aroused.

Calling both his scribes into the gardens at the centre of the house, he sat with his back to the fountain and, at his side, a rolled-up parchment, along with writing implements, lay in a tray. The silence of the courtyard wrapped itself around them as Nahket and Penthu stood before their employer.

The two brothers, at first, appeared to feel no unease in the silence, expecting that the nomarch had things of state to discuss regarding the nome or else wished them to write a personal missive. But as the silence continued and Mysis's stern gaze held them, Penthu slowly suspected otherwise.

He had stood behind the nomarch in the temple as the spirit of Safiya appeared and he had heard all her accusations. He had also seen the quick escape of the lector priests and, thinking they would be caught and his name mentioned, he thought he knew what was coming. Steeling himself, he moved aside from his brother.

On seeing the action, Mysis rose from his seat.

"Have you something you wish to tell me, Penthu?"

The man hung his head. Essam and Ramy, as far as he was aware, were still missing. But in these last days, the scribe had realised they would soon be found, and he had already made provision for his escape, just in case. He had paid for a place on the morning's boat down the Nile for the following day and, having already packed his small belongings, he was hoping this meeting would be

233

the last with the nomarch.

He was soon to recognise his mistake.

"Have you something you wish to tell me?" Mysis repeated, raising his voice in anger.

Penthu felt the chill of fear run through his heart and, looking around, he saw the guards that blocked any escape. He realised he needed to say something in his defence and, hoping for mercy, he dropped to his knees and lifted his hands in appeal.

"I need to unburden my soul, nomarch!"

Mysis ordered him to stand before him and, with two of the guards who had been called forwards, he was told to make clear his dealings with the priests of the island. The scribe knew he must explain and justify his many visits there, and so he stated that Essam and Ramy sometimes called him to the island and gave him packages to send down the Nile. He explained absolutely that he never knew what was in them and, if he had, he would certainly have warned the nomarch.

The governor found this hard to believe and, after taking time to think of the punishment he would hand out, he stood before the man to give his sentence. He saw the likelihood of reckoning rising in the man's agonised face before he duly sentenced Penthu to have both his hands cut off for the robbing of the graves.

For a scribe, losing his everyday work tools was one of the worst penalties imaginable. Yet for an Egyptian, the sentence meant more than the loss of his trade. He would be incomplete in the eyes of the gods and, come the day of his passing, he would be denied entry into the place of unending peace. He would be cast out and never walk the Field of Reeds, and his soul would wander lost forever.

Hearing his punishment, the scribe fell again to his knees. Pleading with his nomarch to lessen the penalty, he placed the fault strictly at the feet of the priests of the island. He repeated he did not know what Essam and Ramy were sending down the river and if he had, he would have brought it to a stop. Mysis heard the apologies in the man's voice but, seating himself back down, he would not lessen the order.

He let the man wait long in his agony of forthcoming misery before slowly coming forwards in his chair and standing. Raised high above the pathetic scribe, he suggested that if Penthu wrote his full admission and cleared the name of Yara from the accusation of tomb-robbing, then perhaps a lesser sentence may be considered. Possibly the loss of only one hand!

Mysis carefully placed the rolled-up piece of papyrus on the ground before him and planted the woven tray containing the reed and ink at its side. Holding out his hand, he indicated for Penthu to make his choice.

The scribe eagerly crawled forwards and, kneeling at the nomarch's feet, he unrolled the papyrus flat across the floor. With a shaking hand, he drew the hieroglyphs stating his involvement in the crime and, beneath this, he wrote the words giving absolution to the governor's daughter-in-law. Finally, he placed his name at its bottom and, knowing this to be the last time he signed a document, he wrote alongside, *ánuk pau ḥem.tã* – I am your servant.

Mysis stood as witness to the man's guilt, and nodding his head satisfyingly, he promptly stooped to pick up the damp papyrus. Waving it to dry, he instructed Nahket to take notice of his brother's sentence and have it made known throughout the village.

The incriminating document was handed over, and the papyrus duplicated. And Nahket swiftly sent the announcement to the priests on the island. Along with that, a message stating retribution would be quick was attached, and the punishment was to be enforced the next morning.

***

High Priest Teos, along with three of his Priests of *Isis*, took the boat over in the early hours to stand witness to the penalty for tomb robbing. The Nile was running heavy in the dawn's light, and the boatmen struggled in the flow. But as they reached the waterside of the village, the force lessened and the boat came to a sudden stop against the sandy bank.

Teos straightened his robes as he got out and, walking the short distance with his retinue bringing up the rear, he came out into the main village. The street was deadly quiet, yet around the homes a blaze of lights met them as the people turned out to testify to the punishment.

Mysis led the assembly as Penthu was brought out, and the crowd of silent watchers fell in behind as the prisoner was taken beyond the village to a place in the east. Here the land dipped into the shape of an amphitheatre and a smooth granite block stood upright out of the sand. It drew the eye of the terrified scribe and, as the dawn light was growing, he was unceremoniously dragged towards it. Held tightly by his guards, his right hand was brought up from his side and placed out on the coldness of the block.

Without looking at the frightened man, Mysis swiftly conducted the punishment and the blade of the axe was raised and brought swiftly down. The sound of it hitting the stone rang out in the arena as the edge of the blade scored deep into the granite and the scribe's blood streamed down the side of the stone.

An agonising scream hit the morning air before Penthu passed out in shock. Beside him on the sand, the fingers of his severed hand lay twitching, before slowly stopping as the blood drained from the wrist, leaving the immaculate fingernails turning white.

Mysis turned away. He saw no great joy in doing this, and throwing the bloodied axe down on the sand, he stalked off, leaving the villagers to deal with the unconscious man.

Later, as he sat alone in his garden with a cup of wine at his side, Mysis's thoughts turned away from the activities of the morning and focused on doing his duty regarding the Priestess Safiya. It was difficult, knowing one of his close family had somehow been involved in her murder, and he spent the remaining day and night-time hours in thought and uncertainty before reaching a conclusion. He hoped it would be a fair retribution for Yara's involvement and would also satisfy the gods.

***

The following day, as the sun began its rise in the east and the birds flitted in and out of the reeds, the worshippers gathered at the river's edge and the nomarch joined them to take the ferry across the Nile to the Island of Philae.

Mysis followed in the parade's rear and passing the Temple of *Hathor*, he saw Nofret standing tall at the house of the goddess, her hand raised in welcome.

Turning aside, he was greeted at the doorway and urged to observe the morning service from within its walls. The ceremony was now being well attended by the villagers, and the nomarch, proceeding to the front of the body of worshippers, took the time to notice those who dropped their heads in his recognition.

The rising of the sun was welcomed and rejoiced in the service to *Hathor* and at the last, the petitioners' offerings were carried forwards and left at her feet.

The nomarch stayed long after the ceremony ended and, leaving the priests to clear away the temple, he and Nofret walked the banks of the island. The priestess kept close at his side as they stopped to look out over the water and the man sensed the woman had something to say. He let her take her time, and eventually, she turned to face him.

"I hope you have found some kindness in your heart, Mysis?" she asked. "It would bother me if I thought you held a grudge in my findings against your family."

"I hold no ill will against you, priestess," Mysis honestly answered. "You've solved a mystery which needed to be brought into the light. Yet, I must be seen to be fair in my administration. Without that, my ruling of the nome is weakened, and any authority given to me by pharaoh is in doubt."

"I see that, Mysis. But please think kindly of Yara!" Nofret had heard about the scribe's punishment and feared the girl might receive the same fate, if not worse.

"I've already made my decision on that." The man smiled, hoping his lightness might ease her fear. "And I'm here to put it forward to Teos. If he agrees, then there should be no worry on your part, Nofret."

He touched the priestess reassuringly on her bare arm

and, leaving the woman to stare out over the water, he strode the island's middle. Passing the palms which sat at its centre, he went to meet with High Priest Teos at his home in the north. There, over drinks of wine and plates of sweetmeats, he put forward his proposal for dealing with Yara.

He reasoned it was not his daughter-in-law's intent to murder, and the violence was done in the heat of the moment. With that, he felt he should spare the life of the young woman. However, he still had to appease the growing outrage of the villagers.

Therefore, he put forward that she should be banished from the village as punishment and, along with her husband, be sent down the Nile to Thebes, where they could start afresh without the stigma of the past.

He hoped for the blessing of the gods in this and High Priest Teos, after taking a short time to think, found the suggestion reasonable in the circumstances. However, he thought the nomarch may eventually come to regret his action.

"You'll be losing your firstborn son, Mysis, along with a grandchild. You realise that, don't you?"

"I know, but I've many other sons." The nomarch took a long drink of the sweet wine, his mind already having reached its closure concerning Yara and Abasi. Dropping his hands to his lap, he let the liquid settle before quickly adding, "My wives have blessed me in abundance on that score, Teos, and my second son, Ramose, in my eyes, is more in keeping with my thoughts of governance."

Teos could only nod his head on hearing the nomarch's resolution and, realising as High Priest on the Island of Philae he had little to say in the nome's overall governance, he gave his blessing and the two men let their talk turn to affairs of the Nile.

***

On the day of Yara's leaving, Nofret travelled across the river to wish the young couple farewell and to bestow the blessing of *Hathor* on the forthcoming new arrival. Her mind had already dealt with the girl's betrayal better than some around, who continued to hold it against her. She had reasoned that Yara had struck out in utter frustration. *And, yes, she had caused injury. But it was not this blow that ended Safiya's life!*

Seeing the couple stood alone in wait for the boatman at the reed-lined edge of the Nile, the priestess walked the fringe before taking the arm of the pregnant woman. Leading her away from the bustle of the waterway, they stopped some distance up the bank.

"I wouldn't have you go without giving you my blessing." Nofret smiled at Yara as the river breeze ruffled the young woman's hair.

For a moment, the heaviness lifted from around Yara's heart and, smiling back, she replied, "You've always given me hope, Nofret." She grasped the priestess's hand and brought it up to her lips. "And thank you for the kindness you have shown me."

Seeing the woman standing there, her extended belly wrapped tightly with her shawl, Nofret accepted the thanks but added, "However, Yara you must remember to continue to give thanks to the Goddess *Hathor*, and rejoice her name out loud for her bountiful gift."

The two walked arm in arm as the valley's silence followed them up towards the village before Yara stopped at the top of the bank. She would go no further;

her mind made up that a new life awaited her in the north. Turning, both women looked over the Nile and, in their amicable silence, they watched the feluccas move back and forth, their bright white sails sitting starkly against the green of the far bank.

Suddenly a voice split the stillness. The boat was waiting for them and seeing the raised arm of Abasi as he called out to his wife, Nofret said her goodbyes.

Kissing the girl on the cheek, she whispered the blessings of *Hathor* in her ear and, wishing her well, raised her hand as the girl walked away.

Nofret returned to the Island of Philae, knowing there was little more she could do for the couple. Her own life, she reasoned, concentrated on her service to the goddess and the daily prayer of the temple. Yet, thankful that the world's cares could be left aside for the moment, she dropped before the statue of *Hathor* and spent her time in quiet contemplation.

***

The elderly *sem* priest, Atsu, passed away before the next Nile flood and he missed out on an inundation like never seen before. The fields that spread out from the river were awash with the rich, dark saturation and, along the banks of the waterways, all the gods were praised for their blessings.

Garai, Atsu's apprentice, took over the business of mummification on the island, his first full embalming being that of his tutor. He had been taught well and excelled at his work, and the pride in which he washed and wrapped the body of his old friend and mentor, was noted by his own new apprentice.

In the Temple of *Hathor*, Nofret gave a small service to the work of Atsu alongside her usual ceremony to the goddess and, after seeing the villagers leave to cross back to their lives on the riverbank, she and her priests walked the stretch of the island and joined a distinguished gathering in the Temple of the Triad.

Teos was conducting an extra special service for the long years Atsu had served as *sem* priest and all the priests and priestesses of Philae attended. They lined the hypostyle hall to pay their respects and, as his sarcophagus rested before the altar, they watched and gave their approval with many shouts and songs as the embalmed body was given the tradition of an Egyptian burial.

At its end, the ceremony finished with the sarcophagus being raised and, lifted in the sight of the gods, carried through the hypostyle hall and taken out into the forecourt of the temple. Turning right, it was borne along the colossal front of the building before reaching the water's edge. Here, it was carefully fed down the side of the island before reaching the entrance into the crypts.

The door to the catacombs was opened and the sudden outrush of stale air met the warmth of the riverside. High Priest Teos led the way in and followed by the wrapped body of Atsu, encased in his ceremonial coffin, the small burial party lifted their torches and trailed behind. It was the first time Nofret, or anyone for that matter, had entered this place since the event in the temple.

Atsu was deposited with some finesse in the niche below the one where past *sem* priests of the temple lay and, pushed to the very back of the ledge, a space was left at the front for two further coffins. Garai, standing back and letting the flame of his torch warm his face, knew this was where, one day, his own wrapped and perfumed body might also lie.

The High Priest of *Isis* led the ceremony, but once over, the torch party turned to leave. However, feeling the closeness of Safiya's burial, Nofret could not leave the crypt without showing her respects to her predecessor. Letting Teos know she would remain a while longer, she took the twisting, sloping tunnel of the catacombs. Lifting the light of the torch and passing the many chiselled ledges and their encased occupants, she let her shadow fall at her feet.

Reaching the bottom of the slope, she paused for a moment, not knowing what she might find. She was unsure if either Essam or Ramy would be found there, or if their bodies lay lost in the labyrinth. Steeling herself and pushing aside her anxiety, she stepped to the left.

In the raised light of the torch, the desiccated body of Ramy lay at the base of Safiya's sarcophagus, the leathery remains held together by the dried-out skin and the mouldering clothing he wore. His blackened head had fallen to one side, resting on his right shoulder, and his viscid eyes had shrunk small into his skull. The teeth protruded from the black taut lips and between them, his tongue had first swollen to fill his mouth before shrivelling to a strip of withered flesh.

Around him in the sand, his inner fluids had seeped out as his body purged itself in his death. Drying on the ground, the liquid had formed a pool of rancid drippings in which he sat. He was holding in his wizened hand, one of the circular flat wooden senet pieces which bore the teeth marks of the desperately hungry. Other pieces lay scattered around, each gnawed around the edges, and the throwing sticks were eaten down to stubs.

Nofret lifted her scarf and covered her mouth and,

feeling no remorse for his ending, left the man to lie. Raising the torch to shine its light into the corners, she looked around for Essam.

Over on the far side, a pile of clothes lay thrown about, as if tossed aside in some frenzy. Here the discarded clothing of the lector priest lay in evidence of his being there, but any further sign of the man was not seen. There were no bones or dried-up corpse of Lector Essam lying around and, after giving her blessing to Safiya's remains, the Priestess of *Hathor* left behind the tomb and searched the older crypts. It was the same. Essam had just disappeared, but Nofret thought she knew where he had gone.

Suddenly, a fear took hold of her and the dark confinement within the catacombs closed in. Feeling the rising panic that so easily gripped her, she needed to escape and leave behind the dead. Quickly, she headed upwards.

The light at the doorway shone clear like a beacon before her and, stepping out onto the banks of the river, she breathed in the freshness of the new Nile day. On the water, a felucca floated past with its net thrown overboard and, seeing the figure on the bank, the fisherman raised his arm. Nofret lifted her hand to the heavens in reply and turned her face up towards the clear sky. The familiar sound of the hippos greeted her with their chorus and the blessing of *Ra* shone down from on high.

***

Many, many weeks ago, beneath the Temple of the Goddess *Isis*, Lector Essam had eventually left behind the sound of Ramy gnawing hysterically at the wooden pieces of the senet board and had returned to the labyrinth. In desperation, he again tried the door into the Temple of the Triad, but it remained closed to him. However, he felt there was one last hope.

Grasping this last flicker of optimism, he made his way blindly through the dark and, in his madness, blundered into the walls that enclosed him. Around he could hear his breathing, but on the very edge of his perception, a sound kept coming and going. Stopping and letting his head rest on the walls of the labyrinth, he eventually heard, far away behind him in the distance, the tinkle of the anklets of Safiya.

The sound brought him to his senses and, desperate to leave his madness behind, he forced himself onward. Blindly racing through the tunnels as fast as he could, he eventually reached the stairs up to Trajan's Kiosk. He clung on fiercely to the expectation that Penthu would have realised where they were hiding and would come across the river to rescue them. Or else, the person who had barred their exit into the temple may have felt remorse for their actions and left the doorway open.

He was soon disappointed. The slab was closed securely over his head and would not move. After pushing hard and beating his hands against the barrier, and the echo of his desperate screams rolled around the temple structure above, he let his bruised hands fall at his side and he hung his head. He was trapped. Blindly fumbling his way down the stairway, his fists took out their misery on the labyrinth walls. He was so close to freedom.

Stumbling through the passageways, he aimed to return to the crypts, but the convoluted maze of corridors held him tightly and fed him this way and that through their weave of tunnels. The sound of the bells filled his mind and followed his stumbling steps, but although they were constant and forever at his back, they never caught up. Finally, exhausted and weakened by hunger, he lost his way within the knot of passages and could walk no longer. Falling to his knees, his breathing came harshly in the surrounding stillness.

Sitting naked in the dark, the feeling of inevitability caught at Essam's dry throat. In his crazed mind, he returned to the Temple of the Triad and, recalling the great service he had performed before the three greatest gods known to the kingdom, his imagination placed him back before the gathering of people. A smile crossed his gaunt face as he remembered their devotion. He had done his service to *Hathor* and *Horus*, and the Sky Gods were reunited under his supervision.

Suddenly the voice of the spirit that appeared in the temple ran through his subconscious and in its character and pitch he at last recognised it. *It was Nofret!*

But she was dead, he reasoned. *Left to die in the labyrinth.*

Knowing his energy was leaving him and the same fate awaited him if help did not come soon, he replayed the words she had said over and over until he aimed to push them aside. The voice, however, stuck fast in his brain and would not go away as the slow realisation fell over him. *It had to be her*, he finally accepted. *It could be no one else!*

He knew she had found one of Safiya's anklets and had worn it around her leg in the Temple of *Hathor* and, he now reasoned, that was what they must have heard as the ceremony ended. *It was no avenging spirit of Safiya that haunted their ceremony and gave judgement on the gathering,* he bitterly thought. *It was just Nofret who had somehow escaped from the tunnels.*

Knowing this could be the only answer, his anger grew. He should have made sure she was dead. Banging his skinny, cold hands heavily on the ground in frustration and despair, he felt no pain as the small bones broke beneath his manic violence. The echo of his outright failure rolled around the enclosure and, as it dulled and grew distant, the jingling of the priestess's anklets slowly took its place.

Essam knew there was no escape. Seated slumped in the chilled air, he wrapped his arms around his emaciated naked body and let his legs stretch long across the labyrinth's floor. Letting his head drop, he could only accept his fate and, waiting for the tinkling of the bells to grow closer in the dark, he whispered his pitiful prayers to the gods.

THE END

About the Author

Glennis Goodwin is a British author who has long held an interest in the myths and culture of the Ancient Egyptians. Along with that, the people of southern Africa have also been of interest and in the early 1980s, she was fortunate to live and work in Zambia.

In her working life, she has gone from nursing to retail and from academic publishing to PA, but during that time, she never lost the feeling that Africa gave her, and, in those years, had holidays in Egypt and Kenya.

In 2004, she aimed to return to her nursing career and enrolled in New Zealand on a refresher course. Settling into life on the other side of the world, she continued to further her career, met her husband and made her home there.

Sadly, a brain haemorrhage and slight stroke ended her study, but after her recovery, she found herself wanting to write, something she had longed to do but never seemed to have the time for. Returning to the UK in 2017, she settled down at her computer, and over the following months, the tales of the Eight Deities of the Primordial Chaos came to life in the story of Malian, the altar tender. Her first book, *The Eighth Deity*, then came into being and *The Gods of Chaos*, a fantasy adventure series, was born.

Now living in a Nottinghamshire village, she has since written a further four books in the series, *Brotherhood of Apep*, *In the Footsteps of Ra*, *The Papyrus of Ma'at*, and

The Bow of Horus. Looking to expand her writing while using the knowledge gained from her trips to Egypt, she is now working on a series of Ancient Egyptian murder mysteries set on the banks of the Nile.

Other Books

by

Glennis Goodwin

The Gods of Chaos Series

The Eighth Deity

Brotherhood of Apep - Book Two

In the Footsteps of Ra - Book Three

The Papyrus of Ma'at - Book Four

The Bow of Horus - Book Five

www.blossomspringpublishing.com